THE PHEASANT PLUCKER

First published in 2006 by

Logan Books
17 Rocklands Drive
Four Oaks
Sutton Coldfield
West Midlands B75 6SP

e-mail: logan.books@wanadoo.fr

ISBN: 0-9552405-0-6
(978-0-9552405-0-8)

The Pheasant Plucker

Bill Daly

LOGAN BOOKS

For Harriet and Blakey

CHAPTER 1

Kilbirnie was where I first saw the light of day some twenty-five years ago. For those not familiar with the town, Kilbirnie rates right up there alongside Milton Keynes as a place people come from, but no one in their right mind ever goes to. Leaving aside alliteration, Kilbirnie and colour have no known connection. When coal mining in Scotland was at its peak a permanent pall of black soot hung over the town and ever since the last of the pits closed down everything about the place has been redolent of grey; from the tarmacadamed roads and the slate-coloured bricks of the terraced housing to the clothes of the stooped, Lowry-like figures who struggle up the High Street leaning into the teeth of the ever-present wind.

When I was born, my late father, Jimmy McClure, was pushing seventy. Big Jimmy had spent his entire working life at the coal face until he was made redundant in his early sixties and while his decision to sink his lump sum into opening a pub in the centre of Kilbirnie could hardly be deemed spotting a niche in the market place, at least he had sufficient nous to realise that the only way he'd ever be able to afford bar staff would be to employ an au pair.

In response to his advert, Monique Carrière, a twenty-four year old Parisienne, came to Kilbirnie in order to improve her English – not an inspired choice. After two years slogging away behind the bar in The Plucked Pheasant she was disappointed to discover the accent she'd acquired didn't travel – not even as far as Glasgow. However, Monique was nothing if not pragmatic and she accepted Jimmy's proposal to share with him the intrinsic advantages of the indigenous Kilbirnie lifestyle – uncrowded shops, traffic-free streets and five customers in the pub on a busy Saturday night; such a pleasant change from the never-ending bustle of the thirteenth *arrondissement*.

My father was a bear of a man. With his shock of flaming red hair and unkempt beard he bore an uncanny resemblance to the picture of William Wallace on the cover of my primary school history book. I don't remember very much about him, other than he spent most evenings in the pub, propped up on a high barstool, playing dominoes and cribbage with the regulars. One thing that did stick in my memory was the way he drank his whisky. When I was five, I used to think whisky was the adult equivalent of castor oil as I would watch my father pinch a shot glass between thumb and forefinger and tense his whole body before throwing the contents down his throat. Screwing up his face, he would tip the whisky dregs into his pint glass, then wipe the back of his hand slowly across his mouth. This ritual was invariably followed by a long, slow swallow of lager, presumably to kill the taste.

Jimmy drank a lot, smoked a lot, laughed a lot, coughed a lot and popped his clogs two days before my sixth birthday, having taught Monique everything he knew about running a pub, which, to be frank, was little more than how to fiddle the optics and the VAT.

My mother had a slim, petite figure with a swanlike neck, a fine bone structure and long, ash-blonde hair which she usually wore plaited to her waist. Her kind, pale-blue eyes were set in a heavily freckled face and a deep dimple indented the point of her chin. Her nose was turned up slightly, but she had the most perfect teeth and she could look incredibly beautiful when she smiled.

I take after my father in that I'm over six feet tall, broad-shouldered and, at a charitable estimate, a couple of kilos overweight – mostly in form of an incipient beer gut. I inherited my father's flaming red hair, though I keep mine cropped short. From my mother's genes, as well as the dimple in my chin, I acquired the mass of freckles which cover my cheeks, nose and forehead.

After Jimmy died, Monique dedicated herself to my bilingual education with an all-consuming passion, inculcating in me her passion for language and literature, both English and French. I attended secondary school in Kilwinning, but my mother flatly refused to allow me to study French because she was paranoid about me speaking her native language with an Ayrshire accent, so she devoted herself to all aspects of my French tuition, cocooning me in her private world of subjunctives and gerundives, of *passé composé* and *passé historique*, of Rimbaud and Voltaire.

Monique actively espoused Marshall McLuhan's theory which postulates that *the school is the gap in the child's education*. Not so much from McLuhan's philosophical standpoint that the medium of television, by creating a global village, has made conventional education irrelevant – more from the practical point of view that, in her not-so-humble opinion, she was more competent than all the teachers in the local educational establishments put together.

During each of my teenage years, Monique would nominate a book as compulsory reading and she'd set a written test a week before my birthday to make sure I'd absorbed it, with the sanction looming of birthday presents being withheld. Having started me off on stories which had stimulated her childhood imagination, *Through The Looking Glass* and *Le Petit Prince*, she moved on to novels which had influenced her adolescent thinking, such as *Zen and the Art of Motorcycle Maintenance* and *Jonathan Livingston Seagull*. When I was older she introduced me to books she considered to be classics, her all-time favourite being *Ulysses*. One of her pet sayings was: 'Every time I open Ulysses, I re-Joyce'. For an intelligent woman, Monique had a dreadful line in puns.

I inherited my mother's love of language and, as a result of my somewhat unconventional education, I ended up speaking fluent French with an accent the Académie Française would have drooled over – a sure-fire recipe for being labelled a smart-arsed, wee prat by my Kilwinning classmates.

Although my forte was sport, I got little encouragement along those lines from my mother and it was a bitter blow when, at the age of fifteen, a clumsy tackle resulted in a multiple fracture of my left leg.

This put paid to any football aspirations I might have had and I spent the next two months confined to a hospital bed with my plastered leg hooked up to a Heath-Robinson contraption of pulleys and weights.

Throughout that summer, while my classmates were taking their first, tentative steps along the path of sexual awakening; fumbling fingers trying desperately to master the black art of bra-unfastening; testosterone-tortured bodies begging for the nirvana of the first knee-trembler behind the school bike shed – mother ensured I was thoroughly fitted out for adult life by having the declension of every French irregular verb at my fingertips.

I was shy at school and, despite being one of the few males in my class to avoid the tribulations of teenage acne, I was gauche and naïve in matters pertaining to the opposite sex. That all changed on the eve of my sixteenth birthday, when serendipity smiled.

It was a Friday night and I was working on my own behind the bar in The Plucked Pheasant while the solitary customer, Sadie Mason, the wife of the local undertaker, was working her way through her fourth large gin and tonic. Although she must have been twice my age, Sadie had a still-youthful, voluptuous figure. Dark roots were visible beneath her crinkly, peroxide curls and her wide mouth was plastered in ruby-red lipstick which was becoming noticeably more smudged with every passing gin.

As we were chatting away, Sadie happened to mention that her grass badly needed cutting but, unfortunately, Mr Mason was still in hospital recovering from his double hernia operation and the lawnmower was too heavy for her to handle. Offering to help seemed to be the least I could do and, the following morning, I went round to her house and mowed her lawn. Sadie was delighted. She said she didn't know how to express her gratitude but she had a fertile imagination and when she found out it was my birthday she insisted we do it again, but this time it was her turn to be blindfolded and handcuffed to the bedposts.

During the weeks and months that followed, Mr Mason's slow

convalescence meant he had to make do with trusses of a different kind and there were many occasions when Sadie had to call upon the services of her *strapping lad*, as she endearingly referred to me.

Despite the fact she hadn't allowed me to study French at school, my mother was determined that I should get a qualification commensurate with the work she had put into educating me, so she browbeat my headmaster into allowing me to take French as part of my final year exams. I obtained good grades in Higher French and English, along with respectable results in maths and science. I desperately wanted to escape from Kilbirnie to go to university, however, it wouldn't have been fair to leave Monique to handle the pub on her own so I enrolled on an Open University course, studying literature and philosophy. This suited my mother down to the ground as it meant she could continue to oversee my education and for the next three years my life was a curious hybrid of Plato and ploughman's, of Burns and bar towels, of Descartes and darts, of Macaulay and McEwan's, of Sadie Mason and sadomasochism, although all of this did little to resolve what for many Ayrshire lads is life's most momentous decision – whether to support Ayr United or Kilmarnock.

Although my father had been a lifelong Killie fan, I opted for Ayr because I'd fallen in love with the ocean. After every home match, no matter the weather, I would wander off on my own and trudge for miles along the sandy beach. My favourite time of year was the depths of winter when the shore was deserted, the tide was in, and huge, sand-saturated, Atlantic rollers would come crashing over the esplanade. I'd happily spend hours on end huddled in a shelter, hypnotised by the waves and gazing out to sea, daydreaming of adventure and romance. Deep down, I knew I was different from my peers. Having spent my adolescence closeted with Daniel Defoe and Jules Verne, I craved a broader outlook in life and travel beyond away matches in Berwick.

When I graduated from the Open University I had no idea what career I wanted to pursue. In order to postpone making a decision, I spent the following year commuting to Jordanhill College of Education in Glasgow, returning to Kilbirnie each evening to work behind the bar in The Plucked Pheasant.

One particularly wet May morning, right out of the blue, Monique announced that she'd formed a meaningful relationship with Me Sung, the owner of the Chinese take-away in the adjoining street and, to the best of my knowledge, the only other foreigner ever to take up residence in Kilbirnie. Me Sung was a slightly built man with narrow, sloping shoulders, slim arms and delicate, bony hands. He had engaging, twinkling eyes and a generous smile.

I got on very well with him and it was he who introduced me to the ancient Chinese practices of energy healing. He taught me to understand my *qi*, the life energy that permeates all living beings. He patiently explained the relevance of *qigong*, the way to control and purify one's body and mind and thus achieve physical and mental peace. He taught me the *ying* techniques of meditation and he schooled me in *dong gong*, the exclamatory cries and striking, mannered poses of *qigong*. On Sunday mornings, during long walks in Kilbirnie's public park, Me Sung and I would practise The Five Animal Frolics of *dong gong* which, it has to be said, did little for the inner peace of the pensioners snoozing on the park benches.

That summer, Monique and Me Sung went off on holiday to Peking and a week later I received an unexpected letter:

Dear Frank,

I hope this doesn't come as too great a shock, but Me Sung proposed to me last night and I accepted. We've decided to settle in Peking. As you know, Me Sung's uncle died last month and left him his haberdashery store. Well, we had a family conference this morning and we've decided to convert the premises into the city's first real ale and karaoke bar. It's a fantastic opportunity. I'll be able to use my contacts in Scotland to order the beer, Me Sung will take care of the food and his brother, Ho, who has spent the last ten years in

Manchester, has the most incredible collection of karaoke tapes.
I'll send you all the details later – and I'll sort out your finances.
For now, I just wanted to give you the news. I'm so excited.
Lots of love,
Mum.

Over the weeks that followed, Monique and I corresponded regularly and I could tell from the tone of her letters that she was idyllically happy. She sent me instructions about which clothes and books she wanted shipped out to China and she took great delight in telling me she'd taken to Mandarin like a Peking duck to water. Monique and Me Sung had a quiet wedding ceremony and Me Sung's cousin, Lok Chan, who came to Kilbirnie to take over the Chinese take-away, brought me a bulging album of wedding photos.

My mother set me up with an adequate monthly income and she arranged for the premises of The Plucked Pheasant and the pub licence to be transferred to my name. I wasn't convinced this was the lifestyle I wanted but for the next few months I kept the pub ticking over. When I got round to balancing the books and realised I was drinking more beer than I was selling, I reckoned it was time to make a clean break. My first thought was to board up the pub and just take off. Then I remembered cousin Lachlan – he of the sheepdog look and the hangdog expression. Lachlan McClure, the only son of my father's twin brother, was several years older than I. He lived on his own in a council flat on the outskirts of Ayr.

The following Saturday I went through to Ayr an hour early for the match. The ring on Lachlan's bell roused him from his bed and he shuffled to the front door in dressing gown and slippers. Using both hands, he parted the mane of scruffy, blonde hair tumbling over his forehead and tucked it behind his ears as he stood in the doorway, blinking, his bloodshot eyes struggling to adjust to the daylight.

"Och, it's yersel', Frank. Whit the hell are you wantin'?"

"Thought you might fancy goin' tae the gemme?"

"Whit are you bletherin' aboot? Whit gemme?"

"We're at hame tae Clydebank this afternoon."

"Huv you lost yer fuckin' marbles, or somethin'?"

"Are you no' askin' me in?"

"Suit yersel'!" Lachlan turned on his heel and scuffed his way back along the unlit corridor, scratching at the back of his head with one hand and at his bum with the other. I followed him into the lounge where the curtains were still tightly drawn. He flicked on the top light. The stale stench filling the room said cheap wine, the clay pipe in the ashtray and Lachlan's sunken, bloodshot eyes said crack cocaine.

"Any news o' a job yet, Lachlan?"

"Couple o' things in the offin'." The stock response. "There's a vacancy fur a night watchman comin' up in Prestwick next week an' there's maybe the chance o' a janitor's job, but that wid mean movin' up tae Glesca."

As far as I was aware, Lachlan had never done a day's work in his life. By now, he was probably unemployable. "I'm thinkin' o' goin' away fur a wee while," I said.

"Aye?"

"I wis wonderin' if you might fancy movin' intae The Plucked Pheasant?"

He looked at me uncomprehendingly. "Whit the hell are you witterin' on aboot, Frank?"

"I'm no' suggestin' you run the pub or nothin' like that. I jist thought you might want tae make use o' the livin' quarters. There's a lot mair room than you huv here – an' there widny be any rent."

He looked me up and down as the drug-addled remnants of his brain struggled to assimilate this proposition. "Aye." He nodded and again parted his unwashed mane with both hands, tucking his hair more firmly behind his ears. "Aye, that's no' a bad idea, son." He scratched vigorously at his backside.

My gaze wandered around the room. Buckled beer cans lobbed behind the settee, numerous cigarette burns in the nylon carpet beside the armchair, overflowing ashtrays, greasy plates stacked on top of the television set, thick dust on the coffee table, God only knows how many fish supper wrapping papers stuffed into the fireplace. I was already beginning to regret my burst of altruism. "Huv a think aboot it then, Lachlan. Come roun' tomorrow afternoon if you like, and huv a look ower the place afore you make up yer mind."

Lachlan pulled a battered packet of cigarettes and a book of matches from his dressing-gown pocket. "Aye, I'll dae that." He lit up, dropping the spent match on to the carpet, then inhaled deeply. Pursing his mouth, he blew an almost perfect smoke ring. "By the way, that wis nice o' you, son. I mean – thinkin' o' me – an' that."

I was in a chirpy mood when I got home. Ayr had recently added a couple of French players to their squad and I'd spent an enjoyable afternoon participating in the banter when they came to the touch line to collect the ball for a throw-in. I'd even picked up a couple of new expressions. To round off an excellent day, we'd come back from a goal down at half-time to scrape through two-one, although our winning goal was clearly offside.

I spent that evening sorting out my possessions in preparation for my departure. Having gathered together all my items of sentimental value, I laid them out neatly on my bed and I spent a nostalgic moment with each one before packing them carefully into a dented biscuit tin; the autographed match programme the year Ayr United reached the semi-final of the League Cup, my medal for winning the under-fifteens' Ayrshire football league, the tiny gold locket containing a black and white photograph of my mother when she was eighteen, my father's wedding ring. Having fetched a stepladder from the basement, I climbed up to the loft and stowed the biscuit tin in the far corner, underneath a black tarpaulin.

A week later, I bade good-bye to the comatose Lachlan stretched out on my settee and, taking my courage and my Larousse in both hands, I caught an overnight bus from Glasgow to London.

CHAPTER 2

I managed to find a bedsit I could just about afford in Kilburn High Road, but I never really adjusted to city life. Soon after I arrived I applied for a job as a supply teacher in an inner-city sink school but, even though they were three teachers short, the Bangladeshi headmaster turned me down because he couldn't understand my accent and he reckoned the kids would have the same problem. I had a similar reaction when I enquired about a teaching vacancy in Barking and I quickly came to the conclusion that an educational career in London was going to be a non-starter, not without a sense of frustration that I, who had never knowingly split an infinitive or ended a sentence with a preposition, could barely make myself understood beyond the confines of my native town.

I signed on the dole and for the next few weeks I spent most mornings browsing the situations vacant in the local Labour Exchange and most afternoons slouched in front of the television in my bedsit, a can of lager clamped in my fist, letting the afternoon soaps wash over me. I quickly became bored with these programmes and I actually spent the whole of one drunken afternoon watching a debate in Parliament, baying and bleating away with the best of them, apparently to the consternation of the old bat in the flat upstairs who reported her suspicions to the RSPCA.

Eventually I realised I'd have to stop feeling aggrieved with the world and get a grip of my life, otherwise I'd have to face the prospect of crawling back to Kilbirnie with my tail between my legs. Redoubling my efforts to find employment, I studied the vacancies where communication skills were not of the essence, finally opting for a job as a traffic warden in Kilburn, my contribution to my roots being never to give a parking ticket to any car displaying an *Ecosse* sticker.

The thing I missed most about being away from Scotland was going to football matches, but there was no obvious solution to my predicament as my upbringing had made me congenitally incapable of supporting any team containing an Englishman. My dilemma was resolved when the landlord in my local told me about Chelsea.

Despite this, I wasn't happy with my lot. I hadn't made any real friends in London and to say my sex life was intermittent would be erring on the side of exaggeration. One evening, sitting on my own in a pub in Swiss Cottage, flicking through the *Evening Standard* while debating the meaning of life with my pint of lager, a small advert caught my eye: *Are you a University Graduate? Do you speak fluent French? Have you ever considered a career with MI6?* I was, I did, and I hadn't, but Sean Connery had instilled a bit of the 007 in me, so I jotted down the phone number in the back of my diary.

I called the following morning. The person who answered couldn't provide me with any details about the vacancy over the phone, but he took my name and address and made an appointment for me to see a Ms Kathleen Morrison in a week's time.

I felt as if I was entering a forbidden world as I walked up to the entrance of the brown, marble-clad building on the south side of Vauxhall Bridge. The guard at reception checked my name against the appointments' register and I was escorted through a maze of brightly lit corridors to a small office in the bowels of the building.

Kathleen Morrison turned out to be the personal assistant to Stanley Frobisher-Allen, the Director-General of MI6. She was about my age, perhaps a little younger, smartly dressed in an off-white blouse, velvet jacket and matching knee-length skirt, but her otherwise efficient manner was betrayed by her straggly, mousy-brown hair which was piled on top of her head in an old-fashioned bun from which several strands had escaped and entangled themselves around the legs of her black-framed spectacles.

Kathleen informed me that her involvement in the selection process went only as far as the initial screening and that my main interview would be conducted by the Director-General himself.

"Is that no' a bit heavy?"

"You could say that. Mr Frobisher-Allen doesn't normally involve himself in hiring decisions, but he's got a specific interest in this mission so he's decided to interview all the prospective candidates personally."

I listened attentively while Kathleen spoke and I thought I detected a slight accent. "You're no', by any chance, frae Ayrshire, Ms Morrison?"

"Well spotted! My family come from Ardrossan, but I moved south four years ago. I thought I'd lost my accent," she added with a smile. "And you're from Kilbirnie," she continued. "Your father was a coal miner, turned publican, and your mother's French. After your father died your mother remarried and she's now running a karaoke bar in Peking."

"Bloody amazin' whit you people can tell frae an accent!"

Kathleen laughed. "You've been positively vetted, Frank. I even happen to know that you were in the same class in school in Kilwinning as my brother, Andrew, and that you and I are practically neighbours in Kilburn."

"You lot dae yer homework," I nodded. "I'll gie you that."

"We have to. The job you're being interviewed for is very sensitive so we need to run a thorough check on all prospective candidates before we divulge any details of the mission."

"That a' sounds very intriguin', Ms Morrison. Whit's the mission, then?"

"I'd better leave Mr Frobisher-Allen to explain that."

Kathleen smoothed down her skirt as she got to her feet, then she led the way to a top floor suite on the other side of the building, where she paused in front of a solid, wooden door. "Don't be put off," she whispered. "His bark's a lot worse than his bite." Giving me a quick, reassuring smile, she pushed open the door and ushered me inside.

I stepped across the threshold and found myself in a spacious, air-conditioned office with floor-to-ceiling windows which gave a magnificent view across the Thames towards Millbank and the Tate Gallery. Stanley Frobisher-Allen, CBE, was seated behind a wide, mahogany desk. I stood in the doorway and cleared my throat but he continued to peruse the document he was studying without acknowledging my presence. When he eventually glanced up, he peered at me over the top of his half-moon, gold-rimmed spectacles as he rose slowly to his feet, signalling to me to come across. My footsteps made no sound on the plush carpet as I approached his desk. He stretched across, shook my hand and indicated a seat for me. Eyeing me carefully, he sank back down on his black-leather, swivel chair.

Frobisher-Allen wasn't a particularly tall man but his ramrod-straight bearing gave him an aura of authority, as did the narrow, clipped moustache which looked as if it had been stencilled to his upper lip. He was dapper in a blue pinstripe suit, starched white shirt and MCC tie, however, his complexion was an unhealthy shade of grey, bearing witness to a lifestyle which rarely saw natural light. Our initial contact was difficult because he seemed to be struggling to keep up while I gave him a résumé of my background.

"Perhaps you might care to repeat that for me in French, Mr McClure?" he suggested. "So I can get a feel for your competence in the language."

I obliged and he was so impressed he insisted we conduct the rest of the interview in French.

"*Pas de problème.*"

When I asked what the job entailed, Frobisher-Allen informed me that MI6 were in rapid-expansion mode in response to the increased threat from global terrorism. Experienced agents were being transferred to front-line hotspots and graduate trainees were being brought on board to backfill them and also to support the new missions MI6 had been allocated, one of which was to monitor the British expatriate community in France. To that end, he was in the process of assigning an operative to each French *département* to carry out a surveillance mission – and there was currently a vacancy in the Hérault.

"What, exactly, does a surveillance mission entail?" I asked

"Surveillance?" He raised his eyebrows. "Not too difficult a concept to grasp, I wouldn't have thought? You watch." He spread his fingers wide and drummed his manicured fingernails on the polished desk. "And you listen." He drummed again rhythmically in time to his words. "And you report back what you find out. It's hardly rocket science," he added with a condescending smirk and a final rat-a-tat-tat.

I wasn't sure if this was some kind of test, but it felt more like I was being patronised. "You mean you want to know the number of Sloane Rangers I see sunbathing topless? How many cars with GB stickers drive in bus lanes? Number of Brits farting in public? That sort of thing?"

"Don't be facetious, McClure," he snapped. "I mean people indulging in anti-British activities that might be of interest to Her Majesty's government."

"Such as?"

"Such as whining about the British government's attitude towards Europe, such as complaining about the level of the British state pension, such as praising the French national health service and the railways in comparison with their British counterparts."

"That's anti-British?"

Frobisher-Allen's bottom lip sucked hard on his pencil moustache. "It's the thin end of the wedge, McClure. It's a small step from grumbling about British institutions to writing to *The Times*, petitioning Members of Parliament, organising protests and mobilising public demonstrations. The present government is very image-conscious and it believes in nipping such things in the bud. The Hérault is a particularly sensitive assignment because we have reason to believe there are political activists in the Montpellier area and we want to smoke them out. We need an agent who can infiltrate the

British expatriate community while pretending not to speak English. Got a bit of a head start there," he muttered, half under his breath, but loud enough for me to hear. The condescending smirk returned. He totally ignored my attempt at a withering look.

Frobisher-Allen went on to ask me various questions about my family background and work experience and, as the interview progressed, I came to the conclusion that he was everything you'd expect from a senior civil servant – smooth, confident, arrogant, opinionated, sarcastic, cynical and overbearing.

"What will be done with the information I send back?" I asked.

"We'll use it to deal with the troublemakers, as appropriate."

"What'll happen to them?"

"We'll make their life untenable. It doesn't take a great deal. Little things like reporting their undeclared Channel Islands' bank accounts to the French tax authorities can be extremely effective."

"What if they don't have any?"

"Don't be naïve!"

I looked at him quizzically. "Is that legal?"

Frobisher-Allen looked genuinely puzzled. "I'm not at all sure you understand the political processes, McClure. We are MI6. We're leading-edge. We try out new ideas on behalf of the government of the day and, if they're successful, we make them legal. Now I do admit we're in the dog days of a pretty tired administration." Frobisher-Allen stroked his chin reflectively as he spoke. "It's a long time since this lot came up with the vestige of an intelligent idea. With the general election imminent, they're in what we professionals call 'straw-clutching mode'. But that's neither here nor there." Pulling off his glasses, he breathed heavily on to the lenses as he tugged a monogrammed handkerchief from his breast pocket. There was a far away look in his eyes and a faint smile played at the corners of his mouth as he carefully polished each lens in turn. "I'm just a humble civil servant, dedicated to serving my political masters." I imagined a vision of a parchment containing the next New Year's Honours list to be unfurling before his eyes.

Replacing his spectacles, Frobisher-Allen snapped out of his reverie. "Well, McClure, as I was saying, there's currently a vacancy for a surveillance operative in the Hérault. I've interviewed several candidates for this position, but none of them had your competence in the language. As you would appear to be eminently qualified, I'm prepared to offer you the post. The initial contract would be for a period of twelve months, attracting a salary of thirty thousand pounds, plus expenses."

"Sounds a damn sight more interesting than doling out parking tickets in Kilburn," I said with a quick nod of the head. "I'll give it a go."

"Good chap!"

"Are the French authorities aware of this activity?"

"Most certainly not!" Frobisher-Allen's eyes narrowed. "Do not underestimate the delicacy of the situation, McClure." There was an edge to his voice. "This is an *extremely* sensitive mission. If the French were to get wind of the fact that we have agents on their territory they'd kick up the most almighty political stink. Without wishing to appear melodramatic, if you fall foul of the French authorities, for any reason whatsoever, we'll disown you." He coughed harshly and fussily adjusted his tie knot.

"After you've signed the Official Secrets Act," he continued, "you will be issued with a new identity. You'll be given a fax number to which you will transmit a status report every week, detailing whatever subversive comments you have overheard, together with the identities of the perpetrators. You will also be given a phone number which will allow you to make contact with headquarters, but this is to be used only in an emergency. You will commit both of these numbers to memory. One further point. Do not, under any circumstances, use a mobile phone for your communications." He caught my puzzled frown. "Cell phone signals are incredibly easy to intercept and trace.

"As cover," he continued, "we've organised a job for you in The Book Cellar, which is a retail outlet for English language books in the centre of Montpellier. The shop is run by an Englishman called

Charles Benson. Benson knows nothing of your identity or your mission. Last month he placed an advert in the local press for a trainee sales assistant and, via an agency, we submitted an application informing him there was a candidate from Alsace who was keen to move south and who would be prepared to work for the national minimum wage. Benson accepted the application on condition that the person would be available to start by the beginning of August. We'll fax him today and let him know you're on your way."

Frobisher-Allen half-rose to his feet and stretched across the desk to take my hand in a firm grip. "Welcome on board, Mr McClure – or, I should say – Monsieur Jérôme Dumas."

Following my interview, Kathleen helped me fill in the official application forms and I had to sign a mound of confidentiality agreements. When the paperwork was completed she suggested we have lunch together and she took me to a quiet salad bar on the opposite side of Vauxhall Bridge.

"Whit dae you recommend?" I asked.

"Do you like tuna?"

"Sure."

Kathleen held up two fingers in the direction of the waitress.

"Is this your regular haunt?"

She gave a wry smile. "I know I'm in a rut when they don't even bother giving me the menu any more. Monday's tuna salad, Tuesday it's cottage cheese, Wednesday's quiche, Thursday's chicken and on Fridays I splash out and have scallops. And every day, a chilled Perrier. Always the same table, always twelve thirty on the dot." She broke off as the waitress brought across two tuna salads and two bottles of Perrier. "And, apart from once in a blue moon," she added with a sigh, "always on my own." Casting down her eyes, she fiddled with the side of her fork to cut through a lettuce leaf, then she dropped the fork on to her plate while she tucked away a flopping strand of loose hair.

When we got back to the office, Kathleen organised a month's salary advance for me in cash and I was issued with a passport, *carte bleue* credit card, cheque book, *carte d'identité* and driving licence in the name of Jérôme Dumas. An account was opened in my name at the main branch of the Crédit Agricole bank in Montpellier, into which, I was informed, my salary would be paid on the twenty-sixth of each month, using an agency as an intermediary to ensure there could be no link back to MI6.

I was instructed to hand in my British passport and driving licence the following morning and told to report to the MI6 technology unit for a briefing on my equipment. I was sort of hoping 'Q' might be there in person to explain the rocket-launching controls in the Aston Martin, the laser-beam in the pen and the bullets concealed in the cigarette case. It turned out to be Tom Ivinson.

"Good morning, Jérôme." Ivinson was looking past me as I walked into his office. I glanced back over my shoulder. "First mistake, son."

I felt my freckles redden. "Sorry, Mr Ivinson."

Ivinson's cheery, ruddy features beamed back at me. "The name's Tom," he announced in a deep, West Country accent as he bounded across the room to pump my fist. "Don't worry about it. Your reaction was natural enough, but you have got to get used to your new identity as quickly as possible. Responding to 'Jérôme' has to become second nature. This is the dossier on Jérôme Dumas," he said, tapping a thick, manila folder lying on his desk. "It tells you everything you might ever need to know – where you were born, what schools you went to, what your father and your grandfathers did for a living. Your whole family history's in there, even down to your cousin Albine who abandoned her husband and five kids to run off with a butcher from Grenoble. You have to live the part, so study it carefully," he said, handing me the folder. "As well as responding automatically to 'Jérôme', there are a few other things you'll find tricky at first, such as not reacting when someone speaks English. You've seen the second world war movie where the Germans trap the escaping British officers by wishing them 'good luck' when they're off guard?" I nod. "Watch out for that. This isn't a nine to five job, Jérôme. You have to be on your toes at all times.

More agents blow their cover by a simple, careless mistake than anything else."

"Will you be snippin' the labels aff ma underwear, Tom, so ma nationality canny be identified if I'm captured?"

"I'm not sure that would prove too difficult a task for an experienced interrogator, son."

"Whit will I do aboot accommodation in Montpellier?"

"That's taken care of. You'll be staying in a gîte in a village called St Martin de Londres, which is about forty kilometres north of Montpellier." He took a set of keys and a slip of paper from his desk drawer and handed them to me. "That's the address. It's actually a converted farmhouse, which is owned by MI6. Make sure you leave the place tidy," he added. "Frobisher-Allen and his missus often go there on holiday when the place isn't being used for official business." I smiled. "There's a car available to you," he added. "A Peugeot 206. It's in the garage adjoining the house. You'll find the keys hanging on a hook in the kitchen."

From the same desk drawer, Tom produced a cellophane-covered package and unwrapped it carefully to reveal a small, cardboard box. "This may look like an ordinary wrist watch, Jérôme," he said, prising open the lid and handing me the watch. "It does, of course, tell the time, but it also incorporates a miniature microphone and recording device. There's five hours' playing time on each cassette and there are half a dozen spares in the box. You can overwrite the cassettes when you've finished with them."

Tom proceeded to show me how to operate the record and playback functions by depressing various combinations of buttons on the side of the watch.

Not exactly licensed to kill. Still, it was a start.

CHAPTER 3

It's a scorching Saturday afternoon in late July and the sun is directly overhead. The engine note changes abruptly and we bank steeply, allowing me an unobstructed view of the plane's flitting shadow as it smudges its way across a succession of parched vineyards and inland waterways. I continue peering through the scratched cabin window as the almost full Ryanair flight crosses the southern French coastline and loops out over the sea before swinging back for the long, low approach to Montpellier's Meditérranée airport. Through the shimmering heat haze it looks as if the whole airport complex, runways included, would fit comfortably inside Stansted's terminal building.

I join the queue for passport control, then I tug my heavy suitcase from the carousel and load it on to a luggage trolley under the watchful gaze of three heavily-armed military personnel. I pass unmolested into the arrivals' area and I'm looking around for someone to ask directions when it suddenly strikes me that I've never actually communicated in French with anyone other than my mother, Stanley Frobisher-Allen and the Ayr United midfield. I go across to the newspaper kiosk and speak hesitantly to the assistant and I'm relieved when my accent is readily understood. Having purchased a street plan of Montpellier town centre and a large-scale map of the surrounding district, I catch a shuttle bus into town.

The journey takes about twenty minutes and throughout the trip I trace the route we're taking on my map. Ten minutes on the motorway to the outskirts of town, then we cross the river Lez and drive through the Antigone, an ultra-modern complex designed in the architectural style of ancient Greece. All the buildings – offices, houses, shops, restaurants, even the imposing public library – are built from slabs of the same off-white stone, a colour my mother would have referred to as 'pale biscuit'. I shield my eyes from the glare reflecting off the buildings and I continue to gaze through the window as we speed past a succession of sweeping terraces, well-watered lawns, high archways, towering pillars, Greek statues and spacious courtyards.

We leave the Antigone behind and enter the old part of the city and I alight at the bus terminus, not far from the railway station. I'm not due to start work until Monday but I've arranged to drop into The Book Cellar this afternoon to introduce myself to Charles Benson so I unfold my street map in an attempt to orient myself. Having figured out the approximate general direction, I lug my case up Rue Maguelone, stopping for a breather when I come to the busy, café-lined Place de la Comédie. An ornate statue of Les Trois Grâces dominates the middle of the square. The moss-covered plinth is studded with stone figures – hard to tell from this distance whether they're cherubs or gargoyles – and water is gushing out from several small fountains around the base. I make my way across to the statue and cup cold water in both hands, splashing it on to my face and neck. With my suitcase in one hand and my street plan in the other, I then thread my way through a maze of narrow, criss-crossing alleyways until I reach the cobbled lane where The Book Cellar is situated. My right arm is aching as I push open the squeaky door.

Slouched behind the horseshoe-shaped counter, to the left of the doorway, a fifty-something, bespectacled, basking walrus is dozing in a faded, Paisley-pattern armchair from which twisted springs and dirty, brown stuffing protrude through various punctured seams. A thick, black moustache curves round the corners of his top lip and horizontal folds of rutted skin ripple upwards from his eyebrows – taut ridges of flesh which traverse his forehead and encroach on to his scalp before burrowing beneath his thinning, grey hair which is stretched back tightly and tied at the nape of his neck with a satin ribbon. He has a ruddy face with heavy, slack jowls and tufts of black nasal hair, sprouting from his vein-lined nostrils, merge into his dense moustache.

I glance around the cavernous bookshop with its high, vaulted ceiling and stone walls thick enough to insulate the place from the heat of the sun. Little natural light penetrates the small, bevelled windows and the solitary, low-voltage electric light bulb, dangling from the ceiling, serves to cast shadows rather than illuminate. Stretching back from the counter, five narrow aisles separate rows of high, dusty bookshelves crammed higgledy-piggledy with an assortment of new and seemingly very old volumes. Stacked against the far wall are piles of boxed video cassettes and DVDs. The atmosphere is dank and heavy with the smell of stale tobacco.

Roused from his slumber by the squeak of the door hinges, Charles Benson's head jerks up and his rheumy eyes start blinking rhythmically behind the thick lenses of his spectacles. When he pulls himself to his feet I see he is a tall man, quite a bit taller than I, but his posture is poor, his slouched shoulders and curved spine concertina-ing his neck into his corpulent frame. He is wearing an open-necked, short-sleeved, patterned shirt and a pair of garish Bermuda shorts strain to cover his flabby belly. His puffy, bare feet are encased in sweat-stained, leather sandals and a red, silk handkerchief is dangling foppishly from the expanding watch bracelet on his left wrist.

"Monsieur Benson?" I enquire. He nods. When I introduce myself, he comes out from behind the counter and shambles towards me, taking my proffered hand in a limp handshake, fingertips only. He greets me in excellent French, almost as fluent as my own, albeit with a pronounced north of England accent. "None of this *Monsieur Benson* nonsense, Jérôme, the name's Charles," he gushes. We've hardly exchanged pleasantries and he's already addressing me in the familiar *tu* form – mother would certainly not approve.

Charles shuffles to the back of the shop to fetch an upright, wooden chair and, when we're both seated, he asks me about my background. I recount Jérôme Dumas' résumé, which I've learned by heart. Born and brought up in Alsace, son of a pig farmer, recent messy divorce from an unfaithful German wife, love of sunshine so moving to the

Midi to make a fresh start; Celtic blood somewhere in the lineage – hence the red hair; very keen to learn English, so hoping to make contact with the British expatriate community.

Charles listens attentively and as soon as I've finished he suggests a cup of tea. Without waiting for my response, he pulls himself to his feet and waddles down one of the aisles to the accompaniment of creaking floorboards. I watch him duck low as he passes under the lintel of the doorway leading to the storeroom and I hear the sound of a kettle being filled. I stand up to stretch my spine, still stiff from being cramped in the plane, and I browse through the bookshelves, pausing when I come across a battered copy of *Ulysses*. My eye is skimming down a familiar passage when Charles' call from the storeroom interrupts my train of thought.

"Do you take your tea weak or strong, Jérôme?"

"I'm no' fussy – it's a' the same tae – " I break off and bite painfully into my bottom lip. Distracted by reading the text, I'd replied in English. I screw up my eyes as an image of Tom Ivinson, shaking his head reproachfully, invades my consciousness.

"Sorry, Jérôme!" Charles shouts. "I didn't catch what you said." I heave an enormous sigh of relief. The car engine revving up outside must've drowned my response.

I revert quickly to French. "I take it as it comes, thanks." With a trembling hand I close *Ulysses* and replace the volume carefully on the shelf, at the same time remonstrating with myself and resolving to maintain one hundred per cent concentration on my role from now on.

Charles returns a few minutes later with two brimming mugs on a tray, along with a saucer containing several slices of lemon. Plucking a half-smoked cigar from the ashtray on the counter, he lights up and, as we sit sipping our tea, he fills me in on the history of Montpellier: three universities, including the oldest medical faculty in Europe, a resident population of two hundred and thirty thousand, swollen during term time by over sixty thousand students, of which well over fifty per cent are female. I notice him drool at this latter statement and his eyes start to glaze over. After a few frozen seconds he twitches his neck muscles, which seems to kick-start his blinking. Using his silk handkerchief, he wipes away the traces of saliva from the corners of his mouth before continuing.

"The Book Cellar's only been going for a couple of years, but we're in a real cut-throat business, I can tell you. In the whole of London there are only a couple of outlets for French books, but Montpellier has three English bookshops within a square kilometre. And we're all after the same market – the student population. The Book in Bar, which is just round the corner, is comparatively new, but The Bookshop in the Rue de l'Université is well established. It's owned by a street-wise Londoner who's managed to corner most of the student market. The bugger teaches English at the university as well, so he's got all the right contacts. Text books are the real money spinner. Ninety per cent of my turnover comes during September when the scholastic year begins. The rest of the time the shop ticks over by selling popular fiction to the British expatriate community, with a bit of video and DVD rental on the side."

Charles breaks off to sip his tea. "The pattern of sales is nothing like a bookshop in England where you'd carry a few copies of everything and operate on a sale or return basis with your suppliers. If I tried to run the business along those lines I'd go bust within a month because the cost of shipping and returning books is more than the profit margin." He takes a long pull on his cigar. "The key to success is selectivity and understanding the snobbish nature of the expatriate market. If a book is trendy, I'll sell fifty copies in a month, if not, sweet bugger all. The trick is being able to forecast when a particular novel's about to take off and then get fast deliveries.

"I even have clients in Spain who place orders through me and whose sole criterion for wanting a book is that I've already taken twenty orders – which, as you might imagine, does leave scope for a bit of creative market manipulation!" Charles grins and rubs his thumb and forefingers together meaningfully. "The sangria set can't bear to miss out on the latest fad. Not that they've got the remotest intention of reading any of the stuff, you understand. They're more than happy to pay a bit over the odds, just so they can say they were the first in Malaga to have the book on their coffee table. As an aside, when consignments of books arrive from England, you'll sometimes find packages pre-addressed to customers in Spain. When you come across these, just take them to the post office and pop them into the mail as quickly as possible."

Charles shuffles back to the storeroom to refill our mugs before continuing with my briefing. "As for your duties, Jérôme, The Book Cellar's opening hours are from ten till one and three till seven, Monday to Saturday. I'll be here next Monday morning to give you a handover, but once you're up to speed with how things operate I'll leave you to get on with it, apart from the busy period in September when I'll work alongside you."

Charles asks me for my bank details so he can arrange for my salary to be paid directly into my account and, having sorted out that and a few other administrative matters, he proceeds to tell me about British activities in the city.

"Most of the events are run by the British Expatriates' Club, which is an association that organises soirées for Brits and French anglophiles. There are various themes, ranging from wine *dégustations* and pastis parties to Guinness guzzling gatherings and whisky tasting evenings. Unfortunately, you've missed this year's Vicars and Tarts party. It was a real hoot. Here, let me show you."

He rummages under the counter until he comes across a flimsy, amateurish newsletter entitled the *BEC Thunderer* which contains barely recognisable, badly photocopied, black and white photographs of a collection of debauched, middle-aged vicars and over-ripe tarts. "That's me," he says, pointing proudly to a supine figure, eyes closed, dog-collar popped, vodka bottle clutched tightly to its bosom. "It was a smashing night. You've also just missed our annual Burns' Supper which we held in July this year because it took me until then to smuggle the haggis across. The French are paranoid about importing British meat products and if they ever found out that I'd sneaked in ten kilos of haggis in a shipment of books they'd go ballistic!" He grins broadly. "Anyway, I don't reckon you'd have understood much of what goes on at a Burns' Supper, Jérôme. It's way beyond me, I don't mind telling you." I have to struggle to hold back a smile. "Besides," he adds, "I don't think a bunch of rat-arsed Jocks stuffing their faces with haggis and whisky while rabbiting on about their Tam O'Shanters and their Holy Willies would exactly be conducive to teaching you the Queen's English, eh?" He slaps my back and laughs heartily. I have to struggle to hold back a punch.

"The BEC have a regular get together on Friday evenings in Fitzpatrick's Irish pub in the Place St Côme," Charles says. "You should go along there once you've settled in."

"I might give it a try."

"Talking about settling in," Charles says. "What are you going to do about accommodation?"

"That's all sorted. I've rented a gîte in a place called St Martin de Londres. Do you know it?"

"Sure. It's a nice enough village, if a bit remote. You'll be needing transport if you're going to be staying there."

I nod. "That's organised, too. My car in Alsace was clapped out – no way it would have made the journey south, so I've arranged to take a car on a three-month lease until I find one I can afford. If everything's gone to plan, the car should've been delivered to the gîte by now. Do you live in town, Charles?" I ask.

"I should be so lucky! Property prices in Montpellier are prohibitive – they've gone through the roof in recent years. When I arrived in this part of the world a couple of years ago, I bought a shell of a farmhouse with a view to renovating it. It's in a place called Le Vigan, about seventy kilometres north of here. If I'd realised what I was taking on I'd have thought twice about it. There's an unbelievable amount of work still to be done just to make the place habitable. The house doesn't even have a roof, for God's sake! There's a caravan on site which

I'm actually living in for now. However, by the time I've finished a day's work here and driven up to Le Vigan, I'm usually too knackered to do anything to the house, so I've taken to kipping down on a camp bed in the storeroom during the week and only going up to Le Vigan at weekends. That's the main reason I decided to take on an assistant, so I can spend more time working on my house. Before I forget, I'd better leave you my phone number in Le Vigan in case you need to get in touch," he says, scribbling a number down on a post-it and sticking it to the side of the horseshoe counter.

"Have you always been in the bookshop business?" I ask.

Charles drains his mug and smacks his lips. "As a matter of fact, this is my first venture, though I've always been into buying and selling in some shape or form. I'm a bit of a nomad. I started out trading coins and stamps in Munich, then I had a toy shop in Barcelona for a couple of years and after that I tried my hand at flogging jeans and T-shirts in Auxerre, but there was no money in that. My last enterprise was a record store in Bordeaux."

Charles proceeds to show me how to operate the telephone answering machine and the fax and he explains the intricacies of the stock control system on the computer. "Do you surf?" he asks, smiling at my blank expression. "I don't mean Bondi-beach style. The Internet. Do you surf the Net?"

I shake my head. "I've never got involved."

"You really ought to give it a go. It's a fascinating old world. Occasionally, orders for books come in via e-mail, but don't worry about that. I'll download them when I drop by. Anyway, the Internet access is password protected and you've got enough on your plate to be going on with. Hey, is it that time!" he exclaims, glancing at his watch. "Time we were shutting up shop." He pulls himself to his feet. "How are you getting to St Martin de Londres?"

"I'm going to pick up a taxi."

"No need for that. I can drop you off."

"Are you sure?"

"No problem. I'm heading up to Le Vigan now and St Martin is more or less on my way."

"Thanks a lot."

Locking up the premises, Charles hands me a duplicate set of keys before leading the way to an underground car park near the Préfecture.

It's a thirty minute drive to St Martin de Londres where we find my gîte with no great difficulty, an isolated, stone-built cottage situated at the end of a twisting lane, some two hundred metres back from the main road. I've invited Charles in to sample the whisky I'd picked up at Stansted Airport before it strikes me that one wouldn't normally acquire a litre bottle of malt while travelling between Alsace and the south of France. To pre-empt any awkward questions, I invent the fact that I'd stopped off to visit friends on my way south and had found Isle of Jura malt whisky to be available on promotion in the Jura district of France – on a sort of twinning arrangement. Charles finds this fascinating. I sincerely hope he won't have the occasion to put it to the test in the foreseeable future. Charles isn't a connoisseur of malt whisky so he has to try two or three small measures before he can decide whether or not he likes it. Having concluded he does, he opts for large ones.

Two hours and four large ones later, Charles rises unsteadily to take his leave. Having confirmed my start date in The Book Cellar to be Monday, the first of August, two days hence, he climbs behind the wheel of his battered Volvo. As he's fumbling to wind down the window he reminds me he'll be there on Monday morning at ten o'clock sharp to give me a handover and after that he'll drop in on Friday afternoons to check everything is going all right and collect the week's takings. He roars off in a cloud of dust and diesel fumes, waving out of the window and tooting his horn as he goes. I keep waving until the car has slalomed from sight.

I rise early the following morning and set out to explore St Martin de Londres – a collection of narrow, winding streets, all of which seem to lead to the twelfth century church. The village square is compact with several cafés and small restaurants huddled around a fountain in the shade of towering plane trees.

I stock up with provisions from the various shops, all of which are open and bustling on a Sunday morning. In each establishment I'm studied with curiosity by the proprietor and my fellow customers. However, I'm deliberately vague in response to the casual enquiries as to whether monsieur's accent is from Paris? Is he enjoying his vacation? Where is he staying? How long is he planning to be in the district?

I spend the rest of the morning getting unpacked and settling into the gîte which seems to be very well equipped, apart from the fact that there's no phone. I think about dropping a line to my mother, but decide against it. During my time in London we'd kept in regular contact but, bound by the terms of the Official Secrets Act, I've mentioned nothing to her about my new job, my last letter merely stating that I was planning to do some travelling so I'd probably be out of touch for a while.

In the afternoon I decide to try to get my bearings. I'd come across a set of car keys hanging on a hook in the kitchen and, in the adjoining garage, I find a red Peugeot 206, not more than a couple of years old, with '75' number plates, indicating the vehicle was registered in Paris. To my pleasant surprise the engine kicks into life on the second turn of the key. However, this is my first experience of a left-hand drive car and my first time driving on the right-hand side of the road and I cause a fair amount of consternation as I weave my way down the main street of St Martin, my nearside wheels frequently bumping up on to the pavement as I struggle to adjust to the unfamiliar alignment of driving position and kerb. Fortunately, this evokes nothing more damning than: 'Bloody Parisian drivers!' from the local populace.

I decide to go for a spin to get the feel of it so I check my map and, taking a towering, overhanging cliff face, the Pic St Loup, as my reference point, I navigate a circular route which takes me in a clockwise loop through several sparsely populated villages before bringing me back to St Martin some forty minutes later.

I park the car in the garage and wander into the village. Stopping off for a beer in the bar in the main square, I ask the barman if there are any good restaurants in the vicinity. He recommends Les Muscardins, on the outskirts of the village. I return to the gîte for a quick shower and a change of clothes, then I stroll the kilometre or so to the restaurant where I have one of the best meals I have ever eaten, washed down with a half-bottle of the local, red wine.

The night air is still warm and I feel content with life as I amble back to the gîte. After a quick nightcap, I turn in for an early night.

CHAPTER 4

Monday morning is hot and very humid and I have the air conditioning in the car going at full blast as I set out for Montpellier before eight o'clock in an attempt to beat the commuter traffic. It's plain sailing as far as the walls of the old city, but I then become entangled in the most tortuous road system ever devised by man – a succession of one-way streets, bus-only lanes, dead ends, narrow, cobbled, twisting roads, blocking delivery lorries, interminable road works and a series of diversions where a new set of tram lines is being superimposed on the existing chaos.

Every time I pull into the side of the road to consult my map, I'm treated to a blaring cacophony from the horns of my impatient fellow-commuters. Hopelessly lost, I drive down the slope of the nearest underground car park where I abandon my vehicle and, with the aid of my street map, negotiate the two kilometres across town on foot.

It's well after ten when I arrive at The Book Cellar to find Charles waiting impatiently. He doesn't look at all happy.

"I hope this isn't going to be your normal standard of timekeeping, Jérôme?"

"I really am sorry, Charles. I thought I'd set out in plenty of time, but the traffic system defeated me totally."

"I can understand that. It does take a bit of getting used to." He seems to be mellowing. "Now let me take you through how things work around here so I can be on my way."

We get through the explanations quickly enough as we don't have the inconvenience of being interrupted by any customers. Before lunchtime, we've covered everything Charles thinks I need to know.

"Give me a call at Le Vigan if you run into any problems," Charles states as he gets to his feet. "If I don't hear from you before then, I'll drop by on Friday afternoon."

When he's gone, I wander down to the storeroom and make myself a cup of instant coffee, then I settle down behind the horseshoe counter, thumb poised over the 'record' button on my watch, eagerly awaiting the opportunity to register unsuspecting expatriates bitching about British government policies while they browse through the bookshelves. The only problem is – no one complains. Or, to be more precise – no one appears.

During my first week in the bookshop the entire custom comprises two Japanese tourists seeking directions to the railway station, three squeaky-clean Mormons trying to persuade me to stock their American language version of the Bible and, late on Thursday afternoon, just as I'm about to close, an attractive, third-year university student waltzes in and demands a refund on the video of *Henry V* because the sound track's fuzzy. The fact that the tape plays back perfectly on the shop's video machine only serves to reinforce her argument that there's something wrong with my tracking equipment because she lent the video to several other students in her class and they all experienced the same problem. To keep the peace, I give her a refund but, as there's no cash float – a point I must mention to Charles – I have to fork out the fifteen euros myself.

The one heartening aspect of my first week in The Book Cellar is that my navigation skills are coming on in leaps and bounds. On Wednesday, I managed to find my way to a car park within a couple of hundred metres of the shop, however, a new diversion was introduced the following day and I was back to my two kilometre foot-slog across town. I spent most of Thursday afternoon huddled behind the counter, poring over my map, trying to figure out a route to the car park at the bottom of the lane and, this morning, I actually succeeded in finding it.

I take out my diary and make an entry. Summary of first week in The Book Cellar. Subversive recordings – zero. Shop takings – minus fifteen euros. As Charles is due to drop in this afternoon I jot down an *aide-mémoire* to suggest we might improve profitability by closing a bit earlier on Thursdays.

Charles comes whistling through the door on the stroke of four o'clock. He doesn't seem in the least perturbed when I give him the news. "Not the best week we've ever had, certainly, but by no means the worst. I remember one time I had to give four Jocks refunds on their copies of the Braveheart video because they claimed they couldn't understand Mel Gibson's accent." Inwardly, I sympathise, but I'm sufficiently into my role by now to let the comment pass without a flicker.

"There's a couple of things I need to check out on the Net," Charles says, switching on the computer. "Be a good chap, Jérôme, and put on the kettle."

I trot off to the storeroom while Charles busies himself at the screen and by the time I return with two mugs of tea he's finished whatever he was doing and has logged off.

"Are you planning to go to Fitzpatrick's tonight?" he asks.

"I haven't really thought about it," I lie. "Will you be going?"

"You betcha! I've been trying to acquire a taste for Guinness for some time but I haven't quite got there yet, so I don't like to miss out on an opportunity to practise. It should be a good night. Come along, why don't you?"

"I don't really like to."

"Why not?"

"I feel as if I'd be a bit of a drag on the proceedings as I don't speak any English."

"Don't be daft! It's a chance to meet some Brits and get your ear attuned to the cadence of the language. Anyway, everyone who goes there can speak French, so you'll make out all right."

I allow myself to be coaxed. "Okay, I'll drop in for a while – if you're sure the others won't mind."

"Not at all." He nods enthusiastically. "Actually, I might be a bit late this evening, so I'd appreciate it if you would get three pints lined up for me. I like my Guinness to be well settled before I quaff."

Before I can commend him on his single-minded dedication to acquiring a taste for Guinness, he hurriedly takes his leave because he's running late for a Château Margaux *dégustation* in the Caves de Notre Dame. I notice he didn't even touch his tea. Damn! I meant to ask him how to negotiate the one-way system round Le Peyrou.

There's still a lot of heat in the evening air when I lock up The Book Cellar just after seven o'clock. Referring constantly to my street plan, I make my way along the crisscrossing lanes towards the Place St Côme, a small, cobbled square nestled deep in the old part of town. I see the sign for Fitzpatrick's on the far side of the square and I walk into an Irish theme pub, decked out in Celtic memorabilia. Displays of Irish bank notes adorn the walls, alongside framed photographs of Padraig Pearse and Eamon de Valera and an original road sign, attached to a pillar, indicates it's twenty seven miles to Kilkenny. A haunting, Gaelic, female voice, singing unaccompanied, is filtering out from concealed speakers.

At this early hour there are few customers. I ask the welcoming barman, in French, if any British Expatriate Club members are present. He responds in English, with a heavy Australian accent, to the effect that he hasn't seen any of them yet, but they should be gathering soon at the large wooden trestle table, which he points out, against the far wall. I look suitably puzzled, then smile and nod when he repeats his answer in French. I'm definitely getting into the swing of this role.

I order four pints of Guinness – one for myself and three for Charles – and wait by the bar until my carefully poured pint, with shamrock skilfully etched into the froth, has settled. I pay for the drinks and wander across to the table, sipping my pint. It's in excellent condition – perfect temperature and creamy smooth. With this quality of Guinness available, I'm surprised Charles is having any difficulty in acquiring the taste. I sit down on the carver chair at the head of the table. I'm rather looking forward to the evening, hoping I might encounter some convivial female company.

Over the next hour or so, the motley crew of BEC stalwarts arrive in dribs and drabs. First on the scene is Tracy, a stocky, mid-twenties, larger than life creature with straggly, blonde-streaked hair. She slips her jacket from her shoulders as she strides up to the bar, revealing a tight-fitting, luminous-green tank top which is struggling against heavy odds to contain her wobbling bosom. Stout, farming-stock legs protrude from an unflattering, black lycra mini-skirt to which hangs Anna, her whingeing progeny. Anna's clutching a battered teddy bear by the ankle, its already disfigured head bouncing off the tiled floor as she drags it unceremoniously behind her. Tracy has the unusual physical characteristic of buck teeth which protrude further than her flattened nose, an attribute the unfortunate Anna seems well on the way to inheriting.

George Davies, the BEC president, a bald, squat, middle-aged Welshman follows close on Tracy and Anna's heels and the three of them come across to where I'm seated and stare at me in silence. When I look back blankly, George explains politely, but firmly, that this particular table is reserved for British Expatriate Club members on Friday evenings. I introduce myself, tell them I'm working for Charles Benson, and ask if it's all right if I stay to listen to the conversation because I'm keen to learn English. George agrees enthusiastically. Whipping out his business card, he tucks it into my shirt pocket while informing me that he's a part-time teacher in one of Montpellier's biggest language schools and, when Tracy's attention is distracted by Anna eating a peanut she found on the floor, he whispers in my ear that he can get me a fifteen per cent discount if I book English lessons through him.

Tracy flops down on the wooden bench by my side, the snotty-nosed Anna dangling from her knee, and for the next fifteen minutes she chatters away, non-stop, in execrable French, more at me than to me and by the time the rest of the BEC regulars put in an appearance she's taken me under her wing. She introduces me to a married couple in their forties: Linda, twee Home Counties, tall, thin as a rake inside a loose-fitting, purple shell-suit and sporting a most improbable bouffant hairstyle, and her French husband, Daniel, a second-hand car dealer with a thick, Marseilles accent. Daniel conforms to everyone's worst preconception of a second-hand car dealer: shifty eyes, slicked-back black hair, leather bootlace tie with a buffalo clasp, not to mention a blue, patterned shirt which screams at his red-checked trousers.

When Emily Abercrombie arrives, as if pre-programmed, the language switches seamlessly from French to English. Emily, of some indeterminate age on the high side of seventy, flicks at the bench seat with her lace handkerchief before deigning to sit down. I get the impression I've been dismissed out of hand before Tracy has even completed the introductions. Raj is written all over the glowering, condescending, wizened features which give me the full benefit of their 'foreigners are only good for servants' look.

"I don't suppose, by any remote chance, that you play bridge?" the pinched mouth intones in my direction. Tracy whispers a translation in my ear and my quick shake of the head is met with a superior sniff which confirms that no further communication will be deemed appropriate.

Paul Sharp, a twittering, spotty, youthful Portmuthian turns up next with girlfriend and poodle in tow – Fifi and Floosie – I never did find out which was which, followed by Keith something-or-other, a surly, boorish, bearded, exchange student from Sunderland University, which I quickly infer has to be an oxymoron.

Charles is next on the scene. Waving across to the assembled company on his way to the bar, he loads up a tray with six pints of Guinness and carries it gingerly to our table. As he lowers his precious cargo he explains that, when he asked me to get three pints in, he'd forgotten he'd already asked George Davies to do the same thing. "Still, all grist to the taste-acquiring mill." Selecting a glass at random, he toasts the table. "Cheers!" He smacks his lips and proceeds to down the pint in one long, Adam's-apple-wobbling swallow, then he pulls out a packet of cigars and lights up. Below the level of the table I surreptitiously depress the 'record' button on my watch and sit back, sip my pint and wait for the political debate.

Three hours and three pints of Guinness later I'm feeling thoroughly depressed. It's going to be hellish difficult cobbling together a status report for Frobisher-Allen from the material I've recorded, unless he happens to have a particular interest in the cost of lace knickers in Tati's sale, the most effective treatment for nappy rash or the fact that Linda's au pair, Inge, was the first person, to the best of anyone's knowledge, to bonk a real vicar at a Vicars and Tarts party.

The nearest we get to any political discussion is when George Davies asks Charles what he thinks the effect of Britain's deferred entry to the euro might be on the long-term future of the British economy. Charles ponders this while he drains his fifth pint.

"In my conshidered opinion." Charles clears his throat harshly as he struggles to his feet. Balancing his cigar on the edge of the wooden table, he holds his hands aloft for silence. "In my conshidered opinion," he slurs again. "All politishans – " He pauses until he's sure he has everyone's undivided attention. "All politishans – are complete wankers!" With a self-congratulatory smirk frozen to his features, hands still held on high, he squints and blinks his way round the table, looking for any sign of dissent. Apart from Anna prodding her mother and demanding to know what a 'wanker' is, his statement evokes no reaction. He shrugs his shoulders. "I resht my case." Lowering his flabby arms, he slumps back down on the bench seat and picks up his cigar to take a long, slobbery drag before turning his attention to his sixth pint. I suppress a groan at this missed opportunity. While Charles' opinion is one which might well find favour with Frobisher-Allen, it can hardly be deemed a significant contribution to the fount of human knowledge.

I've had as much of this as I can take for one evening and I get to my feet to take my leave, hoping no one will notice the hot flush which comes to my freckles as I can't help but overhear Tracy's graphic explanation to her daughter.

When I get back to Saint Martin I change into my pyjamas and pour myself a large measure of Jura, then I sit up in bed and play back my recording, cringing at having to listen again to the stream of grammatical atrocities, hoping against hope that there might be something relevant I'd missed in the flood of merged monologues. I estimate the ratio of talking to listening at a BEC gathering to be of the order of five to one.

However, I find nothing new, apart from, in Tracy's explanation to Anna, a couple of detailed points regarding the female anatomy that I hadn't fully appreciated. There is also the not-uninteresting fact that Linda's au pair, Inge, is Swedish, eighteen, has long blonde hair, legs to die for and finds anyone in uniform totally irresistible. I file this fact away and drain my whisky glass before switching off the bedside lamp.

The following morning, life at The Book Cellar is relatively hectic. By ten-thirty I've already sold a calendar with twelve scenic views of the Lake District – reduced to half-price – and two Wallace & Gromit videos, when a Chronopost delivery van pulls up outside the shop. I sign for the bulky parcel which the courier deposits on the counter.

When I unwrap the packaging I find forty copies of the latest John Grisham novel, together with three separately wrapped, brown-paper parcels pre-addressed to customers in Spain. I put these to one side to take to the post office, then I manage to update the stock control data on the computer successfully. While I'm arranging the newly arrived volumes in an attractive window display I hear the fax machine chunter into life. I cross to the counter and rip off the message: 'To Monsieur Jérôme Dumas: Aunty Hilda hasn't received a postcard from you this week. Would you please make sure you send one today'. I groan. The not-unexpected reminder from London that my status report is overdue.

I stare blankly at the fax machine as I consider my options. I have to submit a report, but my conscience is struggling with the ethics of what I have in mind. Semantically, it's justifiable – extrapolation from the general to the specific being a logical sequitur. Nevertheless, I do feel a bit of a heel as I start to type.

CHAPTER 5

I read the message I've typed: 'Greetings to Auntie Hilda from Jérôme in the Herault. Last night, Charles Benson stated that the Prime Minister is a wanker'. Squeezing the transmit button, I send the fax winging on its way. Perhaps I'm being rotten to Charles, but it irks me that the bugger never even offered to pay for those three pints. A few minutes later I receive an acknowledgement of my fax.

I place the 'back in five minutes' sign in the shop window before hurrying down to the main post office with the Spanish parcels to make sure they catch the Saturday morning collection. When I get back to the shop I make a note that Charles owes me twenty four euros for postage.

The month of August settles into a routine. I spend every Friday evening in Fitzpatrick's, ensconced at one end of the trestle table with Tracy and Anna by my side, listening to a varied assortment of Brits and French anglophiles massacring my mother, if not my mother's, tongue. Charles turns up regularly at these gatherings but he contributes little to the discussions, preferring to dedicate himself to his quest for acquiring a taste for Guinness. To this end he invariably works his way through at least six pints, occasionally knocking Anna's teddy bear to the ground as a diversion so he can ogle the oscillations of Tracy's breasts when she bends down to retrieve it.

I listen, I record, I go home, I play back and I listen again for any hint of political activism. It's soul-destroying. The tapes invariably comprise nothing more than local gossip, scandal and calumny of any BEC member who inadvisedly failed to put in an appearance.

My hopes are raised briefly when Linda announces one evening that Inge will be joining us later on, only to be dashed by the au pair's non-appearance. The following week Linda explains that Inge stopped off en route to ask a *gendarme* for directions and was waylaid.

The only redeeming feature of this mind-bending boredom is that I'm beginning to master various English regional accents. By the end of August I can make a fair stab at Welsh and Yorkshire and, even if I say so myself, my Home Counties is rather impressive. However, while there's an element of aesthetic satisfaction in all this, for my weekly status reports I have little option but to eke out my one quotable quote with as much variation and imagination as I can muster.

Fax for week 2: 'Charles Benson stated that the Foreign Secretary indulges in frequent masturbation.'

Week 3: 'Charles Benson announced that the Chancellor of the Exchequer is a confirmed onanist.'

Then, mindful of the fact that Charles hadn't actually indicted any particular political party: Week 4: 'Charles Benson claimed that the Leader of the Opposition practises self abuse.'

I realise I'm transmitting utter rubbish but, to my amazement, Frobisher-Allen doesn't seem disillusioned with the garbage I'm sending across. Between my Week 3 and Week 4 missives he sends me a message requesting that I try to get my hands on a photograph of Charles Benson and fax it across so they can run a check against central files of known political activists. This seems way over the top, but I remember the photo of Charles at the Vicars and Tarts party and I search under the counter for the battered copy of the *BEC Thunderer*. I ring Charles' shadowy figure and transmit the page to Frobisher-Allen. To my astonishment, his acknowledgement is fulsome.

The following Monday morning Charles turns up unexpectedly at The Book Cellar.

I can tell straight away there's something seriously wrong. Apart from the fact that he's unshaven, his hair hasn't been combed and his blink rate is in overdrive, his glance barely strays in the direction of the

47

tight, denim miniskirt moulded around the curvaceous buttocks of a student bending low to examine a volume on the bottom shelf.

Charles leans across the horseshoe counter and whispers in my ear. "Jérôme, I know we're about to hit our busy period, but I'm going to have to make myself scarce for a while. Do you think you could handle things on your own?"

"I… I suppose so. Why? What's up?"

Charles jerks his thumb in the direction of the student and places his index finger across his lips. "After she's gone," he mouths before disappearing into the storeroom to put on the kettle.

By the time he returns with two mugs of Darjeeling the curvaceous buttocks have left empty-handed.

"What's the problem?" I ask.

Charles pushes the shop door closed to deter any potential customers. "The tax authorities are on to me. I got a letter this morning. Here, see for yourself." He tugs a crumpled sheet of paper from his hip pocket and thrusts it at me. I unfold the official-looking, headed notepaper and read:

Monsieur René Verdu, Chief Inspector of Taxes for Languedoc-Roussillon, requires Monsieur Charles Benson to explain the following apparent anomalies in his tax return for last year:

1. No declaration of interest from Channel Islands' bank accounts.

2. Deductions for wife and four children.

3. Deductions for providing support for aged parents.

4. Deductions for double glazing his principal residence.

5. Deductions for staff wages in The Book Cellar.

Would Monsieur Benson please contact this office and arrange an appointment as soon as possible to discuss these matters.

I feel a pang of guilt as I re-read the first point. "How serious is this, Charles?" He shrugs noncommittally. "Do you have a lot of undeclared interest in the Channel Islands?" I ask.

"Not a bloody sausage!"

"Then it's just an administrative cock-up, isn't it?" I try to sound cheerfully optimistic. "Surely that can be sorted out without too much difficulty?"

Charles tugs at his moustache. "I may have no bank accounts in the Channel Islands but then again, neither do I have a wife, never mind four kids. And it's going to be a bit awkward justifying the eight hundred euros a year I claim towards my parents' living expenses."

"Doesn't sound excessive."

"Probably wouldn't be if they hadn't both been cremated."

Charles runs his fingers through his dishevelled hair. "And the double glazing is going to be a real bugger to explain away considering my house doesn't even have a roof, never mind a fucking window! By the way, if anyone comes nosing around here asking questions, you worked here all last year and I pay you three thousand euros a month. Right?"

I bite into my bottom lip. It seems a churlish time to mention that the thirteen hundred euros due to me for the month of August hasn't been paid into my bank account yet. "What are you going to do?"

"What do you think of this?" Charles reaches into his inside jacket pocket and pulls out a single, typed page, which he unfolds and hands to me.

To Monsieur René Verdu, Chief Inspector of Taxes for Languedoc-Roussillon. With reference to your recent letter to Monsieur Charles Benson, I must regrettably inform you that Monsieur Benson departed this world last week, victim of a tragic skiing accident in Estonia. I attach a copy of his death certificate for your records.

I gulp when I see the letter has been prepared for my signature. "Hey! Just hold it right there Charles! I don't know about this! Putting my name to this letter could land me in a hell of a lot of trouble."

"Don't be daft. It's nothing to get worked up about." He produces a fountain pen from his jacket pocket. "Just sign it."

"I doubt if there's even any skiing in Estonia at this time of year," I protest.

"So what? Who cares? French bureaucrats never follow anything up. All they're concerned about is having the right paperwork."

"How in the name of God are you going to conjure up a death certificate from Estonia?"

"I'll knock something together. I've got an old golfball typewriter with Cyrillic characters and I know a few Russian phrases. I'll add some hieroglyphics and a bit of mumbo-jumbo. What with that and an official-looking stamp, Bob's your uncle."

"Just hang on a minute! It's all right for you to talk. I'm the one who's facing the prospect of doing time in some stinking jail."

"You do exaggerate, Jérôme. Jails are quite hygienic these days. Anyway, it's a doddle. I've done it before. Twice, in fact."

"What!"

Charles tugs his silk handkerchief from his watch strap and uses it to wipe the perspiration from his glistening forehead. "Variations on the theme, of course. A few years ago, when things were getting a bit uncomfortable in Auxerre, Michael Struthers – that was my moniker at the time – was swept away by a freak summer avalanche in the foothills of Mont Blanc. Actually, that proved to be a bit of a bugger to sort out," he says, tucking his handkerchief back into his watch strap, "because I hadn't thought through the implications. I couldn't dredge up a rationale for anyone being competent to sign a death certificate and without the appropriate paperwork the French bureaucrats hang in there like leeches. They're still after me. Can you believe that? They still pay the occasional visit to my old flat in Auxerre and, every six months or so, they send a letter to my next of kin, poor old Uncle Godfrey, pestering him for information about my whereabouts.

"Still, you live and learn – or rather, you *die* and learn," he smirks. "When Andrew Mitchell had to disappear a bit smartish from Bordeaux a couple of years back, everything went like clockwork. His canoe capsized in an expedition up the Amazon and his body was instantly torn to shreds by a pack of man-eating alligators. By an extremely fortuitous coincidence, a Swahili doctor in an accompanying canoe witnessed the whole grisly incident and was able to provide confirmatory documentation.

"I haven't heard a dicky bird about that since. As a matter of interest, if anyone ever gets round to translating Andrew Mitchell's death certificate, they'll find they've got the Lord's Prayer in Swahili. Rather a nice touch, don't you think? I copied it out of a Swahili Bible I found in a second-hand bookshop."

"I don't believe I'm hearing this!" I jump to my feet and stride the length of the aisle, my tea-mug clutched firmly in my fists. "And talking of bookshops," I say, swivelling round and marching back towards the counter. "What the hell's going to happen to this place – and to me – if you do a runner?"

Charles raises an eyebrow. "I dunno. Haven't had a chance to figure that out. If you like," he adds cheerfully, "I could leave you this place in my will. It's a nice little earner."

"That's bloody decent of you!"

"Think nothing of it, old boy. No need for you to get messed about any more than necessary. After you've signed this letter," he continues, thrusting his pen into my fist, "be a good chap and dash off my last will and testament. The authorities like these things to be hand-written. Keep it simple. The bookshop I leave to Jérôme Dumas, everything else goes to Uncle Godfrey in Richmond – that sort of thing. While you're doing that, I'll rattle off my death certificate."

I take the proffered pen and, with considerable misgivings, sign my name at the foot of the page. Plucking a sheet of paper from the stacker on the fax machine, I write out a will along the lines Charles had indicated and place it on the counter by his side. He breaks off from changing the golfball on the typewriter to squint at my page and nods approvingly. "Just the job!" He backdates the will to the fifteenth of August and signs it with a flourish before turning his attention to creating a pseudo-Russian text on a sheet of thick, yellowing parchment. When he's finished typing he rummages in his desk drawer for an ancient John Bull printing set and, having carefully applied the embossing stamp to the top of the parchment, he produces a fountain pen from the same drawer and appends a totally illegible squiggle in black ink. He holds the document at arm's length to admire his handiwork, waving it back and forth to dry the ink.

"Pretty classy, if I say so myself. The French'll go a bundle on this."

"What are you planning to do?"

"Play it by ear." He scratches his head. "Probably lie low for a while. I've got a mate, Mel Hoggard, who lives in Paris. He's got a spare room. I'll be able to kip down at Mel's place till the heat dies down. After that, who knows? I've always fancied trying my hand at running a delicatessen in Italy and – "

Charles' flow is interrupted by the squeak of unoiled hinges as the shop door is forced open. A tall, gangly, slightly stooped figure stands in the doorway, his disproportionately large head balanced precariously on top of his spindly neck with its prominent Adam's apple. Straight, black hair, parted in the centre, reaches to the tips of his pointed, pixie-like ears. He has bushy eyebrows over hooded, sunken eyes, his cheeks are chalk white and his narrow nose is tapered. He's wearing an expensive-looking, cream linen suit with the jacket unbuttoned, showing off an immaculate white shirt and striped tie. A bulging, leather document case is clamped underneath his left arm and a filter-tipped cigarette dangles from the long, bony, nicotine-stained fingers of his right hand.

Charles and I both stare enquiringly. Eventually I break the silence. "How can I help you?"

"My name is Verdu, René Verdu." I feel the hairs on the back of my neck stand proud. "I'm looking for a Monsieur Charles Benson." The voice is deep with the gravelly quality of a three-pack-a-day man. I incline my head towards Charles.

"I haven't seen Charles for a couple of weeks," Charles states casually. "I believe he's off on holiday somewhere. Isn't that right, Jérôme?"

"Er, yes… That's right…" I stammer. "He's… gone skiing, I think."

"Estonia, if I recall correctly," Charles adds. "Can I take a message?"

"Whom do I have the pleasure of addressing?"

"George Davies," Charles states with a beaming smile. "I'm an old friend of Charles Benson's."

Verdu fixes me with his dark, piercing eyes, striking a perfect balance between vulture and Vulcan. Had he not been up and about during daylight hours I might well have added vampire. "Are you also a friend of Monsieur Benson?" the rasping voice enquires.

My mouth goes completely dry and I swallow hard, trying desperately to generate enough saliva to respond. "I… I work for him," comes out in a half-croak.

"Ah, yes. And you are?"

"Dumas. Jérôme Dumas." Verdu's eyes remain locked on to mine and I feel his psychic forces drilling into my skull, probing my innermost thoughts. I blink and deflect my gaze.

"When is Monsieur Benson due back?" he demands.

"Eh? Tomorrow, I think…..... "

"That's good. He'll be trying to get in touch with me when he returns. We have some business matters to attend to." His tone is matter of fact. "When you see him, could you please inform him that I won't be available for the next couple of days as I have to go to Lille on business."

"Of course. I'll make sure he gets the message."

"Thank you." Verdu drops his cigarette on to the ground and crushes it beneath his heel as he turns round. Tugging the shop door closed behind him, he heads off down the hill.

"Hey! This is much too hot for my liking, Charles! That was no social call. Verdu was sizing up the situation."

"So what? By the time he gets back from Lille, your letter and my death certificate will be waiting in his in-tray and that's the last we'll hear about it."

"I'm not so sure about that. He doesn't look the type to back off.

And if he ever suspects that you were here when he called, I'm the one who'll be up shit creek."

"You do go on, Jérôme. Stop fussing. Put on the kettle and make a fresh pot while I address this envelope. By the way, you'll find a bottle in the cupboard underneath the sink," he calls out as I'm trudging towards the storeroom. "I take mine fifty-fifty, Darjeeling-Cognac."

Ten days have passed since Charles' disappearance and during that time things have gone from bad to quite decidedly worse. The so-called 'busy period' never gets beyond two or three customers a day and my 'nice little earner' turns out to comprise six months' back rent due on the premises, five hundred unpaid-for books, a final demand from France Télécom for the outstanding telephone bills and a lawyer's letter threatening legal action if the invoice for two hundred video cassettes isn't settled within a fortnight.

I've come to dread Friday evenings at Fitzpatrick's. It's pure purgatory. While Tracy's scope of conversation rarely ventures beyond scurrilous gossip, bargain-hunting in the sales and the intimate, scatological details of bringing up Anna, Linda's contribution, if anything, is even worse; an endless regurgitation of the same old, boring anecdotes – a weekly version of a verbal menstrual cycle with no relieving menopause in sight.

To add to my problems, Frobisher-Allen is getting shirty. Since Charles' quotes dried up I've had nothing to put in my status reports and last week's effort consisted of: 'Her Majesty's government is well respected in the Hérault and no adverse political activism is evident among the local community'. This was clearly not to Frobisher-Allen's liking and his acknowledgement included a not very subtle hint that if this was the best I could come up with it might be better all round if I were to pack it in and free up the gîte so he and Mrs Frobisher-Allen could use it for their autumn vacation.

When I return to the bookshop after lunch, I slump down behind the counter and stare despondently at the fax machine, wondering what on earth I'm going to put into this week's report. I'm fast coming to the conclusion that Frobisher-Allen might be right. Although life in St Martin is agreeable enough – and the money is certainly good – maybe it would make sense if I were to jump ship. The letter I sent to the French authorities announcing Charles' demise is constantly preying on my mind and, who knows, perhaps I might be able to negotiate a different posting with Frobisher-Allen, maybe even Paris, in return for freeing up the St Martin gîte?

I'm wrestling with my options when the shop door squeaks gratingly and I feel a sinking feeling in the pit of my stomach when I see Verdu framed in the doorway with a young, squat, officious-looking individual hovering by his side.

"Ah, Monsieur Dumas!" Verdu's gruff voice intones. "I was hoping I might catch you. It's my lucky day!"

For some reason, I have a premonition that Verdu's lucky days and mine are not necessarily destined to coincide. Although my heart's thumping, I force myself to be the epitome of outward calmness. "It's Monsieur Verdu, isn't it?"

"Indeed it is. And this is my colleague, Monsieur Serge Sinègre." Verdu and the surly-faced Sinègre step across the threshold and stand in front of the horseshoe counter.

"What might I interest you in today, gentlemen? Joyce's *Ulysses*, perhaps? Or maybe Tolstoy's *War and Peace* might be more to your liking?"

Verdu's features bend into what's probably meant to be a smile. "You wouldn't happen to have *War and Peace* in the original Russian version, by any chance?"

The vulture's henchman emits an ominous cackle. I'm already regretting opening up this line of conversation and I try a carefree laugh which emerges as a strangulated cough as a vision of an overcrowded, sweaty prison cell flits before my eyes. "I'm afraid we stock only English language books. But, if you like," I add enthusiastically, "I'm sure I could order the Russian version for you."

"That won't be necessary – as I don't speak any Russian." Verdu exchanges a meaningful glance with his sidekick. "And you, Monsieur Dumas? Do you speak Russian, or perhaps, Estonian?"

"Not a word of either," I bluster. "I'm not much of a linguist, I'm afraid."

"That's a pity. So you weren't able to read poor Monsieur Benson's death certificate?"

"Charles'… death certificate?" I stammer. "No. But I believe it just gave details of the skiing accident."

"Really? And how would you know that?"

"Er… Monsieur Davies told me. You remember Davies? He was here the last time you called." I can feel the cold sweat trickling down between my shoulder blades. "Now he's what I call a linguist," I enthuse. "He speaks four or five languages fluently. I really admire people like that, don't you? He translated Charles' death certificate for me."

Verdu sucks noisily on his teeth. "I suppose, when you speak as many languages as Monsieur Davies does, it's inevitable that you're going to get them muddled up from time to time." He pauses, sniffs and scratches at the side of his tapered nose with a long, pointed fingernail.

"What do you mean?"

"I'm afraid Monsieur Davies doesn't appear to have done a very good job on this one. You see, I arranged to have Monsieur Benson's death certificate translated into French. I do like everything to be neat and tidy – all the i's dotted and all the t's crossed." He nods towards Sinègre who immediately produces a single sheet of paper from his briefcase. "Would you care to see the translation?"

As the truthful answer of 'no' doesn't seem appropriate, I take the proffered page and read: *Mary had a little lamb. There's no truth in Pravda and no news in Izvestia. Charles Benson's postillion has been struck by lightning. [The remainder of this text comprises jumbled Cyrillic characters which do not form any known Russian or Estonian words].*

56

"Difficult to see where Davies picked up the details of the skiing accident."

"I… I don't understand."

"Of course you don't. You don't speak Russian, do you? Monsieur Davies translated the death certificate for you and you just wrote the covering letter. Is that what happened?"

"Exactly! That's it exactly!"

"In which case, I think I'd better have a word with Monsieur Davies. You wouldn't happen to have his address or phone number, by any chance?"

I can feel the colour ebbing from my cheeks and I'm on the point of being physically ill. "I'm sorry, I don't think I – "

"Not to worry," he interjects. "Not too many Davieses in this part of the world. I'll be able to track him down without any difficulty." Verdu takes the sheet of paper from my limp fingers and hands it back to Sinègre who files it fussily in his briefcase. They move towards the door, then Verdu stops with one hand on the doorknob and looks back over his shoulder. "Oh, one more question, Monsieur Dumas. How well would you say you knew Charles Benson?"

"Hardly at all," I blurt out. "I just started working for him a few weeks ago. Got the job through an agency, as a matter of fact. Benson and I were practically total strangers."

Verdu releases his grip on the door handle and steps back towards the counter. "Really?" He raises both eyebrows. "You mean to say – you only met Monsieur Benson quite recently?"

"That's correct. End of July."

"Is that a fact?" I nod vigorously and he shrivels me with an ice-cold stare. "Would you say that you and Monsieur Benson hit it off straight away?"

I don't like the way this conversation is going but I can't see any way to jump off the treadmill. "We got on all right, I suppose." I shrug. "Just a typical employer-employee relationship, I guess."

"Nothing more than that?" My mouth is hanging open as I shake my head slowly from side to side. Verdu's grin exposes a row of uneven teeth. "How very odd!" He pauses and strokes his chin reflectively before continuing. "How often does it happen that someone employs a total stranger, then, within a couple of weeks, makes him a major beneficiary in his will?"

I'm struck dumb. Verdu continues to stare at me for what seems like an eternity before turning to Sinègre. "Serge, when we get back to the office, remind me to have the handwriting on Monsieur Benson's will authenticated." His piercing eyes flick back to me. "You're not planning to leave the district in the next few days, are you, Monsieur Dumas?"

"No, I... I've no plans to go anywhere. Why?"

"I may have some more questions for you, after I've spoken to Monsieur Davies." He slides a card from his breast pocket and places it on the counter. "Do give me a call if your travel plans change for any reason."

As Verdu and Sinègre head off down the hill, I feel an urgent need to use the loo. As I squat and agonise about my plight, little do I realise that, at this very moment, the British Government is falling.

CHAPTER 6

Although it's still early afternoon, I position the *Closed* sign in the bookshop window, yank down the blind and double-lock the door from the inside. I hurry to the storeroom to find Charles' Cognac supply and help myself to several large swigs from the bottle as I pace up and down the aisle, trying to figure out what to do next.

I think it might help focus my thoughts if I were to write down the problems I'm facing so I pluck a sheet of paper from the fax machine, slump down behind the counter and pick up a pen.

1. When Verdu makes contact with George Davies he'll realise it wasn't Davies who was with me in the bookshop during his previous visit and he'll conclude that yours truly was party to the deception.

2. If Verdu checks out the residents' permit files at the Préfecture he's bound to come across a photo of Charles Benson and he'll realise it was he who was with me that day.

3. When Verdu has the handwriting on Charles' will analysed he'll find out it was forged – and it won't take him a month of Sundays to figure out who forged it!

I could continue, but I've already written enough to confirm my gut reaction that it's time to make myself scarce. However, I reflect, as I crumple the sheet of paper and lob it in the general direction of the waste paper basket, that might not be so straightforward. I consider how I would play it if I were in Verdu's shoes. Clearly, I'm his number one suspect. It will be obvious to him that I'm an accessory before, during and after the fact – even though he might not have the remotest idea what the 'fact' is. So why haven't I been arrested? Maybe he's hoping I'll lead him to Benson, in which case it's a racing certainty I'll be tailed from the moment I set foot outside the shop. Might Verdu also suspect the MI6 connection? If so, perhaps I should be giving the St Martin gîte a wide berth. Frobisher-Allen wouldn't take it at all well if I were to permanently bugger up his autumn vacations. (I chide myself, but I think it's an indication of the pressure I'm under that I'm starting to think in split infinitives). I have to make contact with Frobisher-Allen, but calling from the shop phone is too risky. By now, the line may well be bugged.

On the assumption that I'll be able to give my hypothetical tail the slip, I consider whether I should risk going back to St Martin. On reflection, I figure Verdu probably doesn't know I'm staying there – another reason for setting a tail on me – because I didn't register at the *Mairie* in St Martin and, apart from Charles, I've given the address to no one. In fact, St Martin might well be the safest place to head for right now. I down another slug of Cognac, then almost jump out of my skin when the shop doorbell suddenly clangs. I peer through the bevelled window and see a Chronopost delivery van with its wheels mounted on the pavement, engine idling. The bell jangles again noisily and I unlock the door.

"You had me worried there, mate," the cheerful courier announces. "I thought you didn't close until seven?" I'm not in the mood for small talk. I indicate a corner where he can dump the package, then I sign for it quickly and usher him out.

Six o'clock is chiming as I lock up the bookshop. I hurry to the nearest Crédit Agricole cashpoint and use my *carte bleue* to withdraw three hundred euros, then I head for the Place de La Comédie, stopping off en route at a *tabac* to purchase a telephone card and a newspaper. I find an empty table outside the Grande Brasserie, at the far end of the square, adjacent to the Gaumont cinema, and when the waiter ambles across I order a draught beer. I've seen no sign of anyone following me – no one acting in any way suspiciously. However, the Place de la Comédie is crowded and I give my putative tail credit for being a professional.

I pay for my beer as soon as it arrives and I sip it slowly, pretending to be engrossed in the newspaper. All the while, the cinema queue by my side is building up. As soon as the pay kiosk opens the line surges forward and I make my move. Forcing a gap in the queue, I burst through and race as fast as my legs will carry me, past the post office, wheeling right at the top of the street and sprinting along Rue Jacques Coeur. A sharp left turn, past Simple Simon's tea room, up the steep Rue Collot and already I'm in a quiet, narrow lane where anyone trying to follow me would have to make themselves conspicuous. My lungs are on fire. I spin round and stand, hands on knees, gasping for breath – I hadn't realised I was so badly out of condition. I manage a wan smile as I stare back down the deserted street. As soon as I've recovered sufficient wind I make my way in a staggering run towards the steep flight of steps leading to the car park underneath the Marché aux Fleurs.

On the way to St Martin I stop off at the Carrefour Hypermarket on the Route de Ganges. Although my instincts tell me to put the maximum possible distance between me and Verdu in the shortest possible time, I have to allow for the fact that Frobisher-Allen might not see it that way, so I pile a shopping trolley high with enough provisions to survive an extended siege.

By the time I get back to the gîte it's almost nine o'clock, which means eight o'clock in the UK. I reckon the chances of catching Frobisher-Allen in the office at this hour are remote so I decide to leave the call until morning.

I defrost a pizza, wash it down with a few glasses of red wine, then turn in for an early, but disturbed, night.

Land of Hope and Glory plays incessantly while my call is queued. Five minutes later, when I finally get a connection, I hear a high-pitched, computer-generated voice:

Press '1' if you would like to receive information about specific MI6 activities. Press '2' if you wish details of current vacancies. Press '3' if you would like to apply for a particular position. Press '4' if your requirements are not met by any of these options.

I bang on '4' and repeatedly kick the glass door of the St Martin telephone booth as I watch the units flooding out of my Telecarte. After being treated to two more renditions of *Land of Hope and Glory* the disembodied voice returns.

Thank you for contacting MI6. If you have any further enquiries, please contact our general information service which is available from nine to twelve and two to five, Mondays to Fridays, on – a pause and a whirr precede the singsong, metallic voice – '0171 23 – '.

My Telecarte expires and the line goes dead. I slam down the receiver. So much for Frobisher-Allen's emergency number.

I plod across the square to the café and, even though it's not yet ten o'clock, I order a pastis at the bar. With no fax machine readily available, I'm trying to figure out how I'm going to be able to make contact with Frobisher-Allen. As I'm tipping iced water into my drink I suddenly remember I have another phone number for MI6 – the one I copied from the Evening Standard when I first applied for the job. Searching feverishly through my diary, I find it. I throw back the pastis in one swallow and I stop off at the *tabac* to purchase another Telecarte before hurrying back to the phone kiosk. A polite, male voice answers my call.

"Good morning, sir. How can I be of assistance?"

I treat him to my best Home Counties. "Would you put me through to Mr Frobisher-Allen, please."

"Mr Frobisher-Allen?" His voice sounds incredulous. "I'm very sorry, sir, but this is a public information line. I'm not authorised to connect you with the Director General."

"You have to!" I snap. "I'm an MI6 agent and I can't get through to headquarters on my emergency number."

"That's very unfortunate, sir." I'm sure I hear a suppressed snigger. "But there really isn't anything I can do to assist you."

I slam down the receiver and drum my fingertips against the glass panel for a full minute before picking up the handset and re-dialling the number. The same male voice. The same greeting.

"I'd like tae speak tae Kathleen Morrison, please."

"I'm afraid personal calls aren't allowed on this line, sir."

"Aye, I ken that, Jimmy, but this is important. This is Kathleen's uncle Tommy from Ardrossan." I lower my voice to a respectful whisper. "There's been a death in the family." He hesitates. "I'll only keep her a minute, pal."

"Well... I suppose. Kathleen!" I hear him call out. "Line two, personal call for you."

"Hello?" I recognise her voice.

"Is that you, Kathleen?"

"Who is this?"

"It's Jérôme Dumas. Och, whit the hell am I witterin' on aboot! I mean it's Frank, Frank McClure. You remember me, Kathleen. I went tae school wi' your brother, Andy. You and Frobisher-Allen interviewed me fur a job."

"Who is this?" she screams. "What do you want with me?" It sounds as if she's on the verge of hysteria. "I've never heard of you! I don't know anyone called Frank McClure!"

"O' course you know me, Kathleen! We hud lunch thigither. It wis a Monday – it wis tuna salad, fur fucksake!"

The line clicks dead in my hand. For the second time this morning I resort to kicking the phone booth. What's Kathleen playing at? Why is she pretending not to know me?

I call International Directory Enquiries and ask for the phone number of a Miss Kathleen Morrison who lives in Kilburn. No, I don't have the exact address. I'm informed there is a Kathleen Anne Morrison listed, but her number is ex-directory. Thinking quickly, I request the number of a Mr Andrew Morrison who lives in Ardrossan in Ayrshire. I'm duly given Andy's number.

"It's Frank McClure, Andy. Dae you remember me? We went tae school thigither in Kilwinning."

"Frank who?"

"Frank McClure. Ma mother hud a pub in Kilbirnie – in the High Street."

"Och aye – The Pheasant Plucker."

"The Plucked Pheasant."

"Naw." He laughed. "You – The Pheasant Plucker. That wis yer nickname at school – on account o' yer mother's pub. Did ye no' ken that?" He's chortling away at the other end of the line.

"O' course I did, Andy," I lie, dredging up a laugh.

"You were the right wee swot, weren't you? I remember you aye kent a' thae weird figures o' speech an' stuff. The only wan I ever remembered was yon Mala-somethin'." It's not even half-past ten – half-past nine for him – and he sounds as if he's had a skinful. "Whit wis it called again? Yon Mala-thingmyjig? Malaprop – "

I'm watching the units on my Telecarte spiral downwards. "Andy," I interject, doing my best to sound relaxed and casual. "The reason I'm callin' is that I'm goin' tae be in London fur a couple o' days later in the month and I hear that your Kathleen's workin' doon there. I thought it would be a nice idea tae look her up. You widny happen tae huv her phone number handy?"

"Aye. Sure. It's in my jaicket. Haud on." He drops the receiver with a bang and I hear his strident whistling recede, then become piercingly loud. "Malaprop- somethin'-or-other, wasn't it? I'm sure it wis somethin' like that."

"Dae you huv Kathleen's number, Andy?"

"Aye, aye! Haud yer fuckin' horses!"

I manage to extract the number from him just before my Telecarte gives up the ghost.

There's nothing more I can do now until Kathleen gets home from work. I recall someone in Fitzpatrick's, I think it was Tracy, mentioning that there was a very good Friday market in Ganges, a small town fifteen kilometres north of St Martin. As I don't want to risk going anywhere near Montpellier, I might as well spend the morning in Ganges. I trot back to the gîte to pick up my car and, noticing the fuel level is low, I pull into a service station.

The assistant tries several times to process the payment using my credit card but, despite rubbing the metallic strip furiously on his shirt sleeve, the card refuses to register. Eventually a message appears on his display panel to the effect that the card is no longer valid. I check the expiry date – no problem there. Not wanting to create a fuss, I pay for the petrol in cash and as I continue on my journey I surmise that Verdu must have somehow contrived to have my *carte bleue* invalidated.

To work off my frustration I put my foot down and I touch a hundred and twenty kilometres an hour on a straight stretch of the quiet road. I drop down a gear on the steep climb towards a cutting in the rocks, flicking down the sun visor to protect my eyes from the reflected glare, and when I drive through the narrow fissure, I catch my breath when the vista suddenly explodes in front of me and I'm presented with a stunning panorama of the Cévennes mountains sprawling in a patchwork of sunlight and shade. The effect is on a par with the southern approach to Glencoe. I decelerate sharply to soak up this incredible scenery as I sweep down the hill.

When I get to the outskirts of Ganges I see several signs announcing that the town is closed to traffic on market days so I abandon my car alongside many others on the ring road and join the crowds streaming towards the market on foot. There are stalls on both sides of the main street with enough space between them to support about half a dozen people abreast. The approaching mass of humanity funnels towards this gap and from here on the crowd moves like a lava flow. The outermost lanes, adjacent to the stalls, are stationary, with people examining the goods and chatting, discussing and haggling with the stall holders. The next lane in comprises shufflers looking for an opportunity to squeeze into the outside lanes and the two or three central lanes are occupied by those moving through the market, constrained by the pace of the slowest toddler or pram.

The sun is beating down fiercely on the back of my neck as I stick to the middle lanes, making steady progress past an incredible variety of stalls: designer jeans, Provençal table cloths, compact discs, outsize bras, live rabbits, chain saws, dried beans, second-hand books, unplucked fowl, personalised name plates carved in wood while you wait (his accent sounds Irish), power tools, pots of home-made honey, notepaper embossed with pressed flowers, artisan sausages, fish tanks, slippers, combat jackets, *foie gras* and spit-roasted chickens.

All the time I'm shuffling along I have an uncomfortable feeling that I'm being followed. Of course, I am – by about five hundred people at a rough estimate – but I sense there are eyes watching my every move. I notice the flow is turning to the right about twenty metres ahead so I drift towards the left hand lane and plop out on the bend, finding myself among the permanent shops and bars. I go into the *tabac* and purchase another Telecarte, then I cross to a telephone booth and ask directory enquiries to connect me with the head office of the Crédit Agricole bank in Montpellier. When the call is answered, I quote the number of my *carte bleue* and ask for an explanation.

"I'm terribly sorry for any inconvenience, Monsieur Dumas, but I'm afraid your *carte bleue* has been cancelled and all funds have been withdrawn from the account."

"On whose authorisation?" I demand.

"Yours, of course, sir," the surprised voice replies. "I have the fax you sent this morning in front of me. Naturally, before taking action on such a request, we checked the signature against the one we have on file. It certainly appears to be authentic."

I replace the handset without further comment. So it must have been Frobisher-Allen who pulled the plug on me. What the hell is he playing at? And, to make matters worse, Verdu's bloodhounds are hot on the scent. I gaze across at the foothills of the Cévennes mountains and contemplate spending the rest of my days wandering the forest trails like a latter day Japanese soldier in the Burmese jungle. It's either that or have a beer.

As I'm draining my glass, I study the other customers seated at the pavement tables outside the Restaurant du Commerce: a teenage couple, fingers interlocked, gazing soulfully into each other's eyes and whispering away in German; three elderly, pastis-swilling locals animatedly debating La Belle Etoile's prospects in the sixteen thirty at Longchamp; two young women fussing over a baby in a carry cot. No one looks in the least suspicious and perhaps I'm being paranoid, but I still have an uncomfortable sensation of being watched. Returning to my car by the route I came is physically impossible so I merge again with the human oil slick and complete the clockwise circuit via the Languedocian wine, summer dresses, DVDs, unpasteurised cheese, children's toys, newly-laid eggs, wicker chairs, second-hand clothes, cutlery, garlic, power tools, fruit and vegetables, hunting knives and garden furniture.

It takes me a few minutes to locate where I parked my car. On the route back I accelerate sharply round a tight bend and pull off the road, cutting the engine in a secluded spot among the pine trees and I wait there for a good five minutes. When I set off again I drive back to St Martin by a circuitous route and park in the garage. I sit slumped in front of the television, letting the afternoon soaps wash over me, until six o'clock, when I walk briskly to the village phone booth and dial Kathleen Morrison's home number.

"Frank McClure! How in the name of God did you get this number? I can't talk to you!"

"Try to stay calm, Kathleen."

"This is completely impossible!"

"You have to tell me what's going on," I insist. "Why did you pretend not to know me when I called the office? What are you playing at?"

"No, Frank!" she whimpers. "I can't say anything. It's more than my job's worth."

"Sod your bloody job, Kathleen!" I regret the insensitivity, but feel I have to force the issue. "It's more than my life's worth *not* to know what's going on!" She's sobbing heavily down the line. "I'm sorry, Kathleen," I say quietly. "I didn't mean to bite your head off."

I hear her blow her nose hard. "I'll tell you what I can, Frank." She's regained her composure and her voice is steady. "First of all, you need to understand the background. It's completely out of character for Mr Frobisher-Allen to soil his hands with anything that remotely smacks of work – his delegation skills are honed to the point of abdication. The reason he got involved in interviewing you for the surveillance job is that, for the past six months, he has dedicated his every waking moment to tracking down the person you know as Charles Benson. That's not his real name, by the way – just the latest in a string of aliases. Frobisher-Allen hasn't told any of us why he's got such a bee in his bonnet about Benson who, as far as I'm aware, isn't actually wanted for anything.

"Having said that, he's been diverting resources from here, there and everywhere – terrorist tracking projects, drug squad enquiries, money-laundering investigations, serious fraud cases – in a single-minded attempt to nail Benson. It must be something really important – paedophilia, most likely – that's Frobisher-Allen's hobby horse. I reckon he's invested more of his personal time in this case over the past six months than Jack Slipper did when he was hunting for Ronnie Biggs.

"The surveillance mission you were sent on?" she continues. "That was just a front. Every time we got an intelligence report of a potential sighting of this Benson character, Frobisher-Allen would send in an agent on a so-called surveillance mission to try to get confirmation. The Montpellier tip-off sounded particularly promising so he decided to plant someone gullible inside the The Book Cellar." Kathleen pauses and blows her nose again. "Sorry about that, Frank." Her voice has dropped to a whisper. "But it's better you know the truth. I typed the job spec. myself. The principal requirement was that the candidate should speak fluent French, but he also had to be easily manipulated. That's why Frobisher-Allen had so much difficulty filling the vacancy. Fluent French speakers who are gullible don't grow on trees. Well, I suppose, in France, they might, but..." Her voice tails off.

"Don't bother about trying to spare my feelings, Kathleen," I grunt. "What else can you tell me?"

"When you faxed across the photograph of Benson, Frobisher-Allen was like the cat that got the cream. But that didn't last for long. His plans, whatever they might have been, were scuppered by the recent change of government. New minister, new policies, new directives. No more spying allowed on friendly nations' territories. So far, Frobisher-Allen appears to have made a favourable impression on the new Foreign Secretary and he wants to keep it that way. So, from his point of view, I'm afraid you no longer exist."

I'm struggling to assess the implications of what she's telling me. "What happened to my emergency phone number, Kathleen? All I got was the happy-clappy MI6 recruitment commercial."

"All agents are given a personalised emergency number, Frank, but when we cut someone adrift, we re-direct any calls they make to their emergency number to the public information services."

"Thanks a fucking bunch!" I pause while I try to collect my racing thoughts. "I'm in big trouble, Kathleen. I have got to get in touch with Frobisher-Allen."

She hesitates for a moment. "I'll give you his private office number, Frank, but he must never find out how you got it."

"Of course."

She rattles off a number which I jot down. "Thanks, Kathleen."

"There's something else you should know, Frank. Whatever you do, don't try to get back into Britain with the passport you're carrying."

"Why not?"

"Frobisher-Allen reckons if would be highly embarrassing if you were to turn up over here and start blabbing your mouth off about MI6 spying missions in France, so – "

Her voice is barely audible. I press the receiver hard against my ear, straining to catch her words. "So? Quickly, Kathleen," I insist, eyeing the units on my phone card. "I don't have much time."

"So he's given your passport details to the immigration authorities on both sides of the Channel," she sniffles. "They've been told you're a member of Aum Shinriyko or the Shining Hand or some such organisation. Frobisher-Allen's left instructions that if you present yourself at the border you've to be held in custody and detained without trial for eight months."

"Eight months? Why on earth eight months?"

"Because he retires in seve… "

Another Telecarte bites the dust. I give the telephone booth another resounding kick. Suddenly, the Burmese jungle scenario doesn't seem so far-fetched.

CHAPTER 7

I hurry back to the gîte, pour myself a large whisky and flop down on a chair. As I guzzle my drink, I mentally tot up the assets I have at my disposal. Two hundred and sixty euros in cash, enough tinned food for a month and a car almost full of petrol. Not bad, but hardly an adequate provision for retirement.

An excellent idea strikes me. Why not flog the Peugeot? I allow myself a wry smile as I imagine Frobisher-Allen's face when he finds out what I've done. I recall that Linda's husband, Daniel, deals in second-hand cars and he didn't strike me as the type who would concern himself unduly with trivial details such as who owns the vehicle. My smile broadens when I realise that contacting Linda and Daniel might open up the possibility of bumping into their au pair, Inge. Much as I would love to sicken Frobisher-Allen completely, I dismiss the idea of selling the gîte as impractical.

I'm reasonably confident Verdu doesn't know my whereabouts, otherwise I would surely have had a visit from the vulture pack by now. All the same, I shouldn't hang about. Flog the car as quickly as possible, jump on a train to Paris and then worry about how to get across the Channel. My immediate problem is how to contact Daniel and Linda as I don't even know their surname, never mind their address or phone number. Then it strikes me. Today is Friday, so Fitzpatrick's is the obvious answer. However, it's by no means impossible that Verdu will have the pub staked out.

En route to Fitzpatrick's I pick up another Telecarte and a newspaper and I pass the first test when I walk up to the bar and the regular barman doesn't recognise me behind my dark glasses. I've blackened my hair with boot polish and flattened my stomach as much as physically possible by knotting a scarf tightly around my midriff, concealed beneath my loose-fitting sweater – this also contributing to the overall disguise by raising my voice by a good half octave. I order a pint of Guinness and carry it over to a seat adjacent to the still-empty BEC table where I bury my face in the *Midi Libre*.

Tracy and Anna are the first to arrive, just before eight o'clock. Student Keith is unlucky enough to appear next and he's treated to a twenty minute diatribe on Anna's scatological idiosyncrasies before, as much to Keith's relief as mine, Linda and Daniel put in an appearance, closely followed by a highly excited George Davies. Before even ordering a drink at the bar, George bustles over to the table and takes his life in his hands by interrupting Linda in full flow.

"Listen to this, folks. I've got the most incredible news. Charles Benson has been murdered." Linda gags in mid-sentence and all eyes swivel towards George.

"What on earth happened?" Linda demands.

"Jérôme Dumas bumped him off."

My fists crumple involuntarily into the *Midi Libre*. I slip a trembling hand underneath my newspaper to fumble for my pint and pull the glass through. My long gulp is followed by a wave of acute nausea as I choke on the beer but my imminent asphyxiation draws no attention from the BEC gathering where everyone is gaping expectantly at George.

Tracy is the first to break the silence. "Well, go on, George, for Christ's sake! Tell us! How did Jérôme do it? Did he chop the slimy, old pimp's balls off?"

Anna's in there, quick as a flash, with her demand for an explanation of *pimp* and use of the word *balls* in this context. For once Tracy shushes her, then clouts her around the ear when she persists.

"Well, come on, George!" Tracy demands. "How *did* he do it?"

"I'm afraid I don't have any details," George mumbles apologetically. "All I know is that a bloke called Verdu came to see me this morning. He's something big in Les Renseignements Généraux."

"What's that?" asks Keith.

"I'm not sure we have an exact equivalent," George replies. "Somewhere between Special Branch and MI6, I suppose."

I feel even queasier. I'd had a nasty feeling all along that there was more to Verdu than a run-of-the-mill tax inspector.

George continues in an animated tone. "It seems that Les Renseignements Généraux have been after Charles for some time, though Verdu wouldn't tell me why. When Verdu visited The Book Cellar a few days ago, Charles and Jérôme were there. However, it seems that Charles claimed to be me and said that he, that is Charles, was away on a skiing holiday in Estonia. Everybody following this?" George glances quickly round the table. "Verdu thinks Jérôme must have had a hidden weapon trained on Charles, forcing him to lie. Can you credit that? Anyway, Charles has now disappeared without trace and Verdu reckons Jérôme has done him in and disposed of his body. It seems that Jérôme created a phoney death certificate in pseudo-Russian and he also forged Charles' will so he could get his hands on the bookshop." George breaks off to take a swig from Keith's pint of lager. "Verdu will be coming round to see all of you tomorrow to take your statements," he blurts out. "I've given him your names and addresses. It seems that Jérôme's done a bunk and Verdu wants to find out if any of us can cast any light on his whereabouts."

Suddenly everyone's babbling at once. I catch snatches of conversation: 'I always thought there was something shifty about that Dumas character': 'His eyes were too close together': 'I suspected all along that Jérôme was up to no good'. Chairs scrape against the tiled floor as the BEC members scramble to their feet, all eager to be the first to spread the most exciting bit of gossip to hit the British expatriate community in Montpellier in many a long day.

I peer over the top of my newspaper just in time to see Linda and Daniel disappearing through the pub door and I scurry out after them, staying about twenty metres behind as they make their way along the pedestrian precinct of the Grand Rue Jean Moulin, across the Boulevard du Jeu de Paume and down towards the railway station. As he's approaching a silver-grey Mercedes parked by the side of the road, Daniel depresses his remote control to release the central locking. I wait until he and Linda have climbed inside, then I break into a trot, yank open the rear door and slip in behind the driver.

Linda spins round. "Who the fuck are you and what the fuck do you think you're playing at?" Linda's colloquial French is impeccable. I whip off my dark glasses and she does a double take. "Dumas! What the hell is going on?"

I glance anxiously out of the rear window for any sign of Verdu's heavies. "If we could drive somewhere a bit less public, I'll tell you as we go."

"A bit less public? So you can find a nice quiet spot to bump us off?" Linda is yelling and the pitch of her voice is rising with every syllable. "Start talking right now, Dumas, or I'll scream my fucking head off!"

"There's nothing to get excited about, Linda." I say this as reassuringly as I can, though I don't get the impression she's going be the easiest of people to convince.

"Tell that to Charles!"

"There's nothing wrong with Charles," I snap. "He's not dead."

"Why did you say *dead*? Who said anything about Charles being *dead*?" There's terror in her eyes. "So you did do it!" By now she's reached soprano, flirting with falsetto. "You murdered Charles!" I see her take a deep breath as she winds up for a top-C, maximum-decibel yodel. She isn't leaving me a lot of choice.

Clamping my hand across her widening jaws, I slam her head against the side window, at the same time jabbing the index finger of my other hand into Daniel's ribs. "Drive!" I demand. "Or I'll blow your guts through the windscreen."

Daniel is nobody's hero. "Where to?"

"Your place."

When we've gathered some speed I release my grip on Linda's jaw but I continue to maintain the pressure on the small of Daniel's back. The journey takes little more than five minutes, the silence being broken only by intermittent sobs from Linda and the odd squeak from Daniel when the pressure from my finger increases as we bump across a series of sleeping policemen on the approach to their house. We turn into a long, tree-lined driveway and pull up outside a detached villa, sheltered from the neighbours' view by a dense bank of conifers. Hanging from a low branch is a twee, ceramic sign proclaiming: 'Bienvenue chez Linda et Daniel Scetbon'.

"Sorry about that, Daniel." Abandoning the pretence of carrying a gun, I throw open the rear door and scramble out of the car. "I couldn't take the risk of Linda attracting attention." The Scetbons get out of the car and stand side by side, eyeing me warily. I hold up both hands in a gesture of conciliation. "Just let me come inside for a few minutes and talk to you. I can explain everything."

"For your sake, Dumas, this had better be good!" Linda's eyes dart towards Daniel and she whispers something to him out of the side of her mouth. When she gets his curt nod, she spins on her heel and her stiletto heels scrunch into the loose gravel as she marches towards the house. "There's no one here," she announces, flinging open the front door. "It's Inge's day off and the kids are at their grandmother's." I feel a tinge of disappointment. As I'm following Linda down the hall I realise that she has just opened the front door without using a key. Strange, she doesn't strike me as the type who would leave her house unlocked. When we walk into the lounge I notice the French windows leading to the terrace are ajar. My suspicion that there's someone else present is reinforced by a faint smell of recently smoked tobacco, vaguely reminiscent of Charles' cigars.

Daniel and Linda plonk themselves down on the settee and sit in po-faced silence while I recount the tale of Charles' self-inflicted disappearance. When I get to the part about Verdu and the forged death certificate, Daniel gets to his feet and starts massaging the base of his spine with both hands.

"If even half of what you're saying is true, Jérôme," he says through a barely stifled grin, "I reckon you're in deep shit."

"At least we're starting to see eye to eye on this, Daniel." He looks at me quizzically. "I need your help," I say.

He furrows his brow, tightens the buffalo clasp on his string tie and fixes me with a doleful stare. "I've got enough problems on my plate without getting mixed up with Les Renseignements Généraux." His Marseilles accent seems even thicker than usual.

"I'm not asking you to get involved."

"What do you want, then?" He picks up a packet of Gitanes from the coffee table and taps out a cigarette.

"I want to sell a car."

"What kind of car?"

"Peugeot 206, two years old, low mileage, very good condition, market value around twelve thousand euros. What can you give me for it?"

He scratches at his bristled chin. "Is it nicked?"

"Of course not."

"Is it yours?"

"Not exactly – "

"Fine distinction, eh?" He smiles a toothy grin as he strikes a match and lights up. "Any hire purchase outstanding?"

"No," I state confidently.

Pulling a pen from his shirt pocket, he scribbles some numbers on the back of his cigarette packet. "For a friend, three thousand euros."

"What!"

"Three thousand," he repeats, nodding his head.

"Oh, come on, Daniel! Give me a fucking break!"

"I'm sorry, Jérôme." He makes a pretence of checking his figures. "Three thousand. It's the best I can do."

"I'd be quite happy not to be a friend if that changes the calculation." Sarcasm isn't Daniel's forte. He starts to scribble some more. "Listen, *friend*," I say, pulling the pen from his hand. "Be reasonable. You could flog this car for ten thousand euros without breaking sweat."

He gives a world-weary sigh. "I really am sorry, Jérôme. Six months ago I probably could have done a bit better, but there's been a glut of second-hand Peugeots on the market recently, so I really can't see my way to going beyond three thous- "

"Save me the salesman's sob story, for Christ's sake!" I interject, waving my arms in front of my face. "Okay! Okay! You win. Three thousand it is – but it has to be cash."

"Of course." As a conditioned reflex he plucks a business card from his hip pocket and thrusts it at me.

"How soon can I have the money?" I ask, stuffing his card into my pocket.

"As soon as you can produce the vehicle."

"How about tomorrow?"

He exchanges a nervous glance with Linda. "Linda and I have to go to Nîmes first thing in the morning," he says. "But our au pair will be here," he adds. "If you drop the car off here, I'll leave the money with Inge."

Suddenly life is looking just a teeny-weeny bit brighter. "Would eleven o'clock be okay?"

"Whenever."

"No need to offer me a lift back into town, Daniel," I call over my shoulder as I'm heading towards the lounge door. "I should be able to pick up a cab without too much trouble."

"Fine." Sarcasm is definitely not Daniel's forte.

I stride down the driveway until I'm out of sight of the house, then I turn round and creep back up the path, dodging from the cover of one pine tree to the next, and I track my way round to the back garden from where I can see the lights from the lounge spilling on to the terrace through the open French windows. There's twenty metres of lawn with no cover between me and the house, but the shadows are deep, so I bend low and sprint towards the building, slamming my face into the ivy-covered, brick wall less than a metre from the French windows. The male voice drifting out is agitated. He's speaking English, but there's no mistaking Daniel's accent.

"I tell you I don't like it! I don't like it one fucking, little bit! Linda and I have to go to Nîmes tomorrow morning and I'm not coming back within a mile of this place in the afternoon. According to Davies, Les Renseignements Généraux will be snooping around here asking questions. Inge will just have to deal with them."

"Get a fucking grip of yourself, Daniel!" This voice is also male, but I don't recognise it. He sounds like a native English-speaker, but my hopes are dashed. Though I have to strain to hear his words, I'm sure the voice isn't Benson's. Despite a weak feeling at the back of my knees, I steel myself to snatch a look inside. Sliding my face along the clagging ivy, I peer round the corner of the window and see Linda and Daniel standing with their backs to me. The other person in the room is in profile. He looks to be middle aged, short and stockily built, his obese stomach straining against his bulging shirt and dangling over the waistband of his trousers. His head is completely shaven and I can see several small rings looped through his left earlobe and a couple more protruding from his eyebrow. He pulls hard on his cigar, then he tilts his head back and takes a long swallow from a can of beer.

"You're the one who needs to get a fucking grip!" Daniel retorts. "You do realise I'm taking delivery of a consignment of Semtex from Gerry Madill tomorrow morning before we go to Nîmes? The *last* thing I need is Les Renseignements Généraux poking their noses in around here!"

"Why the hell is Madill delivering Semtex here?" he growls. "I thought we'd agreed to keep the lid on things for a while?" He swigs from his can and turns towards the window. I jerk back my head, my heart hammering nineteen to the dozen. Suddenly, I remember my watch. Depressing the 'record' button, I twist my wrist and hold it as close to the window as I dare. I'm hugging the wall so tightly I can feel the ivy tickling the inside of my nose.

"Madill got in touch with me last week." That's Daniel's voice. "He said he'd had enough of sitting around on his arse doing nothing. He thinks it's time for action." I hear the sound of a ring-pull being ripped from a can. "Those fucking Arabs gave us a pasting in New York, Madrid and London and it's time we sorted them out once and for all. Gerry has always fancied the idea of going for a spectacular on the anniversary of 9/11 and he's come up with a real cracker of an idea."

"What's that?"

"On Sunday, we're going for a dozen Muslim targets in Britain and France in quick succession – six mosques, four schools and a couple of private houses – and the initial letters of the towns we're going to hit will spell out the message: 'Fuck Bin Laden!'"

"Wow!" I hear a low whistle. "That is a bit special, and no mistake."

"Madill has managed to get his hands on a supply of Semtex and he's coming across in person to deliver the bombs for France. He'll be here first thing in the morning to drop the stuff off, then he's coming with Linda and me to Nîmes to check out the target and let us know where to plant the device to achieve the maximum effect before heading up to Avignon to sort things out there." Daniel bursts out laughing. "We're going to give the towel-heads an anniversary present they'll never fucking forget! It's the only language those greasy bastards understand!"

"Will you two put a sock in it!" That's Linda's voice. "Do you want the world and his wife to know what we're up to?"

I hear footsteps stride quickly across the lounge. My head's reeling. I clench my fists into the clammy ivy – so hard that I break a fingernail. Linda's hand reaches out to within inches of my mine and tugs the French windows closed. My heartbeat's in overdrive.

I cling to the wall for several minutes, hardly daring to breathe, then I bend as low as I can and scuttle back towards the shelter of the trees. As soon as I'm out of sight of the house I break into a run and race hell for leather down the driveway. I'm going flat out when my peripheral vision detects a large, black shadow closing in fast from my right-hand side. A wolf? An Alsatian? I do my utmost to accelerate but whatever it is comes flying through the night air and hits me in the thigh with an almighty thump which drives every vestige of breath from my lungs and sends me crashing to the ground, one side of my face grinding painfully into the sharp gravel. I gulp for air and try to struggle to my feet, but my legs are tightly pinned. As I flop back down, my brain clicks in to inform me that, as far as it's aware, neither wolves nor Alsatians do rugby tackles.

I feign unconsciousness, waiting for his next move. A full minute passes, two minutes, seems like hours. I twist sharply on to my back and his arms slowly unwind from my legs and he rolls away, down a small incline, coming to rest face up in the shallow ditch by the side of the path. I scramble to my feet and bend down to examine him. He's dressed in black from head to foot; jogging pants, trainers and a tight, short-sleeved T-shirt which shows off his muscular biceps. His hair is cropped close to the scalp and I can see a jagged, purple scar running from the corner of his right eye to just beneath his ear lobe. His eyes are open wide and he's staring unblinkingly.

What the hell has happened to him? Did he hit his temple on my kneecap? Is he dead? I lift one of his arms and feel his flopping wrist, but fail to detect any pulse. I run my hands tentatively up and down his body, tugging out the pockets of his jogging pants but, apart from a mobile phone clipped to his waistband, I find nothing. Bending down, I grip him underneath the armpits and, after pausing for a moment to make sure there's not going to be any reaction, I drag him out of the ditch and lug him twenty metres into the dense undergrowth on the far side of the path.

I stand, panting, over the prone figure, half-expecting a bank of floodlights to suddenly blaze and a screeching alarm to sound. When nothing untoward happens, I stagger back to the path and take off down the road as fast as my wobbly legs will carry me. After two hundred metres I flag down a passing cab and slump on to the back seat.

The taxi drops me off at the underground car park where I pick up my car and drive like a maniac towards St Martin de Londres. My head's reeling. Who was that guy? One of Scetbon's cronies? One of Verdu's heavies? What if he's dead? My whole body's trembling and my right hip is throbbing painfully. Questions come lancing into my brain. How on earth am I going to get news of the bombing campaign to Frobisher-Allen? Do I dare go anywhere near the Scetbons' house tomorrow morning?

I screech to a halt beside the St Martin phone booth. I'm not holding out much hope that the number Kathleen gave me for Frobisher-Allen is going to be any use at eleven o'clock on a Friday night, but I've got nothing to lose. The phone rings out unanswered. I try Kathleen's home number with the same result.

I search through my pockets for Daniel's business card and find it has both his work and his home phone number. I dial his house and recognise his gruff voice. "It's Jérôme Dumas here, Daniel," I say as casually as my trembling voice will allow. "Sorry to disturb you again. I said I'd be round at eleven o'clock tomorrow morning to drop off the car, but ten would actually suit me a lot better. Would that be all right?"

"I told you," he snaps. "Come whenever the hell you like. Inge will be here all day."

"Right. Thanks." I hang up. It would appear it wasn't one of his guys I tangled with. Daniel isn't that good an actor.

As soon as I get back to the gîte I play back my recording. It's faint, but it's there all right – the names 'Gerry' and 'Madill' are fuzzy, but they can just about be made out. I'm sure Tom Ivinson will be able to enhance the soundtrack.

I run a hot bath and scrub my scalp vigorously with shampoo, which has the effect of removing more hair than I really would have liked along with the caked boot polish. As I lie soaking in the tub, more unanswered questions come tripping into my brain. Are these nutters the real reason I was sent out here? Is Charles Benson involved with these people? And the one question that won't go away – who was the guy in black?

I stretch out full length in the bath and consider my options. Today's the ninth of September, which means they're planning to bomb their targets on Sunday. I have got to get that information to Frobisher-Allen as soon as I possibly can. I can try calling him first thing in the morning, but what the hell am I going to do if I don't manage to make contact? Reluctantly, I conclude I'll have to throw myself on Verdu's mercy – I don't see I have any other option. However, I don't fancy my chances of convincing him that I've stumbled across a cell of racist murderers.

Despite a very large whisky night cap, I spend most of the night tossing and turning, the little sleep I do get being disturbed by confused nightmares of exploding mosques lighting up the night sky. From high in the burning clouds I become aware of a distant cackling sound and, when I shield my eyes from the glare, I see hundreds of black vultures circling overhead, each with a long, filter-tipped cigarette jammed in its beak.

CHAPTER 8

I rise early and run all the way to the phone booth in the village. My fingers are trembling as I tap out Frobisher-Allen's number and, to my immense relief, the phone is answered straight away, but I don't recognise the voice. I speak tersely.

"My name's Frank McClure. I need to talk to Frobisher-Allen – straight away." There's a moment's hesitation. "And before you try telling me he's not there, tell him that if he doesn't want to see a report on MI6's spying missions in France plastered across the front pages of tomorrow's tabloids, he'd better take this call."

"It is Saturday, sir, and – "

"Don't mess me about, pal," I interject. "I don't give a monkey's toss whether he happens to be sitting next to you or if you have to patch this call through to his mobile on the first tee at Wentworth, just get him on this line! And fucking fast!" He doesn't respond. One click and I'm straight into *Land of Hope and Glory*. Halfway through the first verse the line clicks again.

"Frank, my boy," the familiar, smarmy voice intones. "Stanley Frobisher-Allen here. Good to hear from you. I was starting to get concerned about you – not having had a status report this week."

"Cut the bullshit."

"You sound upset, Frank. What's going on out there? There's a rumour going around that you've bumped off Charles Benson."

"That's a load of crap," I growl. "Now listen to me, and listen carefully. I've got information about a group of extremists who are planning a bombing campaign tomorrow on the anniversary of 9/11. They're going to hit a dozen different Muslim targets in Britain and France."

There's a stunned silence. "Where are you calling from?"

"A phone booth in St Martin de Londres."

"Could the line be bugged?"

"How the hell should I know?"

"Give me the number, Frank. I'll have the line checked out and call you back."

"If this is another one of your tricks, pal, I'll take the greatest of pleasure in blabbing my mouth off to a friendly *News of the World* reporter."

"No tricks, Frank. I'll call you right back."

I read out the number printed on the side of the booth and I replace the receiver. It's a good five minutes before the phone rings out.

"Okay, Frank. The line's clean. Now what the hell is this all about?"

"I stumbled upon some nutters last night in Montpellier. They've managed to get their hands on a supply of Semtex in England and they're planning a bombing campaign tomorrow. I overheard them saying they were going to give Bin Laden's lot an anniversary present they'll never forget. They're going for a dozen Muslim targets and the initial letters of the towns they'll hit will spell out 'Fuck Bin Laden'."

I hear a sharp intake of breath "Do you know which towns?" he demands.

"One of the targets is Nîmes – and I think another one is Avignon – but I don't know any more than that."

"Jesus Christ! Do you know who's involved in this, Frank?"

"Does the name 'Gerry Madill' mean anything to you?"

"Hold on. Let me check." I hear tapping at a keyboard. "There's a Gerry Madill on our blacklist," he says. "Lives in Leamington Spa. Used to be a member of the British National Party but got kicked out for being a troublemaker, which takes some doing. He's one of the morons who follow the England football team abroad in order to stir up trouble. According to his file, he's a cunning bastard who keeps a low profile and lets others do the dirty work. We haven't managed to gather enough evidence to justify confiscating his passport. Do you have any proof that Madill's involved?"

"I overheard two blokes talking about the bombing campaign and I've got some of the conversation on tape. Madill is mentioned in connection with supplying the Semtex for the attack in Nîmes."

Frobisher-Allen whistles softly. "Nice one, Frank! Is Charles Benson mixed up in this?"

"Not as far as I know. I've only got one other name, a Frenchman called Daniel Scetbon who has an English wife called Linda. He's the one who's going to be planting the bomb in Nîmes."

There's a hum of whispered conversation at the other end of the line. "Frank, this is first rate work. Quite outstanding. We'll handle everything from this end from here on in. I'll liaise directly with the French authorities. All I want you to do is send me that recording."

"I can put it in the post. I don't know how to get it to you any quicker than that."

"That'll do fine. Send it straight away by registered post. And when you've done that, I don't want you getting involved in this any further. Your mission is surveillance, remember? I want you to concentrate on Benson."

"You've nothing to worry about on that score," I grunt. "Benson happens to be my number one priority. The bastard set me up. So if you want to get your hands on him," I add, "you'd better start co-operating with me. This isn't for Queen and country any more. I don't know whether you're after Benson for paedophilia, or bombs, or whatever, and, quite frankly, I don't give a shit, but for me, it's personal. I'm going to have his guts for garters, but I need funds. I want my bank account reinstated and my credit card reactivated." I hear more muffled whispering.

"Frank, what can I say? Has there been a problem with your bank account? How very annoying. It must have been an administrative cock-up. Not much I can do about that at the weekend, but I'll have someone look into it first thing on Monday morning." Frobisher-Allen clears his throat harshly before continuing. "I'm sorry you've been messed about, Frank. I'm going to put you in the picture, but before I do, I have to remind you that you're bound by the terms of the Official Secrets Act. What I'm about to disclose is strictly need-to-know information. There are only two of us in headquarters who are up to speed with what's going on with Benson."

"I'm all ears."

"The reason we're after him is that The Book Cellar is a front for an international crime syndicate."

The phone goes slack in my fingers. "What?!"

"It's big-time stuff. The network is Europe-wide, extending as far as the ex-USSR republics. These guys are into everything; hard-core porn, prostitute trafficking, paedophilia, snuff movies, you name it. Internet sites are their prime means of communication. We broke a coded website six months ago and we've been monitoring it ever since, trying to identify the ringleaders. We know Benson's somewhere high in the chain of command, but we don't know if he's top dog. That's why I sent you in under cover. I wanted an operative I could trust inside Benson's camp."

"If you could trust me so bloody much," I grumble, "why wasn't I told all this before you sent me in?"

"It took us six months to get a fix on Benson. He's a slippery bastard. If he'd picked up the slightest vibes that we were on to him, he'd have disappeared before you could say Jack Robinson. I made the decision to send you in cold so you could gain his confidence. Once you were established I was going to brief you on the true purpose of your mission."

"Are the French authorities up to speed on this?"

"There's too much danger of a leak at that end, Frank. We suspect that someone high up the French civil service is a key player in the paedophile ring."

"In that case, why the hell did you let Les Renseignements Généraux scare Benson off? Don't you guys cooperate?"

"I dropped a hint to Verdu that he might want to check out Benson's tax affairs. I thought that if Benson needed to raise cash quickly to pay off a tax bill, he might get careless. I didn't expect him to do a bunk."

"Neither did Verdu. He thinks I've murdered him."

"So I'm led to believe."

"Well, for a start, you can get Verdu off my back."

"I'll see what I can do, Frank." Frobisher-Allen's tone is at its condescending worst. "But it's not as simple as that. Verdu's convinced you've murdered Benson and I can't pull rank and have him taken off the case without suspicions being raised and questions being asked."

"I don't know if you're spinning me a line, pal, but if I find myself in a French jail on a murder rap, a certain wee Scots lintie will be chirping his head off – Official Secrets Act or no Official Secrets Act."

"You can count on me, Frank."

"Sure I can. Well, I've got my own agenda now and as it would appear that the only way I'm going to convince Verdu that I didn't murder Benson is by delivering him on a plate, that's what I intend to do – after I've rearranged his face."

"Frank! We need to work together on this. Stay in contact via this number and use the code word 'Operation Puella' when you call in. That'll make sure you're put straight through to me."

"I've told you – Benson's claimed. If you want to make yourself useful, see to it that my credit card's reactivated immediately – and I need an open-ended expense account."

"Carte blanche on your *carte bleue*, Frank. You've got it."

"And sort out my passport. I don't want any hassle from the French or the British immigration officials."

There's a sharp intake of breath. "How the hell did you know about – ?"

"I'm MI6," I interject. "I'm leading-edge. Remember?"

"Eh? Of course, Frank. Of course. Now listen to me. There's no point in you going off half-cocked. We need to work together on this so we can – "

Kathleen's comment about the requirement for 'someone

gullible' suddenly comes to mind. I replace the receiver. As I'm heading back towards the gîte I hear the phone ringing out again, but I don't turn back.

I dig around in the bureau drawers and find an envelope which I address to Frobisher-Allen. Carefully removing the cassette from my watch, I place it inside the envelope and bind the small parcel tightly with sellotape before hurrying to the post office and mailing the package recorded delivery.

I rack my brain until I manage to come up with the name of the guy Benson said he would be staying with in Paris – Mel Hoggard. With the assistance of the village postmistress I access the on-line directory enquiry system and find there are two Hoggards listed in Paris, one of whom, I'm delighted to see, is Melvin Martin Hoggard, who lives at 14 Rue Daru in the eighth *arrondissement*. I jot down his address and phone number before heading back to the gîte.

It's a huge weight off my mind to have communicated the bombers' plans to Frobisher-Allen and, as I'm running an iron over the trousers, I allow myself a self-congratulatory smile for having had the good fortune to hang on to my traffic warden's uniform. The cap's looking rather sorry for itself, peak curving up rather than down, having spent several weeks stuffed inside my suitcase, but after bending it back into shape I admire the overall effect in the bedroom mirror. Not bad. I'm looking forward to Inge's reaction. I rummage in my toilet bag for a condom which I slip into my hip pocket, then I quickly stuff the rest of my belongings into my suitcase as I've no intention of returning to the gîte.

I park at the bottom of the Scetbons' drive and make my way on foot to the scene of my nocturnal encounter. The drive looks different in daylight but I find the crushed vegetation where I'd dragged the body off the path and I follow the trail through the undergrowth until I come to the patch of flattened grass where I'd abandoned him. There's no sign of life. More to the point, there's no sign of death. I'm not sure if this is good news or bad news. I run all the way back to the car and drive up to the house.

It's just after ten o'clock A quick check in the rear-view mirror, a final adjustment to the rakish angle of my cap, and I stride purposefully up to the front door and depress the bell push. I'm taken aback when the door's answered, but I quickly recover my composure.

"Would you please tell Inge that Jérôme Dumas is here. I'm expected," I add with a confident smile.

My smile is returned. "Hello, Jérôme." The smile widens. "Pleased to meet you." A delicate hand is proffered. "I'm Inge." We eye each other up and down. The accent is undeniably Swedish, the hair is blonde and bouncy and is cascading around the slim shoulders. Indeed, there's absolutely nothing wrong with the legs. However, I do find the goatee beard off-putting.

"I thought – ?"

"You were expecting a girl?" He lets out a high-pitched titter. "Lots of people make that mistake. They don't expect an au pair to be male. Inge's short for Ingemar, by the way." His roaming, pale-blue eyes continue to explore my body. "Nice outfit, Jérôme. Do come in."

Snatching off my cap, I thrust it deep into my tunic pocket. "Just for a minute," I say gruffly. "I'm in a terrible rush."

Inge leads the way to the lounge where he takes a sealed envelope from the top drawer of the desk and hands it to me. Without bothering to check the contents, I stuff the envelope into my hip pocket, flinching when I nick my finger on the tinfoil of the condom wrapper. I drop the car keys on to the coffee table and hurry outside to pull my suitcase from the boot. Having refused Inge's offer of a lift into the city centre, I hail a passing taxi as soon as I'm out of sight of the house.

I alight at the railway station and take the escalator to the upper level. There's no queue in the ticket office and I cross to an empty booth to purchase a ticket for the next TGV to Paris. I find I've got a couple of hours to kill so I go back down the escalator and cross the road to a pavement café where I first visit the toilets to change out of my traffic warden uniform into a blue-checked shirt, jeans, linen jacket and trainers. I empty out my pockets on to the hand basin and gaze wistfully at the solitary condom before thrusting it into my trouser pocket. Wandering outside to a table in the sunshine, I order two croissants and a double espresso.

The guard's whistle shrieks. I've been allocated a window seat and, although the train's busy, it looks as if I'm going to have two places to myself. However, the vision boards just as the train is pulling out.

CHAPTER 9

She appears to be in her early twenties, tall and leggy. Her short, jet-black, gelled hair is swept back from her forehead and sculpted in a tapering wedge which comes to a point against her left cheek bone. She has a slightly retroussé nose and a wide mouth with full lips. Slimly built, with slender hands and wrists, her incredibly long, deep-tanned, bare legs are displayed to full advantage by a scalloped miniskirt and ankle-length boots. Her face is also tanned and she appears to be wearing no make-up, other than a trace of green eye shadow which matches to perfection the colour of her stunning eyes; sparkling pupils surrounded by large, sea-green irises flecked with minute spots of grey. Long, black eyelashes curve upwards towards her plucked eyebrows and there's high colour in her cheeks from the effort of running.

As she flops down on the seat beside me she unbuttons her jacket, revealing a virtually transparent, cream blouse. My gaze is drawn to her small breasts, unencumbered by a bra, rising and falling in synchronisation with her snatched breathing. She catches me gawping and I turn away and stare out of the window at the station rushing past. Her perfume, wafting across, fills my nostrils and makes me feel light-headed. I pinch the top of my leg to make sure I'm not dreaming. For the next three and a half hours this vision will be by my side. The palms of my hands are clammy with sweat.

The first, casual remark is all-important, but timing is everything. I can't leave it too long to break the ice. 'You mean it took you ten minutes to come up with that?' On the other hand, I don't want to go at it like a bull at a gate. My mind goes completely blank.

In retrospect, the downside of catapulting from virgin to bondage fetishist in fifteen minutes is that you tend not to develop much of a chat-up technique along the way – and it does seem a bit early in our relationship to impress her with my mastery of the imperfect subjunctive.

I continue to stare out of the window, rejecting every banal opening line that ambles into my brain. 'Do you live in Montpellier?' 'Are you travelling on business?' 'Are you going all the way to Paris?' 'You almost missed the train, didn't you?' Seriously, McClure, is this really the best you can come up with? If only she'd been struggling with a heavy suitcase, I could have gallantly offered to stow it on the overhead rack, but she's carrying no luggage other than a Gucci shoulder bag. A winning smile and: 'You look out of breath, would you like me to get you a glass of water from the buffet car?' might've been appropriate ten minutes ago. However, as I steal another sidelong glance, while there's no denying that she looks breath-taking, she's no longer displaying any signs of being out of breath.

She pulls a book from her shoulder bag and flicks it open and as the kilometres whip past panic starts setting in. An opening remark I could have got away with when she first sat down would no longer be adequate. She's been by my side for fifteen minutes, for God's sake. She'll be expecting something clever, sophisticated and witty. My brain churns like mad but nothing, absolutely nothing, comes to mind.

I still can't believe what came out. "Excuse me, please, I need the loo." I stand up and squeeze past her and my knees go weak when the backs of my legs brush along her exposed thigh. I can feel my face turning bright red as I sway my way up the aisle. I can't believe I just said that! Why couldn't I have left it at 'Excuse me, please', which would have left open the possibility that I was going to the buffet car for a coffee or a beer? But no: 'I need the loo'! I slam the toilet door closed behind me and, as I'm peeing, I twist round and gaze into the mirror at a sea of scarlet freckles. Jesus Christ, Sadie Mason, you've got a lot to answer for!

Before returning to my seat, I make sure I'm reeking of soap in order to reassure her that I have, at least, washed my hands. Pathetic, I know, but I've only got the imperfect subjunctive to fall back on. She lowers her book when she sees me approaching and she angles her legs inwards to allow me to slide past. I think I might die of ecstasy as I once again make contact with her naked thigh. I sit down and fix my stare on the back of the seat in front of me, too embarrassed to risk eye contact.

As we're approaching Nîmes station she closes her book and gets to her feet and for one dreadful moment I think she's about to get off the train. She touches my arm lightly and smiles when I turn to face her. "Would you mind watching my things for a minute?" she says. "I need the loo."

Whooping is frowned on on TGVs. I settle for a long, silent scream and a few chords of air guitar.

While she's away, I sneak a look at the book she left on her seat. This is incredible! It's *Jonathan Livingston Seagull* by Richard Bach, part of my compulsory reading when I was a teenager. I check her bookmark. She's more than halfway through. To be sitting by her side when she reaches the *dénouement* is a privilege no other human being will ever experience. I replace the bookmark with a trembling hand and reposition the book exactly as she'd left it.

I'm not implying for one minute that she didn't wash her hands, only she didn't make any great effort with the soap to communicate the fact. She smiles at me again as she takes her seat but I make no attempt at conversation, willing her to resume reading. Occasionally, I steal a glance to see where she's reached. On the outskirts of Avignon, Jonathan is banned by the elders of the flock because of his conviction that seagulls are put on this earth to fly and not to scavenge for food. By the time we reach Montélimar, he is capable of attaining incredible speeds and he's come to understand that love and kindness are the raisons d'être of life. He finally achieves transcendence as we sweep past Valence. She closes the book and puts it down on her knee and I notice her eyes are tightly shut. I wait a few moments before I break the silence.

"Have you read *Zen and the Art of Motorcycle Maintenance*?"

"Pardon?" Her huge, startled eyes spring open and her neck twists towards me.

"*Zen and the Art of Motorcycle Maintenance.* It's by an American – Robert M. Pirsig. It's the only other book I know that has an equivalent impact."

"You've read *Jonathan Livingston?*"

I nod. I'm dying to tell her I've read the English version as well as the French translation, but that would be gilding the lily. "What did you make of it?" I ask.

Lyon and Macon flash past in an animated exchange of ideas. By Dijon, having dissected *Jonathan Livingston Seagull*, we've analysed the poetry of Kahlil Gibran and delved into Buddhism, moral philosophy and transcendental meditation.

While we prattle on, her hands never stop moving and her cheeks repeatedly crinkle with infectious laughter, but it's her eyes that are truly exceptional – they have a life and energy all of their own. Everything Me Sung tried to teach me in the Kilbirnie public park falls into place. Her eyes express her *qi* more lucidly than words ever could and her every emotion exudes through these green, limpid pools; wave upon wave of excitement, mystery, sadness, passion, intrigue and amusement.

"Does the word *qi* mean anything to you?" I ask.

She clasps the palms of her hands to her cheeks and cocks her head at an angle. "I've heard of it," she says, "but I couldn't tell you what it means. Isn't it something Chinese?"

I nod. "It's the life energy that permeates everything. You can learn to control it with *qigong*, which is a form of energy healing. It allows you to achieve complete physical and mental peace."

Her eyes are positively dancing. "Will you teach me?"

"Of course."

She starts giggling – the sexiest giggle imaginable. I'm in my element. Opportunities for imperfect subjunctives abound.

The guard's interruption to announce that we're on the approach to Paris Gare de Lyon is the worst moment in my life.

"Hey!" she says. "Are we here already?" Grabbing hold of my wrist she takes my hand between both of hers in a delicate, prayer-like posture. "You do realise we're about to get off this train and we might never meet again?"

My God. She's fondling my fingers and she expects me to be able to speak! Every part of my body that's capable of tingling is doing so in spades. I want to hold on to that moment for ever.

"And we haven't even touched on Pirsig," I croak. "Couldn't we maybe… you know…" I'm at the stammering stage, not a million miles from babbling. "Perhaps we could meet up, like – later on?"

"I'm only in Paris for a couple of hours – for a boring business meeting. I'm heading back to Montpellier this evening."

I don't know what to say. I hear: 'Do you often have to work on Saturdays?', which presumably came from my mouth. At times I'm capable of unplumbed depths of banality.

"Afraid so. In the fashion business it's seven days a week during the season. What brings you to Paris?"

"I'm… I'm here to visit someone."

"When will you be back in Montpellier?"

"I'm not actually planning to go back. I mean, I might," I add hastily. "I'm not sure. It all depends – "

"I am sorry," she interrupts. "I really must go." Her voice is drowned by the whoosh of the train's air brakes. "Someone's meeting me." She's shouting to make herself heard. "If you're ever back in Montpellier you have to call me." I nod. "Promise?" I nod even more vigorously. "We have to exchange something," she states as she's getting to her feet. "I'm superstitious. If we have something belonging to each other, it means we'll meet again."

I'm flustered and I fumble in my trouser pockets, but somehow a condom doesn't seem appropriate. I lick at my right hand furiously and struggle to pull off my signet ring.

"Good God, no! It must be nothing of value. Just something that'll remind me of you. What about that?" She points to the cheap pen jutting from my jacket pocket.

"Of course." I tug it out and hand it to her.

"And you have to have something of mine. Let me see. How about this?" She pulls the pseudo-leather bookmark from *Jonathan Livingston Seagull* and hands it to me. "You mustn't lose it. Otherwise we'll never meet again."

"I'll take good care of it. Don't worry. I'll give it back to you when we meet up. Anyway, you'll need it when you're reading *Zen and the Art of Motorcycle Maintenance*."

Again, that infectious, sexy giggle. She takes her diary from her bag, rips out a blank page and uses my pen to scribble down a phone number. Thrusting the slip of paper into my hand, she closes my fist around it. "Do call me as soon as you get back to Montpellier," she says. "I can't wait to hear all about Pirsig."

I clutch the page and sit transfixed as the vision merges with the mass of humanity shuffling and shoving its way down the aisle. When she's disappeared from sight I study her phone number and, as a conditioned reflex, commit it to memory. Taking out my wallet, I carefully tuck the bookmark and her phone number into the back compartment. It's only then I realise that I don't even know her name.

I'm the last person off the train and when I walk out of the Gare de Lyon the temperature feels a lot cooler than in Montpellier. Although I've never been in Paris before, I feel perfectly at home. Everything about the place is familiar. I know the Métro map and the layout of the main boulevards by heart and I've studied photographs of every historic building and monument at my mother's knee. Mentally, I've walked every inch of this city and the name Rue Daru conjures up an image of the Russian quarter and the ornate, gold-leaf, onion-domed church of Alexandre Névsky.

I take the RER to Place Charles de Gaulle and switch to the Métro for the short ride to Place des Ternes, stopping outside the station to gaze up Avenue Wagram and admire the Arc de Triomphe. I trail my suitcase the short distance to Rue Daru under a rapidly blackening sky and I find a block of modern flats at number fourteen, adjacent to the Russian Orthodox church. The nameplate for Mel Hoggard indicates a third floor apartment but when I press the bell push there's no reply. I cross the street to an ethnic restaurant, La Ville de Petrograd, which is empty apart from a solitary waiter sitting with his feet up on a chair, reading a book. I select a table by the window from where I can observe the entrance to the apartment block. The *carte du jour* is propped up against a vase of artificial roses.

"I'll have the thirty euro menu," I call across. "And a bottle of house red."

"We don't start serving until seven." The waiter replies without raising his head from his book. I check my watch. It's just after six.

"In which case, I'll have a beer to be going on with."

Three beers precede dinner. Rain starts falling between the blinis and the borscht and I have to wipe a gap in the steamed-up window to maintain visibility of the street outside. A torrential downpour greets the stroganoff and barely eases during the pavlova. A fine drizzle and a *fine* Cognac accompany the coffee.

It's midnight and I'm nursing my umpteenth coffee and Cognac, lost in an erotic daydream involving my unnamed creature. No one else has ventured into the restaurant since I arrived and there's been no sign of Benson approaching the block of flats opposite. Since my initial conversation with the waiter, when I placed my order some six hours ago, the sum total of our communication has comprised a *bonne continuation* from him preceding each course and, latterly, several half-hearted enquiries as to whether monsieur would like his bill, met each time by a resolute '*encore un café et un Cognac, s'il vous plaît*'.

My blurred vision struggles to focus on my watch and I finally decide to call it a day. I down my last Cognac in one gulp and call for the bill which appears instantaneously by my side and I wince when I see the size of the dent I've made in my meagre capital. I'm about to ask the waiter if he can recommend a cheap hotel in the neighbourhood when I pick up the slurred strains of *The Blaydon*

97

Races wafting through the window. Pressing my nose hard against the glass, I stare out at the familiar, hunched figure weaving his way along the middle of the road, grey hair centre-parted by the rain and plastered against his flushed cheeks, soggy cigar in his left hand, whisky bottle jutting from his jacket pocket and an open can of Guinness clamped in his right fist. Evidently, Charles is still committed to acquiring the taste.

I leave a considerably larger tip than I'd intended, instructing the waiter to hold on to my suitcase until the morning. I scuttle outside and catch up with Charles as he's fiddling with a set of keys at the entrance to the apartment block and I remain in the shadows until he's stumbled inside, then I move swiftly and catch the door with my toe cap to prevent it swinging closed. Charles doesn't glance back as he lurches across the foyer, past the empty concierge's office, towards an enclosed, internal quadrangle. He staggers across the courtyard, negotiates the three steps with a degree of difficulty and zigzags along the corridor towards the lift, warbling at the top of his voice. I wait until he's inside the elevator, then I sprint up the adjoining staircase to the third floor landing. I'm panting in the hallway when the lift doors slide open to the strains of *'Gannin' along the Scotswood Road'* and I join in with *'To see the Blaydon Races'*.

He spins round.

"Good evening, Charles."

His blink rate is phenomenal. "Who the fuck? What the fuck?"

"One question at a time."

"Jesus Christ! It's Jérôme, isn't it?" he says, pushing his spectacles up on to the top of his head and rubbing at his piggy eyes with the backs of his fists. "God, am I glad it's you." His sigh of relief is almost palpable.

"You might want to reconsider that."

He ignores my remark as he struggles to introduce his key into the lock of the apartment door facing the lift. "Come on in. Mel's away for a few days and I've got the place to myself." After a few more fumbles he succeeds in turning the key. "How did you manage to find me? How's the bookshop doing?" He breaks off and looks anxiously up and down the corridor. "You weren't followed here, were you?"

Having been reassured on that score, Charles kicks open the front door and ushers me ahead of him, across the hallway, into a small, well-furnished lounge. The curtains are open wide, giving a superb view of the floodlit cathedral opposite. Newspapers and magazines are strewn all around the room, the ashtrays are overflowing and several days' unwashed dishes are piled on the coffee table next to the television. Charles tugs the whisky bottle from his jacket pocket, pours two large measures and hands me one before flopping down on the settee. I take the seat beside him.

"Tell me, then," he says between swigs of whisky. "What brings you to Paris?"

"Verdu's hounding me. He thinks I've murdered you and disposed of your body. He's convinced I forged your will so I could get my hands on the bookshop."

Charles' wrestles with this scenario for a moment, then slaps my knee and lets out a raucous laugh, almost choking on a mouthful of whisky that goes down the wrong way. "He doesn't credit you with a lot of common sense then," he splutters.

"This isn't funny, Charles. I'm facing a murder rap."

"You do go on, Jérôme. Don't be ridiculous! Verdu's got nothing on you and without a corpse he can't even begin to build a case."

"Be that as it may," I say in what I intend to sound like a meaningful tone. "But my life would be an awful lot simpler if I had a few thousand euros to be going on with."

He shrivels his brow. "What the fuck?"

"We've done that one, Charles."

He glowers at me and tugs a soggy packet of cheroots from his shirt pocket. "What makes you think I could lay my hands on that kind of money?" He strikes a match and sucks hard on the damp cigar but doesn't succeed in getting it lit. "And even if I could," he slurs, dropping the cigar on to the carpet, "why should I give you a brass farthing?" He pours another belt of whisky down his throat, then shakes his head and cackles.

"What's the profit margin on paedophilia?" I ask quietly. Charles' laughter dies in his throat. "Enough to fund a few kilos of Semtex?" He looks at me in open-mouthed astonishment. "And I might also add that, as well as singing my head off to Verdu, there are certain people in MI6 who would be very interested in knowing your whereabouts."

An eyebrow is slowly raised in my direction. "For a trainee bookshop assistant from Alsace, you seem amazingly well connected." He drags himself to his feet and staggers towards the whisky bottle on the coffee table. "Let's talk about this sensibly, Jérôme. There must be a solution that'll keep both of us happy." Having topped up his glass, he offers me a refill.

When I come to, I'm lying on my back on the carpet and bright sunlight, streaming through the windows, is piercing my eyelids. I drift back to consciousness to the faint strains of ecclesiastical music and my initial impression, that I've sloughed the mortal coil and am being welcomed into heaven by a celestial choir, is quickly dispelled by the excruciating pain in my left jaw. It slowly dawns on me that I'm hearing plainchant floating across from the Russian church.

I have to admit it was a neat move – though it must be said that circumstances conspired against me. I'd held out my whisky glass for Charles to top it up and, as he was approaching the settee, I was startled by a muffled explosion emanating from the street outside. A car backfiring? A bomb? The apartment windows were vibrating and rattling noisily in their frames. I twisted round in my seat to look out of the window and, although I saw it coming out of the corner of my eye, I'd no time to take evasive action. With a dexterous flick of the wrist, Charles smashed the whisky bottle into the side of my face.

I get to my knees and sink my face into my hands, flinching when my fingers encounter a lump the size of a duck's egg above my left temple. I run my tongue around the inside of my furred-up mouth and experience the extremely unpleasant sensation of snagging my tongue on the razor-sharp edge of a chipped tooth. The whisky bottle, which Charles contrived to empty before departing, is lying by my feet. I pick it up and weigh it in the palm of my hand, my befuddled brain juggling with the imagery of this bottle exacting revenge for the number of times I've hit its comrades.

The contents of my jacket pockets have been spilled out on to the carpet. Charles has been considerate enough to leave me my identity papers, my keys, my *carte bleue* and my cheque book. However, the bastard has relieved me of my wallet, and with it all my cash.

I drag myself to my feet and stagger along the corridor to the bathroom where I peer into the mirror at barely recognisable features. I suppose I should be grateful the whisky bottle didn't shatter. However, my left eyelid is purple, the eye itself is practically closed and the bruising has spread down the side of my face as far as my chin. I spit a mixture of congealed blood and chipped tooth into the sink, then I run the cold tap and cup water in both hands, wincing when I splash it on to my face. I squint at my watch. Ten to three. Through my blurred vision the date on my watch seems to be pulsing, screaming at me that today is the eleventh of September. A cold shiver runs down my spine when I remember last night's explosion. That was after midnight. Is there a district nearby with one of the initial letters the bombers are targeting? What had Benson been up to before he came home last night? Might he have been planting a bomb? My brain's hurting.

I go through to the kitchen and find a radio which I switch on and tune to *France Inter* and I sit at the kitchen table with my head in my hands, waiting anxiously for the three o'clock news. They lead with a road accident and follow it with a story about a corrupt politician who's due to appear in court tomorrow but, thank God, nothing about terrorist attacks in Paris or anywhere else. I heave a huge sigh of relief. Bizarrely, I suddenly feel famished. Using the entire contents of the fridge, I cobble together a meal which comprises a three-egg, cheese and tomato omelette and two cans of Guinness. Eating is a laborious process as I can chew on only one side of my mouth. Drinking is even more awkward as my swollen jaw is devoid of feeling.

When I eventually finish eating I search the flat for any clue as to where Benson might have gone and, from among the cracked eggshells in the kitchen pedal bin, I extract a credit card receipt, dated yesterday, made out to the SNCF for sixty three euros and twenty centimes – a sum I know to be the price of a single TGV ticket between Paris and Montpellier.

If it is his intention to head back south, it must be for something pretty important if he's prepared to run the risk of crossing swords with Verdu. I come to the conclusion that fate has ordained that I follow him back to Montpellier and, despite the ache in my jaw, I manage a weak smile as I conjure up a vision of those sparkling, sea-green eyes.

I take the lift to the ground floor and cross the street to La Ville de Petrograd where the same waiter is clearing tables. He doesn't look in the least bit pleased to see me.

"Don't worry. I know I'm too late for lunch. I'm only here to collect my suitcase."

His gaze locks on to my battered face and I see fear in his eyes. "It was the cops' decision, monsieur," he mutters. "Nothing to do with me." I raise an enquiring eyebrow, lowering it immediately when a vicious stab of pain pulses through my forehead. "When you left last night," he mumbles, "I was worried about your case – thought it might be a bomb, so I called out the CRS. They took it out back to examine it and they decided on a controlled explosion."

"Jesus Christ! The CRS blew open my case? Where is it now?"

He shrugs uncomfortably. "When I said *controlled*, I was speaking relatively. What I meant is they don't seem to have done any structural damage to the building."

I recall the vibrating window frames. "And my things?" I ask quietly.

He lowers his eyes and shakes his head. "There's only that." He jerks his thumb towards the counter. "I was going to keep it as a souvenir but, of course, you can have it back."

I emerge from the restaurant with a badly scorched traffic warden's cap perched at a jaunty angle on my head.

I stop at the corner of Rue Daru to count the change in my pockets. Forty centimes. Not even enough for a Métro ticket. Look on the bright side, I say to myself as I stride out down the Faubourg Saint Honoré. At least it's dry and if you still had your suitcase you'd have to have lugged it all the way to the Gare de Lyon.

Walking briskly, it takes me just over an hour to reach the railway station. I use a cheque to purchase a ticket for the 18.53 TGV to Montpellier, then I go to the station buffet and annoy the waiter by asking for a glass of tap water and a straw. I position myself on a bench from where I can observe the passengers funnelling towards the platform on the off-chance that Benson might be catching this train and I wait there, recognising no one, until a couple of minutes before the train's due to leave. Having validated my ticket in the machine at the top of the platform, I board just as the guard's sounding his whistle.

I doze fitfully throughout the journey until I'm hit by a sudden surge of adrenalin when the guard announces we're on the approach to Nîmes station. I stare through the window into the inky blackness, half expecting a ball of flame to erupt at any moment in the overcast sky. The scheduled stop of four minutes seems to last a lot longer than that before we continue on our way to Montpellier, pulling into the station two minutes ahead of schedule.

I'm tempted to phone my unnamed creature, but decide against it. Apart from the lateness of the hour, I want to get myself cleaned up before I arrange to meet her. The bistros on the Place de La Comédie are all still open and I choose an Italian restaurant where I order fettuccini with cheese sauce as I think this is the most my fragile jaw can handle. When I ask the surly waiter if there was anything important in the news today he gives a dismissive shake of the head. While I'm waiting to be served I reflect on how one's options are restricted when one has a cheque book, but no cash. Whereas buying a beer or a coffee is nigh on impossible, paying for a meal is no problem. I wash the pasta down with a half bottle of Valpolicella and finish off with a peach melba and an espresso.

As I'm stirring sugar into my coffee I consider the immediate problem of a bed for the night. I still have the keys for the gîte at St Martin, but taxis are notorious for not accepting cheques and the car rental offices have long since closed. I could pay for a hotel room with my credit card, but I don't want to attract unnecessary attention by turning up late at night at a hotel with no reservation and no luggage.

I suddenly remember the camp bed in The Book Cellar. Ideal. I still have the keys and it's only a few minutes' walk from here. I call the waiter across and order another half bottle of wine and when he opens it I stick the cork back in the neck of the bottle. Having settled the bill, I wend my way through the alleyways, swigging from the bottle as I go.

I don't switch on any lights when I get to the bookshop. As far as I can tell by the illumination from the street lamp filtering through the bevelled windows, everything is exactly as I left it. I slouch down on the chair behind the counter and pour the remaining contents of the wine bottle down my throat. Groping my way to the loo, I pee haphazardly in the gloom. I tug off my jacket, drape it over the back of a chair, then I feel my way to the narrow, rickety camp bed and collapse on to it, fully dressed. Within minutes I've passed out in a drunken stupor.

I jolt myself awake by rolling over and almost falling off the bed. It's pitch dark and I was dreaming about squeaky, unoiled hinges. When I hear the squeak again I sit bolt upright, wincing when I rub at my bruised eye.

CHAPTER 10

I'm wide awake in the inky darkness, frozen to the bed, my ears straining to detect the slightest noise. I pick out what sounds like shuffling footsteps and I catch my breath when a strobe of white light comes flooding underneath the storeroom door.

Despite the pain, I rub again at my swollen eyelids. Everything goes pitch black, then, a few seconds later, another flash of light pulses beneath the door. I deduce that someone must be sweeping the bookshop with a torch. More muffled footsteps, moving more quickly this time, then a ripping, rending sound. Swinging my feet to the floor, I feel my way on tiptoe, through the gloom, towards the storeroom door. I twist the handle slowly and ease the door ajar. Thankfully, no tell-tale squeak. When I push the door open another couple of inches I can make out a shadowy figure in the far corner, at the end of the narrow aisle. He's on his hands and knees with his back to me and his flashlight, propped on the floor, is directed towards the unopened Chronopost package which he's hacking at with a knife. I open the door just enough to squeeze through and, with no clear idea of what I'm going to do next, I creep towards the kneeling figure.

I really should have remembered the creaky floorboards. He wheels round to face me and scrambles to his feet. The torchlight, shining up from ground level, catches him underneath the chin and casts a huge, dancing shadow on the ceiling. He crouches low and I can see what looks like a hunting knife balanced in the palm of his right hand. A handkerchief is dangling from his left wrist.

"Who the fuck? What the fuck?"

"You're getting predictable, Benson."

"Dumas! Well, who would have believed it?" He cackles. "We'll have to stop meeting like this." He bends even lower and starts shuffling clockwise, his knife puncturing the air in small stabbing jerks. I circle away from him, my eyes locked on to his, until I feel the small of my back brush against the horseshoe counter. I reach behind me and my fingers tighten around a heavy, glass paperweight.

Benson stops moving. "We don't have to do this, Dumas. I just need to get something from that package, then I'll be on my way."

"I don't think so, Benson." I start circling again, edging round until I've cut off his access to the front door. "You and I have a score to settle."

I saw the disarming trick in the movies. It's particularly effective in the dark. You hurl a heavy object, in this case a paperweight, high over your adversary's head and, when his attention is momentarily distracted, you lunge at him with arms outstretched, lock your fingers around his throat and throttle the breath from his body.

Unfortunately, it would appear that Benson has seen the same movie. He doesn't flinch when the paperweight crashes off the ceiling and he steps aside nimbly when I throw myself at him, his knife arcing through the air. At first I assume he's missed because I feel no pain, other than a sharp jolt when my right knee smashes into a bookshelf, causing several heavy volumes to come clattering to the floor. When I spin round to face him again I feel warm liquid oozing from my cheek and seeping down the inside of my shirt collar and when I put my fingers to my face it stings. I press the palm of my hand flat against my cheekbone to try to stem the flow of blood, while keeping my eyes glued on Benson. He starts shuffling round again.

"Ah said, we dinny huv tae dae this, Dumas." I do a mental double-take. Did he just speak to me in English? I'm so disoriented, I'm not sure. I struggle to reconstruct his actual words. "Efter a' the time you spent listenin' in Fitzpatrick's, yer English should be pretty good by now, Jimmy." He spits out the last word. The bastard *is* speaking in English – and he's mocking me with a pathetic Scottish accent. The beam from his discarded torch catches his knife and I can see drops of my blood glistening on the blade. He lobs the knife in the air and expertly grabs the spinning weapon by the handle as it falls, then he lurches forward, knife arm fully extended. "Here's a wee test for you, Jimmy," he taunts. "Tae see how much English you really understaun'. If you don't back off right now, Dumas – or whatever the hell your name is," he snarls, "I'm going to fucking kill you."

It's ridiculous, I know, but the split infinitive upsets me more than my split cheek. My brain takes time out to analyse where *fucking* should go in that phrase. Normally, the adverb would follow the infinitive, but 'I'm going to kill fucking you' doesn't sound right and 'I'm going to kill you fucking' doesn't bear thinking about. As I launch myself again at his throat, I fleetingly wonder whether I might be the first person ever to meet his maker while parsing.

Benson jerks his head back and my grasping fingers claw at his face. His knife carves upwards and this time the pain is instantaneous, the scrape of steel against jawbone screeching in my brain. The scything blade bounces off my chin and nicks my top lip before catching the inside of my right nostril and ripping it open. I sink to my knees and clutch my hands to my face, struggling to breathe as I gag on the blood swilling round my mouth and gurgling down the back of my throat. Through a mist of pain I hear a vehicle drawing up outside the shop, followed by an urgent voice shouting muffled instructions. I spread my fingers and, by the faint light of the street lamp, I think I can detect panic in Benson's rapidly-blinking eyes.

Benson takes one pace forward and lashes out with his foot, his toe cap driving into the pit of my stomach. I pitch forward and throw up on the shop floor, a spluttering, retching, gooey mixture of half-digested fettuccini and blood. Dropping to his knees, Benson uses his knife to slash at the binding on the Chronopost package. He picks up his torch and quickly scans the contents, then he grabs a brown-paper package and drops the knife and the torch before hurrying down the aisle towards the storeroom. I hear the dull thud of shutters being thrown open, followed by the sound of running footsteps receding down the lane. I crawl on my hands and knees towards the front door and peer out. There's laughter and a hiss of air brakes as the rubbish collection lorry moves on down the street. I pass out in a dead faint.

I've no idea how long I was unconscious. When my eyelids flicker open they're greeted by the gruesome sight of congealed vomit and blood. It's on my hands, down the front of my shirt, clotted in my stubble and meandering across the shop floor in a coagulated river. I drag myself to my feet and stagger to the bathroom, breathing as best I can in short gulps through my mouth. Switching on the light, I examine what passes for my face in the mirror. An ashen complexion and, on top of last night's bruising, my cheek slashed open, loose flesh sagging from my lower jaw, a swollen, purple top-lip and remnants of my imploded nostril unrecognisable beneath a crust of caked blood.

Groggily, I make my way back to the front shop where I use Benson's knife to hack away the remaining tape binding the Chronopost package and when I spill the contents on to the floor a couple of dozen Barbara Cartlands come tumbling out, together with three brown paper parcels, similar to the one Benson took, addressed to customers in Spain. I rip open one of these packages and, instead of a book, I find a boxed, unlabelled video cassette. I slide the tape into the VCR machine, depress the play button, and collapse on to a chair. Though I've never read any Barbara Cartland, it doesn't take a devoted fan to realise this isn't the film version of the book.

It starts off innocently enough with a hand-held camera taking wide-angled shots of four well-endowed, teenage girls sunbathing topless beside a heart-shaped swimming pool. Two virile pool attendants arrive on the scene and start chatting to the girls and, within minutes, their swimming trunks have been discarded and the scenario develops into a series of close-ups of intertwined limbs and improbably large penises hopping effortlessly from orifice to orifice to the accompaniment of badly synchronised moaning and grunting. Watching these physical contortions is doing nothing for my nausea or my ego. I hobble across to the machine and thump the eject button.

I pace up and down between the bookshelves, trying to figure out what's going on. Why did Benson speak to me in English? Was he trying it on because I'd let slip in Paris that MI6 were interested in his whereabouts? But why the phoney Scottish accent? And why take the risk of coming here in the middle of the night to recover a second rate porn cassette he could have picked up for a few quid in any sex shop? I can't make head nor tail of this, but my first priority has to be to get my face patched up. Trying to focus on the yellow pages through blurred vision does nothing for my thumping headache but I manage to find the number of a local taxi firm. When I pick up the phone I'm relieved to get a dialling tone. I was worried that France Télécom might've cut me off by now. I'm told a cab will be here in fifteen minutes so I go back to the bathroom and clean up my face as best I can, although my nose is too painful even to touch. I also seem to have done some serious damage to my right knee as the kneecap has swollen to twice its normal size.

The taxi driver announces his arrival with a toot on the horn but his smile quickly dissipates when he sees the state of my face. He winds down his window and stares open-mouthed.

"What the hell happened to you?"

"I had an accident."

"There's ambulances for that sort of thing, mate." He starts rolling up his window and glances towards his offside wing mirror as if he's about to drive off. The car bearing down on him gives me just enough time to wrench open the rear door and climb into the back seat.

"Hey! Get out of my cab! I don't want blood all over my seat covers."

"Give me a break, pal. Anyway, the blood's dry."

"No way! Get out!" I glare at him defiantly. "If you don't move your arse this minute," he shouts, "I'll drive you straight to the nearest police station."

"I'll pay double fare."

He hesitates. "Where to?"

"Casualty department."

"Which hospital?"

"You choose."

He stares at me long and hard, then flicks down the handle on the meter and drops the cab into gear. As we're threading our way across town I finger my total worldly assets of forty cents in my trouser pocket. I tap the driver on the shoulder when I spot a cashpoint machine.

"Pull over there. I need to withdraw some cash."

"What are you playing at now?" he demands.

"Do you want to get paid or don't you?" He glowers at me in his rear-view mirror and curses loudly as he pulls up at the kerbside, flicking on his hazard warning lights. He keeps the engine and the meter running, watching suspiciously as I limp towards the cash dispenser. I'm not looking forward to the consequences if Frobisher-Allen hasn't reactivated my card.

To call this my lucky day would be stretching it. However, the machine does spew out three hundred euros in response to my request.

I'm wary about giving the receptionist at the Lapeyronie Hospital my name and address so I identify myself as Charles Benson and request the invoice be sent to The Book Cellar. My explanation for my injuries – tripping when inebriated and crashing head first through a plate glass window – is greeted with a sceptical frown, but the matter isn't pursued.

I'm given a local anaesthetic and my chin is carefully shaved. Four stitches are inserted in my jaw and two more in my upper lip. The slash in my cheek is superficial but some fancy needlework is required around a splint in my right nostril. Apparently the injury to my knee isn't serious, nevertheless I'm advised to rest my leg as much as possible for a few days to allow the swelling to subside. I'm given a prescription for painkillers and told to report back to the outpatients' department in forty-eight hours for a check up.

As I limp out of the hospital I'm feeling thoroughly depressed. I haven't a clue where to start looking for Benson and I can't bear the thought of my gorgeous creature seeing me in this state. For lack of anything better to do, I take a taxi back to the bookshop where I slouch in the armchair behind the counter, feeling sorry for myself. As the effects of the anaesthetic start to wear off a purple haze clouds my vision and intermittent jolts of pain pulse through my jaw. I decide to phone my creature. If I can't meet her, at least I'll be able to talk to her. I dial her number, which is ingrained forever in my memory, and a female answers on the second ring. Voices are often different over the phone but, even allowing for that, this one doesn't sound right. The pitch is too low, the vowels too clipped.

"Hello. Is that – ? I mean. Are you – ?" I'm flustered and I'm slurring my words. Speaking is difficult enough with my stitched lip and I haven't thought through what I want to say. "Have you read *Jonathan Livingston Seagull*?" comes blurting out.

"What the hell are you talking about? Who is this?"

"You don't know me, but – "

"I don't care what you're selling," she interrupts. "I don't want it."

"I'm not selling anything. Honestly! Is there someone else there?"

"Jesus! Who do want to talk to, for God's sake?"

I take a stab in the dark. "Your flatmate."

"Which one?" The voice is laden with suspicion.

"I… I don't know which one, but – "

"Weirdo!" The phone is slammed down. I take several deep breaths before dialling again. "Ye...es?" The same dubious voice.

"Don't hang up on me! Please! I know this sounds crazy but I met one of your flatmates on the train on Saturday."

"Which one?"

"The TGV to Paris."

"Which flatmate, smart arse?"

"Oh! I don't know, but – ."

"Jesus Christ!"

"Please! Let me explain – "

"You'd better not be messing me about," she interjects testily. "Philippe! Bernard!" she yells out. "Did either of you give our phone number to some weirdo you met on the train on Saturday?"

"No!" I scream back down the line. "It wasn't Philippe or Bernard. It was a girl!" My jaw screams back in protest.

I hear a male voice in the background. "It wasn't me, Pascale. But I think Martine went up to Paris by train on Saturday."

There's a pause. "Is it Martine you want to speak to?" she asks.

"It's Martine," I repeat quietly.

"Well she's not here. She popped out to do some shopping. She shouldn't be long."

"Can I leave a message?"

"Go on."

"Would you please tell her… just tell her I called."

"Tell her who called?"

"Robert," I state. "Tell her Robert Pirsig called. Tell her I'll phone her back later."

If anything, the phone call has left me even more depressed. What's the set up in the flat? There's no reason to assume Martine's in a relationship just because she happens to share a flat with a girl and two blokes. All the same, I've taken an intense dislike to both Philippe and Bernard.

I hobble down the street to the pharmacy to pick up my prescription and I stop off at an *épicerie* to buy a litre of milk and a packet of straws, then at a *tabac* for the local paper, before trudging back up the steep hill as quickly as my throbbing kneecap will allow. Using Benson's hunting knife to pierce the milk carton, I stick in a straw and suck at the liquid, at the same time swallowing a random selection of pain killers. I flick quickly through the local pages in the paper but there's nothing about any bomb attack in Nîmes or Avignon. I skim the international section, but find nothing of consequence.

Holding my head in my hands, I gently massage my brow with my fingertips as I contemplate what to do next. Staying put is too dangerous with Verdu on the prowl. St Martin would be a better bet, but that will require hiring a car. Driving up to Benson's farmhouse in Le Vigan would seem to be the only hope of picking up his trail, but I don't even know his address.

My eye catches the post-it stuck to the side of the horseshoe counter. At least I have his phone number. I search through all the drawers in the counter, hoping I might find a letter or something else with his address on it, but I draw a blank. When I come across a tattered, hard-backed address book, buried beneath a stack of unpaid invoices, I thumb through it, but there's nothing listed under 'Benson'.

I swallow another couple of painkillers, almost choking on them when the phone by my elbow suddenly rings out.

CHAPTER 11

Struggling to get my spluttering under control, I lift the receiver and hold it against my ear, but I don't speak.

"Hello!" It's a high-pitched, female voice. Still I say nothing. "Could I speak to Robert Pirsig, please?" I snatch the handset from my face and stare at it in disbelief. "Hello!" the voice trills again. "Is there anyone there?"

"Martine? Is that you?"

"Who were you expecting, *Robert*?"

"How on earth did you get this number?"

"My finely-tuned extrasensory perception detected your *qi* floating in the Montpellier air space and supernatural forces took control of my fingers and made me tap out this number. Isn't that's how it works?" She's consumed by a fit of the giggles. "My intuitive powers also tell me you came back to Montpellier yesterday by train. Am I right?" she demands. "I am! Tell me!" she insists like an overexcited child.

"Good guess. I did come back down from Paris yesterday. But seriously, how on earth did you get this number?"

She laughs aloud. "Nothing magical, I'm very sorry to say. Just boring old technology. We have a gizmo attached to our phone which displays the number of anyone dialling in. Very useful if you want to avoid an unwelcome caller. Pascale noted down your number when you called a few minutes ago."

A thought suddenly strikes me. "Tell me, Martine. If all you had was somebody's phone number, could you find out his address?"

"Ye...es." She drags the word out. "I do believe I could."

"How would you go about it?"

"This is a trick question – right? It's some kind of test?"

"What do you mean?"

"Well… if I had someone's phone number… and I wanted to know his address, I'd phone him up and ask him where he lived. How did I do?"

I chortle as much as my aching jaw will allow. "Ten out of ten. Go to the top of the class. However, supposing, just for the sake of argument, you didn't want to phone him. Could you still find out his address?"

"Sure – with a Minitel."

"Do you have one?"

"Yup."

"Would you do me a favour?"

"What's that?

"If I give you someone's phone number, could you look up his address for me?"

"No problem. What's the number?"

"Do you have a pen handy?"

"I've got one right here that I borrowed from a really nice guy I met on the train on Saturday."

For the first time in my life my heart literally does skip a beat. I feel a warm glow spread throughout my body and I'm almost purring as I squint at the post-it and read out Benson's number.

"I'll have to hang up," she says. "I need to use the phone line to connect to the Minitel service. I'll call you back in a couple of minutes." She pauses. "Are you feeling all right?"

"I'm fine. Why?"

"Your voice – it sounds funny – as if you've got a lisp."

"I had a bit of an accident."

"An accident! Oh my God! What kind of accident?"

"I'll tell you about it later."

"Tell me about it now!"

"It's nothing."

"Are you sure you're all right?"

"It really is nothing."

"I'll call you back in a couple of minutes, er… Robert. Hey, what *is* your name?"

"Jérôme."

"Same as my brother's. Cool." The line clicks dead.

I sit at the counter with a silly grin plastered across my face until the phone rings out a few minutes later.

"The number you gave me belongs to someone called Charles Benson who lives in Le Vigan," Martine states.

"That's the guy."

"Now tell me about this accident."

"Oh, I managed to stumble and launch myself head first through a plate glass window. Made a bit of a mess of my face, that's all."

"That's terrible! Have you seen a doctor?"

"I've got the stitches to prove it."

"Jesus Christ!"

"It looks worse that it feels," I lie.

"Have you got anything planned for this afternoon?" she asks. I hesitate.

"If not, I thought that maybe we could meet up?" she adds.

"I really would like to, Martine, but – "

"But what?"

"Two buts, actually. First, the state my face is in, I don't think you'd want to know me right now, and second, I really must go up to Le Vigan this afternoon to see Charles Benson."

She hardly pauses for breath. "Then why don't we kill two birds with one stone? It doesn't sound to me as if you should be driving in your condition, so why don't I give you a lift to Le Vigan?"

"I must admit that's a very tempting offer. But seriously, my face is a real mess and I – "

"What's a few cuts and bruises between friends?" she interjects with that infectious laugh. "Anyway, you can't go to Le Vigan without me because I haven't given you Benson's address. That's settled then. Where and when will we meet?"

"Why do I get the impression that you're used to getting your own way?"

"Some you win, some you lose," she breezes. "How about four o'clock in the drop-off zone in front of the Corum?"

"That would be fine."

"I should warn you," she adds. "It's a building site around there because they're in the process of laying a new set of tram lines, but if you wait by the traffic lights nearest to the Corum, I'll pick you up there. I'll be driving a red Peugeot."

"I'll make sure I'm on time. Thanks again, Martine," I say. "And if you're driving a 206," I mutter under my breath as I'm replacing the receiver, "I sincerely hope you didn't buy it recently."

I head for Sauramps, Montpellier's biggest bookshop, where I'm delighted to find a French translation of *Zen and the Art of Motorcycle Maintenance*. I have it gift-wrapped. I buy a burger and a milk shake from a fast food stall in the Place de la Comédie and I force down as much as I can as I wander up the Esplanade towards our meeting place.

I get to the Corum just before four o'clock and I've been waiting for ten minutes when a red Peugeot 307 coupé cabriolet with the hood down screeches to a halt in front of me. If anything, Martine looks even more stunning. Not a single hair out of place. Her white miniskirt displays as much of her long, tanned legs as decency will allow and she's wearing a tight, pale blue T-shirt which matches the colour of her eyes.

"Jesus! You weren't kidding!" She throws open the passenger door. "You really shouldn't argue with plate glass, you know. It usually knows best."

I force a smile and climb in, slipping the carrier bag containing the book beneath the passenger seat. I stare into Martine's huge, sky-blue eyes. "There's something different about you." I continue staring. "I could have sworn your eyes were green."

I clip on my seat belt as she accelerates away. "Might well have been.

Can't remember what I was wearing on Saturday, but today it's the blue-tint contacts."

Conversation isn't easy above the growl of the engine as we lane-hop to the top of the Avenue de Nîmes and bump our way along the cobbled, main street of Castelnau le Lez. Threading our way through a maze of narrow roads and quiet villages, we pick up the Ganges road just north of St Martin de Londres.

"You seem to know your way around here pretty well."

"Montpellier born and bred. Where are you from originally?" she asks. "That doesn't sound like a local accent."

"I was born in Alsace." I have to shout to make myself heard. "But my mother's Parisienne," I add.

"Did you see her on Saturday?"

"She doesn't live there any more. She's settled in Peking and - " I break off as I suddenly realise I've slipped out of role.

"Fascinating!" she shouts. "Is that the *qigong* connection?"

"Sort of," I mumble.

"Well I hope you've done the full course." She turns side on to study my face. "That's going to be a bloody good test for your energy healing powers."

I take a deep breath and sit back in my seat, allowing my gaze to settle on her tight-lipped profile as she concentrates on overtaking a lorry.

I'm waiting in anticipation and this time I can admire the full effect of the explosive vista of the Cévennes when we burst through the narrow cutting. We zip round the outskirts of Ganges and the slanting sun is in our eyes as we start the climb through twisting mountain roads towards Le Vigan. Martine leans across me and her outstretched arm seems to linger against my thigh while she snaps open the glove compartment to pull out her sunglasses.

"Who is this Benson character?" she asks as we're approaching Le Vigan. "And why the secrecy about finding out where he lives?"

I'd anticipated the questions. "I used to work for him, but he's trying to avoid me now. He owes me money."

"Oh!" We traverse the centre of the village and Martine pulls up outside an isolated building on the northern outskirts. "Chez Benson," she announces. We're parked opposite what had once been a nineteenth century, dry-stone cottage and is now a roofless, windowless shell. "I hope you didn't lend him too much money," she says, jerking her thumb in the direction of the dilapidated building. "If this is his idea of a good investment."

I get out of the car and make my way up the weed-infested, crazy-paving path towards the front door. Incongruously, it's locked. I scramble over the low arch of the erstwhile bay window into what was probably once the kitchen and when I look up I can see a scattering of fluffy clouds through the gaping rafters. Stepping back outside, I make my way round to the back of the building where I find an overgrown courtyard enclosed by a high, pyracantha hedge. A rusty caravan, supported on four piles of bricks, is propped against the cottage. I try the door handle but it's locked. There are no curtains on the dirty windows and when I peer through I can make out a single bed, a calor gas heater, a fridge and a television. There's an electricity generator in the yard hooked up to the caravan and a telephone cable stretches from a gap in the roof to a nearby pylon.

Martine follows me round to the back. "No sign of life?" I shake my head.

"This place must be a real bunch of laughs in winter." She mimes a shiver. "It can drop to minus fifteen around here – no problem."

Forgetting about my swollen knee, I casually kick a loose stone. My knee reminds me and I hobble back towards the car.

"Are you not going to leave him a message?" Martine asks.

"No point."

"What do you want to do now?"

I shrug. "Do you know a good pub?"

"Sure." There's not a lot said as we head back towards Montpellier. I'm trying to figure out what Benson might be up to, Martine's concentrating on her driving. I have to admire her style; early braking and full use of the camber as she accelerates hard through the tight bends; skilful use of the gearbox as she negotiates the undulating, twisting, country roads. She brings us into Montpellier on a road I didn't even know existed. We seem to be heading for the town centre when she suddenly steps hard on the brakes outside a brightly-lit, Vietnamese restaurant. Glancing over her shoulder she reverses expertly into the parking space she's spotted.

"This is it?" I ask.

"Not the restaurant," she says with a smile. "Just down the road. Best watering hole in town. Limited range of drinks, perhaps, but the ambience is second to none."

"Lead on." I tug my carrier bag from beneath the passenger seat and wait on the pavement while Martine closes the electric hood and locks the car. I follow her across the street, down a narrow lane and round a corner. She stops opposite a *boulangerie* and taps in a code at a panel. Putting her shoulder to the heavy, wooden door, she waves me in ahead of her and when we cross the courtyard she presses a button to summon a tiny cage lift. There's barely enough room inside for two average-sized people, which means we're approximately one *embonpoint* too many. I find myself standing face to face with Martine.

"I like your perfume."

"It's Rive Gauche." She stretches round my back to reach for the lift buttons and I feel her breasts crush into my chest. I squint over my shoulder and see her finger poised over button number five. My prayers are answered. It's a very, very slow lift.

"Strange place for a pub," I say as we're ascending.

"Very select clientele," she whispers in my ear. I can feel her lips touching my ear lobe and I may be deluding myself, but I do believe she's snuggling in closer than is strictly necessary. The lift jolting to a halt has much the same effect on me as the guard announcing our arrival at the Gare de Lyon.

Martine pulls a bunch of keys from her handbag and unlocks the door facing the lift. We're in a dark, high-ceilinged hallway with several doors leading off. "The lounge is the first door on the right," she says. "Go on in. I'll be with you in a minute." Her eyes are twinkling. "I need the loo." She tickles me playfully under the chin, taking care to avoid my stitches, before skipping to the far end of the hall.

I encounter Brutus in the lounge. He's big and black with long, shaggy hair and his piercing, yellow eyes glower suspiciously at my entry. I cross towards the settee where he's sitting and hold out a friendly hand which is greeted with a flashing claw and a hissing spit. I step back quickly and Brutus vaults over the back of the settee and starts shredding the carpet.

I curse under my breath and suck at my grazed knuckles as I gaze round the spacious room, crammed with an assortment of reproduction furniture – a hotchpotch of Louis XV, Louis XVI and art deco. A floor-to-ceiling bookcase runs the length of the far wall and a curtainless, bay window gives on to an internal courtyard garden. The windows are closed and the room is oppressively warm. I pull off my jacket and drape it over the back of a chair and I'm studying the bookshelves when Martine comes breezing in.

"I see you've met Brutus," she says, nodding towards my hand. "Sorry! I meant to warn you. I'm afraid he's a bit of a one-woman moggie. What can I get you to drink? Beer, pastis, vodka or whisky?"

"Whisky sounds great."

"Ice or water?"

"A splash of water would be good."

Martine crosses to the bay window and flings it open wide before heading back down the echoing hallway, whistling cheerfully. I resume my examination of the books. Numerous French classics – Voltaire, Victor Hugo, Rousseau, Molière. Mother would approve. A reasonable selection of poetry – Rimbaud seems to be popular. It looks like the complete works of Marcel Pagnol. I see *Jonathan Livingston Seagull* perched on the top shelf, out of reach without a stepladder. An amazing number of cookery books, mostly French, but also Japanese, Thai, Indian, Mexican and Australian – I didn't know Australian existed. An eclectic collection of paperbacks, mainly translations of American best-sellers. James Joyce doesn't seem to rate.

Martine returns a few moments later with a half-full bottle of *The Famous Grouse* and two tumblers balanced on a tray, together with an ice bucket, a carafe of water, a bowl of peanuts and a straw. She places the tray on the coffee table and sits down on the settee to pour the whisky.

"Do you like the books?" she asks.

I nod. "Are they yours?"

"Most of them." I cross to the settee and take the seat beside her. She pops two ice cubes into her whisky and the straw into mine. "I'll leave you to add your own water," she says, handing me my glass and the carafe.

I laugh when I see the straw. "The lady thinks of everything," I say, tipping in a splash of water.

"Peanuts?" She offers the bowl.

I finger my jaw. "I think I'll give them a miss."

She holds up her tumbler and clinks it against mine. "Cheers!"

I take a long suck of whisky through the straw, then I pull my gift-wrapped parcel from the carrier bag and place in on her knee. "Surprise!"

"What's this?"

"A present for a *chauffeuse.*"

She slams her whisky glass down on to the coffee table. "I love surprises!" she exclaims, tearing excitedly at the wrapping paper. When she sees the book she lets out a squeal of delight and flings her arms around my neck, knocking the whisky from my grasp. The jolt when our cheeks clash might have killed a lesser mortal.

"Oh, I'm *so* sorry, Jérôme! I forgot." She pulls her head away and runs her fingertips ever so gently up and down my bruised cheek. I don't even notice the whisky seeping into my jeans. "That must've hurt terribly." She continues caressing my face tenderly. I don't know which cloud I'm on, but it's significantly higher than nine. Martine refills my whisky glass and makes a fair stab at straightening my straw.

Not wanting to spoil the surprise, I refuse to answer her deluge of questions about what happens in *Zen and the Art of Motorcycle Maintenance*. However, Pagnol, Proust, Plato and *The Famous Grouse* are good for a couple of hours.

"God, I've just realised how hungry I am," she says, springing to her feet. "Shall I fix us something to eat?"

"That would be great, but hey! I hope I'm not in the way? I mean, your flatmates?"

"No problem. Philippe and Bernard are off playing in some bridge tournament in Biarritz all week and Pascale always stays over at her boyfriend's place on Monday nights."

There's a limit to how many blessings one can count after five or six *Famous Grouse* (especially when the tiresome pedant in the right ventricle of one's brain is insisting on questioning whether that should be *Grouses*, or perhaps even *Grice*). Nevertheless, here goes:

Number One: no one's coming back here tonight.

Number Two: Pascale has a boyfriend – who is neither Philippe nor Bernard – which significantly increases the probability that the flat is a sharing arrangement and not a *menage à quatre*.

Number Three: Martine seems to be ever so slightly tipsy.

However, every silver lining has its cloud. The whisky bottle's empty.

"I certainly could do with a bite to eat. Shall I nip out and pick up some wine while you're putting something together?"

"Don't be daft. There's gallons of the stuff in the kitchen. You could pour me another whisky, though. You'll find a fresh bottle in the cupboard in the hall."

Aforementioned cloud explodes in a white puff leaving nothing but silver lining as far as the eye can see.

I don't know how she does it. I just sit at the kitchen table pouring Chablis and Burgundy while she conjures up the lightest of cheese soufflés, *omelette au fines herbes*, spaghetti carbonara, roquefort and runny brie, followed by *tarte aux pommes* with *crème chantilly*. By the time we get to the coffee and Armagnac, Martine isn't the only one feeling the effects. She drags her chair round to my side of the table and slips her arm through mine, her head resting gently on my shoulder.

"I've had a lovely evening, Jérôme."

The Armagnac, which I'm warming in both hands, is in imminent danger of boiling over. "Me too."

She nuzzles at my ear. "I'm awfully tired," she yawns. "Do you think you could carry me to bed?"

I lift my Armagnac to my lips and drain the glass. Blessing Number Four: I have a condom in my pocket.

CHAPTER 12

I'm wakened by the strains of Mahler's Fourth drifting down the corridor. I lift my head and blink slowly. Engulfed in nausea, I slam my eyelids closed and let my head sink back on to the pillow. It's a long time since I've had such a blinding hangover.

I lie motionless for a few moments before forcing my eyes open again and I keep my head pressed hard against the pillow as I take a blurred, magical mystery tour of my unfamiliar surroundings: a high, cream-coloured ceiling with ornate cornicing picked out in gold; closed, full-length, red velvet curtains; various items of antique furniture, looks like oak – an imposing wardrobe against the far wall, a bulky chest of drawers, a cluttered dressing table in front of a large, oval mirror. I see I'm lying in a four-poster, double bed. The pillow to my left is indented and I'm definitely picking up the scent of Rive Gauche. I recognise the blue-checked shirt which is hanging over the back of a chair by the door and the dark green underpants, lying on top of a pair of folded jeans, look like mine. Running my fingertips tentatively up and down my body underneath the duvet confirms that I'm bollock naked. I manage to half sit up in bed and squint at my watch which is propped on the bedside table. It shows quarter past ten.

An eerie sensation hits me when I see the gloating, pink object lying beside my watch and I reach out and pick it up delicately between thumb and forefinger. It's gelatinous, soggy and tied tightly at the neck, with a familiar opaque liquid bulging the bulbous tip.

I hear footsteps traipsing down the hallway and, in a moment of blind panic, I hurl the evidence across the room and let my head slump back on to the pillow. Tugging the duvet tightly to my chin, I feign unconsciousness.

"Good morning, Jérôme!" I open one eye and see Martine limping into the bedroom. She places a tray containing orange juice, scrambled eggs, toast and coffee on the bedside table. She's wearing a white T-shirt and a pair of figure-hugging jeans. Perhaps it's something to do with the angle I'm lying at, but her legs look even longer in jeans than they did in a miniskirt. My gaze travels the length of her body and I notice her left ankle and foot are bound in a white stretch bandage. She sits down on the edge of the bed and runs her fingers through my hair. Her eyes and her mouth are smiling at me. "The shower's through there." She indicates a door between the wardrobe and the chest of drawers. "Use the towels on the radiator."

"What happened to your ankle?"

"Ho, ho! Very funny!" She plants a long, lingering kiss on my forehead, then she nibbles at my earlobe. "I thought you might need some breakfast," she whispers in my ear. "To replace some of that energy." She gets to her feet and hobbles towards the door, turning back in the doorway to blow me a kiss from her fingertips. Tra-la-la-ing to Mahler, she clip-clops her way back down the corridor.

I don't know whether to laugh or cry. I try desperately to recall the events of last night. I remember everything about the meal – and I remember pouring back a lot of Armagnac. The last thing I remember is picking Martine up to carry her to bed. After that, everything's a complete blank.

In the hope that food might reactivate my closed-down memory banks, I stuff my face with eggs and toast before trudging to the bathroom and stepping into the shower. I turn on the taps and close my eyes and as soon as the warm water starts cascading down my back I feel a sharp, stinging pain at the base of my spine. Leaping out of the shower, I twist round to peer into the bathroom mirror and see several raw, jagged weals stretching from the middle of my back down to my buttocks. I dry myself gingerly and go back to the bedroom to pull on my clothes. As an afterthought I search for the condom and flush it down the loo.

My head is still looping the loop as I push open the lounge door and see Martine stretched out full-length on the settee, the sleeping Brutus curled up on her stomach. Her bandaged foot is propped up on the armrest and she's engrossed in *Zen and the Art of Motorcycle Maintenance.* She sits up straight when she sees me come in and she lifts Brutus from her lap and places him down on the floor. He shows what he thinks of that by taking it out on the carpet.

"You forgot the dedication," she says.

"What?"

"On the flyleaf. You didn't write anything."

I grin. "What would you like me to write?"

"How about some of the things you said in bed last night?" She titters. "If I promise never to let the book fall into the hands of impressionable children?"

On second thoughts I decide against asking what happened to her ankle. "Do you have something to write with?" I'm playing for time.

She stretches over the back of the settee for her handbag and produces the pen I gave her on the train. "I'll swap you this for a bookmark."

I laugh. "Fair enough." I start towards my jacket, which is where I left it, draped over the back of a chair. I stop in my tracks. "Oh shit!"

"What's wrong?"

"I haven't got your bookmark, Martine. I've just realised. It was in my wallet when it was stolen. I really am sorry."

"Stolen?"

I let out a sigh. "You remember I told you Charles Benson owed me money?" She nods. "Well, there's more to it than that. When I was up in Paris on Saturday he nicked my wallet which contained, among other things, your bookmark."

She gets to her feet slowly and I swear I can see the sparkle dying in her eyes. She turns her head away. "It's a sign." Her voice is a tremulous whisper

"Hey, let's not get this out of proportion, Martine. I'll get you another bookmark. I'll get you a dozen!"

"It's a sign," she repeats. " It means we weren't meant to – " She breaks off and sinks her teeth into her quivering bottom lip. I grab her by the shoulders and see tears welling in the corners of her eyes.

"Martine, it's just a bloody, plastic bookmark, for God's sake!" I give her a shake. "It can't be that important!"

"I'd like you to leave now, Jérôme." Her body is limp and her voice is bereft of all emotion.

"Not like this!"

She fixes her stare on the pattern on the carpet. "Please go."

I continue to hold her shoulders tightly but she won't look at me, her eyes remaining locked on the floor. Silent tears are channelling down her cheeks. As soon as I relax my grip she takes a step backwards and buries her face in her hands. I walk slowly across the room, pluck my jacket from the back of the chair and fling it over my shoulder as I shuffle towards the door. With one hand on the door knob I turn back, but she still won't meet my gaze. I cross the corridor, wrench open the apartment door and summon the lift. When it arrives I thump the button for the ground floor. As I descend, I knuckle away an intrusive tear. It's a very, very slow lift.

I've been walking for ages. I've no idea where I am but I came across signs for *centre ville* half an hour ago and I've been following them ever since. When I eventually recognise the back of the railway station I pick up the pace and head for The Book Cellar. The fresh air and brisk walk have cleared the worst of my hangover but my right knee is giving me gyp.

I take the bookshop apart looking for any clue as to where Benson might have gone. I search through all the cupboards in the storeroom and I empty out the drawers beneath the horseshoe counter but I unearth nothing apart from a plethora of clutter and a pile of unpaid invoices. I come across his tattered address book and I remember, when I was writing out his will, he said something about his Uncle Godfrey who lives in Richmond. I flick through the pages, vaguely recognising some of the entries: Andrew Mitchell in Bordeaux, Michael Struthers in Auxerre, but no mention of an Uncle Godfrey.

I turn to the front of the book and, on the inside of the hard cover, I find the name *Arthur Hawkey* printed in bold letters. Something clicks. If *Arthur Hawkey* is Charles' real name, Benson being just the latest is a string of aliases, and if his Uncle Godfrey happens to be a paternal uncle – a fifty-fifty chance – his uncle will be called Godfrey Hawkey. I look up *Hawkey* in the address book but the only entry under 'H' is Mel Hoggard in Paris. I recall Charles mentioning that the French authorities were still hounding his Uncle Godfrey about his whereabouts. If anyone knows where Charles is, it's bound to be Uncle Godfrey – and there can't be that many Godfrey Hawkeys in Richmond.

I weigh up my options. Stay in Montpellier, trying to dodge Verdu and moping about Martine, or travel to Richmond at Frobisher-Allen's expense, track down Uncle Godfrey, find Benson, smash his face in and recover Martine's bookmark. No contest. I can taste the warm beer already.

But before I go anywhere, I need some new clothes as I've been living in the same outfit for the past three days. I head down to the morning market in the Place de la Comédie, which is crowded, though not on the same scale as Ganges. The first item I purchase is a rucksack, then I wander round various stalls picking up jeans, trainers, shirts, socks and underpants. When I come across a stall selling toilet accessories I buy a razor, soap, shaving foam and a bottle of after shave, as well as a toothbrush and a couple of tubes of toothpaste.

I cross to the travel agency on the far side of the square and I'm told by the girl behind the desk that there's no direct flight from Montpellier to Heathrow, but I can get there via a connecting flight in Paris. When she confirms on her computer screen that there are seats available this afternoon, I book a ticket.

I head for the taxi rank beside the opera house and, as I've a couple of hours to spare before I need to head out to the airport, I ask the driver to make a detour via the Lapeyronie Hospital. The duty nurse in the outpatients' department examines my wounds and carefully removes the splint from my right nostril. The stitches in my lip and chin are self-dissolving, but she recommends I report back in a couple of days time for another check-up.

The taxi drops me off at the airport and, after I've checked in, I decide to call Martine. Pascale answers the phone and tells me, curtly, that Martine's not there. I don't leave any message.

Martine suddenly appears by my side, looking absolutely stunning. She smiles disarmingly and when I grin back she slowly winks one of those huge, sea-green eyes before tugging her T-shirt over her head. She isn't wearing a bra. She lets her shirt slip from her grasp and her long, painted fingernails reach up to tease out her tousled hair. She's just kicked off her sandals and is twisting to unzip her miniskirt when I'm dragged protestingly back to consciousness by the rumbling growl of the jet engines as we prepare for take off.

"George Hawkey, Gertrude Hawkey, Geoffrey Hawkey – but no Godfrey."

"Would you mind checking that again for me, please?"

The registrar lets out a weary sigh as he runs his index finger slowly down the list. He shakes his head firmly. "Definitely. No Godfrey."

"Could he have died recently?"

To the accompaniment of another heavy sigh, he lugs a voluminous file from beneath his desk and, adjusting his spectacles, he thumbs his way slowly through to 'H'. He looks up, shaking his head. "No one called Hawkey has died in Richmond this year, or last year."

Another fifty-fifty chance bites the dust. "Can you tell me how many Godfreys there are in Richmond?"

"Oh, for God's sake!"

"Why not?" I protest. "There can't be that many. It's not as if I'm asking you to look for someone called John."

"We don't file under Godfrey, that's why." His delivery is laboured. "We don't file under John. Nor do we file under Matthew, Mark or Luke. We only file under surnames."

"Are you trying to tell me that's it?"

"That's it!"

"Is there any way I could find out if there's a Mrs Hawkey who has a relation called Godfrey?"

"No, there bloody-well isn't!"

I get to my feet slowly. "Well, could you at least check the surrounding districts, in case he lives just outside the Richmond boundary?"

"Listen, mate." He tears off his spectacles and flings them down on the desk. "This is Richmond upon Thames. By a strange quirk of fate, I happen to have in front of me the electoral register for Richmond upon Thames. I do not have Brentford, I do not have Putney, I do not have Kingston upon Thames. Neither do I have Richmond Virginia, Richmond North Yorkshire or Richmond South Yorkshire. Have I made myself clear?" He gives a dismissive wave, then seems taken aback when I lean across his desk and plant a slobbery kiss on top of his bald head.

I book into a hotel near King's Cross Station and get up early the following morning to catch the first train to Sheffield. We arrive only a few minutes behind schedule and I pick up a cab from the rank outside the station and ask to be taken to the registry office. When we get there, I tell the driver to wait. The clerk checks the electoral roll for Richmond, South Yorkshire, but draws a blank on 'Godfrey Hawkey'.

"Where would I need to go to check the electoral roll for Richmond in North Yorkshire?" I ask.

"That would be Northallerton."

"How do I get there?"

"The train to Darlington is probably your best bet. You should be able to catch a bus from there to Northallerton."

I trot down the steps to my waiting taxi. "Back to the station?" he asks.

"What the hell! Take me to Northallerton."

He turns right round in his seat, looking completely flummoxed. "Did I hear you right?"

"Sure. I'm on expenses," I announce with an expansive wave of my arm.

Again, I ask the driver to wait for me outside the Northallerton registry office.

"You did say Godfrey Hawkey?" Miss Layfield's polished fingernail tracks down the column. "Just the one." The disappointment of South Yorkshire is dissipated. Miss Layfield's thin mouth smiles at me. "Shall I write the address down for you?"

I beam back. "That would be very kind." The prim registrar copies the information neatly from the electoral roll and hands me the slip of paper. I glance at the address and stuff it into my jacket pocket. "Is there a hotel in Richmond you could recommend?" I ask.

"There's The King's Head."

"Is it the best?"

She blushes. "My sister works there."

There's light drizzle falling when my taxi drops me off in the centre of Richmond, a quiet backwater nestling on the banks of the river Swale. The keep of a Norman castle dominates the sloping town square and the architecture of the surrounding buildings appears to be Georgian. I use my *carte bleue* to dispense a wad of notes from the Barclays' Bank cashpoint machine and, having paid off the cab driver and got a receipt, I sling my rucksack over my shoulder and whistle an upbeat version of *Sweet Lass of Richmond Hill* as I stroll up one side of the square.

The town appears to be frozen in some kind of time warp. The four sides of the cobbled square comprise a disparate collection of stone-built houses, most of which have been converted into hotels, banks, building societies, offices, cafés, pubs and shops. Some of the window displays look as if they haven't been altered since their Victorian heyday. The square itself is a monument to a bygone era – a collection of rounded, highly-polished cobblestones on a steep gradient, guaranteed to provide a regular supply of broken ankles and twisted knees for the local hospital.

Seeing the painted sign for The King's Head and its Tea Shoppe on the opposite side of the square, I set out to traverse the incline, my slip-sliding efforts on the glistening stones bringing me to a teetering halt outside the general store of Mr Coleman and Mr Morris, some fifteen metres downhill from the hotel. As I make my way back up the slippery slope, I'm lost in admiration for the technique of the two arm-in-arm pensioners who are holding the line across the square with their tittupping, figure-skating crossover steps.

I book into The King's Head for one night. Room eight is quite small, but the decor appears to have been renovated recently and the bed feels comfortable.

I drop my rucksack on to a chair and make my way back down the carpeted staircase to the reception desk. "Can you tell me where I'd find Cross Lanes?" I ask the young girl.

She calls across to the hardly overworked porter. "Cross Lanes, Peter?"

"Past the Co-op, up the hill, straight on at the roundabout, past the schools. It's on the left. You can't miss it."

"How far?"

"About a mile, I suppose. Do you want me to call a cab?"

I glance out of the window and see the drizzle has eased. "No, thanks. I could do with the walk."

My knee's standing up well but the hill's steep and I'm out of breath when I turn into Cross Lanes, a wide street of 1960's semi-detached houses. Pausing to recover my wind, I pull the slip of paper from my jacket pocket to check the house number and when I glance up again I see a tall figure with bouncy, blonde curls, attired in a red trouser suit, hurrying down Godfrey Hawkey's drive. I'm not close enough to make out her features. She jumps into a black Audi and roars off up the hill.

I'm yelling because Godfrey Hawkey is very hard of hearing. "Arthur and I go back a long way, Mr Hawkey. In fact, I remember him when he was Michael Struthers and Andrew Mitchell, long before he ever became Charles Benson." I chuckle. "That shows how long I've known him."

Several physical characteristics run in the Hawkey family. The tall, stooped figure, the telescoped neck, the heavy eyelids, the slack jowls.

"What did you say your name was?"

"Pirsig. Robert Pirsig."

"I've never heard Arthur mention you." Uncle Godfrey turns his attention to poking fussily at the smokeless fuel in the small grate. I steal a glance around the room and see what appears to be an airline ticket wedged on the shelf beneath the coffee table. Godfrey doesn't strike me as the type to have ever crossed the Pennines, never mind taken to the air. He hangs the brass poker back on its companion set and stares fixedly at me. "What do you want with me?" he demands.

"I was just passing through, Mr Hawkey."

He cups a hand to his right ear. "What did you say?"

I repeat myself, slower and louder. "I was just passing through Richmond, Mr Hawkey, and I thought it would be a nice idea to look Arthur up as I haven't seen him in ages – not since he moved to Montpellier."

"No one passes through Richmond." Godfrey sucks hard on his dentures. "Not unless they're going from Catterick to Gilling West." He picks up his pipe from the ashtray on the coffee table and taps it out against the side of the fire. "Why would you be going from Catterick to Gilling West?"

I force a laugh. "Not literally passing through, Mr Hawkey. I was actually driving from Glasgow to London and Richmond's not much of a detour from Scotch Corner."

"Where's your car, then?" The old codger doesn't miss much. "I left it in town and walked up the hill. I wanted to stretch my legs after being cooped up behind the wheel all day."

"Hmm." He pauses to blow through his pipe. "What happened to your face?"

"Oh, that." I finger my bruises. "I got involved in a football discussion in a Glasgow pub. Never a good idea." Godfrey turns his attention to minutely adjusting the ornaments on the mantelpiece. "Arthur told me he was planning a trip to Richmond about now," I say. "I was hoping I might catch him."

"He didn't say anything to me about that," Godfrey says, moving towards me and shepherding me towards the front door. "But I'll let him know you dropped by."

"Who was the girl who was leaving when I arrived, Mr Hawkey? I'm sure I recognised her."

"If you recognised her, then you won't be needing me to tell you who she was."

"Her name's slipped my memory."

"That happens to me too."

I go for a change of tack. "When did you last hear from Charles – I mean Arthur." I force a chuckle. "I've got so used to calling him Charles."

"Funny, that. He's only been Charles since he went to Montpellier – and you haven't seen him since then."

"We chat so much on the phone, Mr Hawkey. That's what it is."

"In which case you must have talked to him more recently than I have – what with all the chatting you've been doing on the phone. How's he keeping?"

Game, set and match.

I plod back down the hill and cut through the resident's car park to the rear entrance of The King's Head. In the dusk, I almost miss the black Audi parked head-on against the brick wall.

I stick my head round the door of the lounge bar and see the back of the solitary customer, perched on a high stool, chatting to the barman. She has long, blonde curls and she's wearing a red-leather trouser suit. I'm debating whether or not to approach her when she suddenly lets out a familiar, high-pitched, sexy giggle. I freeze and glance down at her feet, balanced on the ledge of the barstool. She's wearing red, sling-backed, high-heel shoes and, on her left foot, underneath her stocking, I can make out the lines of a bandage.

CHAPTER 13

"It's a small world." Her voice sounds even sexier when she's speaking English and she has the most incredibly sophisticated accent. "Never in my wildest dreams did I imagine I'd bump into you here, Jérôme." She takes a sip from her gin and tonic.

I decide to give it my best Home Counties. "Your English is excellent."

"It ought to be. My mother's from Canterbury," she states casually, "and I took my PhD at Cambridge." She twiddles her swizzle stick.

"Really?"

"Your own English isn't too bad." I let the comment pass. "How's your jaw, by the way?" she asks.

I stroke my chin gingerly. "Still tender. And your ankle?"

"I can walk without too much pain now." She takes another sip of gin. "Your nose is looking a lot better."

"Look, Martine, or whatever the hell your name is! We can play cat and mouse all night or we can put our cards on the table. What's it to be?" She focuses on her drink, swilling the ice cubes round and round, then she puts down her glass and tosses back her head, running her fingers through her long, blonde curls. She gives a quick, affirmative nod.

"Let's move over there," I say, indicating a table at the far side of the lounge.

I order a pint of lager and another gin and tonic and carry the drinks across. Sitting down facing Martine, I take a long, slow swallow of lager while I consider how much I'm prepared to disclose. "Ladies first," I say, placing my pint on the glass-topped table.

"You already know who I am. My name's Martine Rubio, I'm twenty four years old – Montpellier born and bred." She makes an exaggerated display of taking hold of my hand and shaking it up and down. "And whom do I have the pleasure of addressing?"

"Jérôme Dumas."

"Pardon?"

"Frank McClure."

"From Alsace?"

"From Kilbirnie."

"That's better."

"Matter of opinion."

She smiles and picks up her drink, cradling it in both hands. "Would you prefer me to call you Jérôme, or Frank?"

"I'm easy." I shrug my shoulders. "I've sort of got used to Jérôme."

"Fine. Jérôme it is. My father's Spanish, from Madrid," she continues, "and, as I mentioned, my mother's from Canterbury. My parents met when they were both working at CIRAD, which is an international centre in Montpellier specialising in agricultural research." She pauses while she squeezes the juice from her lemon slice into her drink. "I graduated in English language and literature from Montpellier University and I took my PhD at Cambridge." She glances up and looks me straight in the eye. "I'm now a graduate trainee in an organisation called Les Renseignements Généraux." My jaw drops and I find myself doing a goldfish impression. "I believe you might know my boss," she adds casually. I'm sure that's a grin playing at the corners of her mouth. "His name's René Verdu." She cocks her head to one side as she assesses the impact. "You may be wondering what I'm doing here?"

"You could say that." I'm responding on auto-pilot.

"Our department wishes to interview Charles Benson, aliases far too many to mention, with regard to various tax evasion activities," she states. My brain's working overtime, trying to keep up. Either Martine's unaware of the paedophile angle or she's holding back on me. The thought suddenly strikes me that Verdu might very well be the high-level pervert in the French civil service. "Monsieur Verdu

138

received an anonymous tip-off that you had murdered Charles Benson and forged his will," she continues. "That triggered him to have Benson's death certificate translated and when he found out it contained gibberish he kicked off an investigation. Do you recall him turning up at the bookshop and giving you a translation of Benson's will to read?" I nod. "That was just so he could get your fingerprints on the page. When the prints matched those on Benson's will, and when our Alsace division failed to uncover any trace of your previous existence, that was enough to convince Verdu that you'd murdered Benson.

"However, further checks revealed similarities in Benson's disappearance to other mysterious 'sudden deaths' and, having cross-checked files and photographs, we realised that 'Benson' was yet another alias for a guy we already knew as Struthers and Mitchell. Verdu figured Benson was probably still alive and he reckoned you would probably make contact with him sooner or later, so he decided to have you followed. After you gave our agent the slip in the Place de la Comédie, we staked out The Book Cellar and Fitzpatrick's and I was on duty in the pub when you turned up in that ridiculous disguise."

"I don't remember seeing you there?"

"You weren't supposed to!" she retorts. "I followed you when you left Fitzpatrick's in pursuit of Linda and Daniel Scetbon. My car was parked in a side street and I drove round the block and picked up the procession at the end of the pedestrian precinct. I must say, it was all a bit Chaplinesque – you following the Scetbons and me bringing up the rear. By the way, you do realise you have me to thank for saving your life?"

"I do?"

"I dealt with the guy in black who attacked you in the Scetbons' drive. While you were inside the house, I spotted our friend skulking among the trees. I was parked opposite the end of the driveway and I had him in my line of sight. He watched you come down the path and when you turned back and sneaked round the side of the house, he made a call on his mobile. He was waiting for you when you came running down the path a few minutes later and, when he rugby-tackled you, that's when I let him have it."

"Let him have what?"

"A hundred thousand volts in his left buttock."

"You're not serious?"

"Anti-rape device." She taps her handbag. "Effective up to a range of eight metres. Knocks an assailant cold for a couple of hours without damaging his heart."

The rationale for an anti-rape device being effective at a range of eight metres intrigues me, but I don't want to interrupt her flow. "Who was that guy?" I ask.

"Not a clue." She looks at me quizzically. "I was hoping you might be able to fill me in on that?"

I shake my head. "Why did you give him the stun gun treatment?"

"My instructions were to keep tabs on you and he looked as if he was about to complicate my life."

She pauses to take a sip of gin. "When you jumped into a taxi, I followed the cab until it dropped you off at an underground car park, then I picked up your car at the exit and tailed you out to St Martin de Londres. Having spent a most uncomfortable night in my car," she continues, her grimace clearly indicating she considered this to be my fault, "I followed you back to Montpellier the following morning where you stopped off at the Scetbon's place to fraternise with a notorious Swedish male prostitute." Her eyebrows leave me in no doubt as to what she thought of that.

"I then followed the cab you took to the railway station and, after you'd purchased your ticket, I went to the same booth and booked the adjacent seat. There were a couple of hours to kill before the train was due to leave so I went back to HQ and briefed Verdu. It was his decision to bug you."

"Bug me?"

"The bookmark."

"What are you talking about?"

"The bookmark I gave you on the train – it contains a microchip. In fact, it's a sophisticated radio transmitter. It emits a continuous signal which is bounced off a satellite and can be monitored via a tracking device, pinpointing the carrier's position to within a few metres. We've only recently got hold of the technology and Verdu thought it would be an ideal opportunity to road test it – much more practical than trying to follow you around all the time. I was instructed to plant it on you so we would be able to monitor your movements, hopefully leading us to Benson."

I indicate to the barman to replenish our drinks and I drain my pint glass while I let the implications of all this sink in. "So, all that stuff on the train? *Jonathan Livingston Seagull?* Buddhism? The interest in *qigong?* It was just a day's work for you?"

"I didn't say that." She looks genuinely hurt as she places her hand lightly on my forearm.

"All that palaver about exchanging gifts to ensure we would meet again?"

"I had to do that." Her fingers grip my arm tightly. "But I do believe in destiny, Jérôme. I'm convinced there are cosmic forces which bring people together."

I want to believe those stunning brown eyes are sincere.

"Look!" She tugs *Zen and the Art of Motorcycle Maintenance* from her handbag. This isn't a pretence, is it? I was hardly expecting to bump into you today, now was I? She flicks the book open at the folded-down page. "I've read a hundred and eighty pages, for God's sake!"

"What do you make of it?"

"I can't make head nor tail of it!" She slams the book shut. "But at least I'm persevering."

"Quality." I nod. "That's what it's all about. Quality of life. You might have to read it three or four times to get the hang of it."

"Thanks a lot!"

"When did you realise I no longer had the bookmark?" I ask.

"I twigged something was wrong when you phoned me on Monday from The Book Cellar. My tracking device had monitored the bookmark while you were in Paris. It told me you'd gone to a restaurant in the eighth *arrondissement*, then you'd crossed the road to an apartment block and after that you'd spent the rest of Saturday night in a knocking shop in Pigalle," she adds disdainfully, "before returning to Montpellier by train on Sunday morning. When you phoned me on Monday, I checked the origin of your call. The gizmo on my phone told me you were phoning from The Book Cellar, but that didn't match the location of the bookmark, which my tracker told me was on the other side of town. Evidently, you were no longer in possession of the bookmark."

"I had the bookmark when I was in the restaurant and the apartment," I nod. "That was where Benson nicked it."

"When you then asked me to check out a phone number and I discovered it was Benson's," she continues, "I called Verdu for instructions. He told me to tag along with you to find out what had happened.

"Back in my flat, I nearly fell off the settee when you told me Benson had stolen your wallet, including the bookmark. We actually had him bugged without realising it. I had to think of a ruse to get rid of you so I could go after Benson as quickly as possible. There was no way of knowing how long he'd hold on to the bookmark." She looks embarrassed. "Sorry if I was a bit insensitive."

"But you were crying?"

"Special contact lenses," she mutters into her drink.

"Oh!" There's silence as the barman brings across our drinks and places them on the table. I pick up my glass and swallow several mouthfuls of lager. "What about the night before?" I ask tentatively.

She sinks her teeth into her bottom lip. "I spiked your drink," she mumbles.

"You don't say?" She nods quickly. "I had a feeling my headache the following morning was something more than a routine hangover."

"You drank your Armagnac far too quickly," she protests. "You passed out while you were carrying me to bed. Dropped me on the floor – sprained my ankle. It was a real bugger dragging you all the way to the bedroom and getting you undressed."

"I can imagine."

"Glad to see you've changed your socks, by the way," she says, glancing down at my feet. "Not before time, if you don't mind me saying."

I swallow hard and look her straight in the eye. "What about the condom?"

She fiddles with her swizzle stick and casts her eyes down. Her voice is a whisper. "I found it in your trouser pocket when I searched your things."

"Yes, but… it was…used…"

She shakes her head slowly from side to side without raising her eyes. "*Crème chantilly* – "

"Come again?" I interject.

"Unfortunate choice of phrase." She's starting to snicker. "*Crème chantilly*, diluted with a little milk and lemon juice for colour and texture. It's standard procedure."

"You do this sort of thing regularly?" She looks up sharply and tosses her blonde curls. Her face is scarlet. "What about the scratch marks on my back and on my bum? Was that also standard procedure?"

She splutters. "Spur of the moment."

"You keep a spur specially?" She presses her fingers hard into her flushed cheeks as if trying to squeeze her blushes away. Her whole body's shaking with suppressed laughter. "Oh, for fuck's sake, Martine! You didn't let Brutus loose on me?"

She lets out a high-pitched squeal and rocks back and forward uncontrollably, tears of laughter coursing down her cheeks. The barman is staring across. It's several seconds before she regains enough composure to speak. "Just my fingernails," she whispers, wiping the

143

tears from her cheeks with a tissue. She stretches out both hands and mimes jazz piano on the table top. "Perhaps administered with the slightest touch of vengeance for my sprained ankle." I start giggling, which starts her off again. "I seem to have been doing all the talking," she says, dabbing at her streaming eyes with her tissue. "Your turn. How did you get involved in all of this."

I force myself to continue chortling while I figure out what I'm going to say. "I responded to an advert in the newspaper for someone to work in The Book Cellar." I manage to state this with a fair degree of conviction. "That's all there is to it."

"What brought you to Richmond?"

"I found Benson's uncle's address in the bookshop," I lie. "I came here to try to find Benson so I could recover your bookmark."

"You came all the way here – just to get my bookmark?"

"I thought … I thought it mattered to you… to us…" My voice is croaky. Martine blushes furiously. I realise I'm behaving like a complete bastard but I justify it to myself on the grounds that I'm bound by the Official Secrets Act. "Did Verdu send you to England to apprehend Benson?"

"Hardly! Benson's small beer. We'll deal with him if and when he ever sets foot on French soil again. However, recovering the bookmark's a completely different kettle of fish." She checks to make sure the barman's not within earshot. "There's the mother and father of all political rows going on right now," she whispers. "It's all terribly hush-hush. Last month, British intelligence claimed to have caught one of Verdu's guys bugging the Cabinet Office. The bookmark was never intended to leave French territory," she confides. "However, if an electronic bugging device belonging to Les Renseignements Généraux were to be discovered on British territory right now, the shit would hit the proverbial fan and no mistake. I've got to get it back." Her long eyelashes flutter in my direction. "The bookmark's in Hawkey's house, but Benson's not there."

"How do you know that?"

"I rang Uncle Godfrey's doorbell this afternoon and asked if Charles was in town. Told him I was an ex-girlfriend. There wasn't the slightest flicker when he told me Benson wasn't there. I'd have been able to tell if he was lying."

"I wouldn't bet on that. Uncle Godfrey's a crafty old bugger." I take a swig of lager. "What makes you so sure the bookmark's there?"

She opens her handbag and produces a flat, metallic object, the size and shape of a powder compact. Snapping open the lid, she shows me a liquid crystal display of a miniaturised map with grid cross-references and in the middle of the grid there's a stationary, pulsing, green light. "The map is centred on Cross Lanes," she explains. "The pulse represents the position of the bookmark. It hasn't moved during the past twenty-four hours. Will you help me get it back?" The eyelashes are working overtime.

"How?"

"If you could lure Uncle Godfrey out of the house, I could get inside and recover the bookmark."

"At this time of night?"

She thinks about this. "It would be more practical to do it in the morning," she concedes.

"In which case," I say, getting to my feet. "How about some dinner? I'm famished."

There are only a handful of people left in the hotel dining room, most of whom are already at the coffee stage.

"Your hair grows quickly," I say, leaning across the table and running my fingers through her long, dangling, blonde curls.

"Jealous?" She tugs off the wig and drops it on to the floor. "It's bloody warm under that lot."

"Hey! Your eyes don't match your hair any more!"

She gives a weary shake of the head. "I don't give a bugger." She drains her gin and tonic.

The service is fast, the kitchen staff evidently hoping for an early night. I don't mind – I could use one myself. The style of cuisine in

The King's Head is traditional, the portions are ample and the house wine is perfectly acceptable. Conversation is lively throughout dinner, but by the time the coffee and brandy arrive we're both slowing down. We're on our own now and when the waitress leaves the coffee pot on the table and bids us goodnight, Martine flicks off a shoe and stretches her long leg underneath the table, running her stockinged sole up and down the inside of my thigh.

"Did you really come all the way to Richmond just to recover the bookmark for me?"

"Yup."

"That was an awfully nice thing to do." She exhales slowly and dreamily. "By the way, I'm glad it was Benson who spent the night in the Pigalle knocking shop and not you." Her eyes are dancing again. She tilts back her head and drains her brandy glass. "Tired?" she asks.

"Mmm." I tip the dregs of my brandy into my coffee.

"Very tired?" Her tongue is lolling round her slightly parted lips. Something stirs in my jeans. Martine's toes find the bulge and probe gently.

I lock eyes with her. "No secret supplies of *crème chantilly*?" Her mouth eases into a wide grin as she shakes her head slowly from side to side. "No hidden agenda?" I ask.

Slowly and deliberately, starting from the waist, Martine starts popping the studs of her red-leather jacket. She's not wearing anything underneath. "No hidden agenda." Her voice is hoarse. I break eye contact as her jacket gapes, barely covering her nipples. She gets to her feet and drags her chair round to my side of the table. Flopping back down, she cradles my arm in hers, her eyes dropping towards what has now become a very uncomfortable bulge in my trousers.

Sod's law dictates that when you want to do your best Linford Christie impression, your willy invariably contrives to find a tuck in your underpants. She's hoping for an appetising lunch-box and all I've got on offer is strangulated jam roly-poly.

"Do you have a thingy?" Her voice has gone really husky.

I'm not sure how to handle this. "Of course I've got a thingy!"

"Don't be stupid! I can *see* you've got a thingy! What I mean is, do you have a *thingy* for your thingy?"

The penny drops, which is more than can be said for my oxbow willy. "I'm sure I'll be able to get one," I croak.

My open-mouthed gaze meanders from her tongue rolling round her pouting lips, past her firm chin, down the indentation in the crook of her neck, along the cleavage between her small, evenly-tanned breasts before settling on the perfectly formed navel nestling in her flat stomach.

She gets to her feet slowly and when she bends down to pick up her shoe and her wig I get a tantalising flash of nipple. She blows me a kiss from her fingertips as she slips on her shoe. "Room twenty-two," she mouths. "Second floor." She gives an exaggerated wink and steadies herself on the back of her chair before turning and weaving her way towards the staircase.

The old joke about dachshunds comes flashing into my mind – the one about the guy who had six male dachshunds and six females. Wanting to keep them apart while the females were in heat, he took the bitches upstairs and left the dogs downstairs before leaving confidently for an evening in the pub. Have you ever seen a dachshund with a hard-on trying to get upstairs?

Aren't night porters wonderful? Every bit as good as barbers. Having made a quick detour via the loo, I take the lift to the second floor. I knock discreetly, clear my throat and turn the handle to ease open the bedroom door. Room twenty-two is in pitch darkness. "Martine?" I cough louder as I step across the threshold. "Martine, are you there?"

I flick on the top light, to be greeted by an empty room.

CHAPTER 14

I close my eyes in fear and trepidation as the Audi roars backwards towards me in the confined space and my nostrils are filled with the acrid smell of burning rubber as the car squeals to a halt inches from my toes.

"Where I come from, there's a tradition of paying the bill before we leave a hotel," I yell.

She presses the button to lower the driver's window. "They've got my address. They can forward the damned bill. Now get out of the way before you get run over."

"Martine, you can't drive in your condition! It's too dangerous!"

"It's only a hire car." She revs up violently but I hold my ground. Her head jerks out of the window. The blonde wig is back in place, albeit askew, but she hasn't bothered fastening her jacket. Her suitcase is lying on the back seat. "Will you get out of my bloody way!"

"Where do think you're going?"

She rummages in her handbag which is lying on the passenger seat and produces the electronic tracker. "Look!" She flicks open the gadget. "Benson's on the move." I hear a low, rhythmic bleep and see the blinking, green pulse creeping across the map grid.

I snatch the device from her hand and take a quick step backwards. "Well you won't be going very far without this."

She's out of the car at the speed of light and has me pinned against the wall. She's scrabbling behind me, trying to recover the tracker, her jacket flapping open as we struggle. "Will you give that to me!" she whispers forcibly, her bare breasts rubbing up and down my chest. My eyes start to water as my willy finds yet another cul de sac in my underwear.

"You can have it," I pant, "as soon as we're back inside the hotel."

Her temper calms as quickly as it had flared and her arms drop to her sides. I step around her and re-park her car. Pulling her suitcase from the back seat, I take her by the arm and lead her through the foyer, choosing to ignore the knowing wink from the night porter.

Martine sits propped on the edge of her high bed, her long legs dangling, her heels drumming against the base. I hold out the tracker and she snatches it from my grasp. "Why can't we follow him?" she demands petulantly.

"For a start, neither of us is in any fit state to drive. Anyway, what's the rush?"

She falls backwards, swinging her legs up on to the duvet, and places the tracker on her bedside table, balanced so she can observe the hypnotic, pulsing light. She tucks both hands behind her head on the pillow, not seeming to notice, or care, that her jacket is flapping wide. Her eyelids flutter.

"Think it through," I say. "Tomorrow, either Benson will still be in England and we'll be able to track him down or else he'll have crossed back to France, in which case your primary concern will be resolved." She doesn't respond. "Martine?" I'm answered by the softest of gentle snores. I gaze at the steady rise and fall of her breasts for a couple of seconds – okay, it might have been a tad longer – then I gently fold her jacket across her chest. I call the night porter and book an alarm call for six a.m. for rooms eight and twenty-two. He sounds disappointed.

Rummaging in my pockets, I find the slip of paper with Hawkey's address on it and I print: 'I'll meet you for breakfast at six-thirty' on the reverse side and prop the note against her phone. When I kiss the tips of my fingers and press them lightly against her forehead, she stirs, moans softly, and rolls over on to her side. I ease the duvet from underneath her and tuck it up to her chin. Switching off the light, I pull the door closed behind me and plod down the staircase to room eight, fingering the condom wrapper in my trouser pocket.

I allow myself the luxury of an extra twenty minutes in bed after the alarm call, then I run a hot bath and lie soaking in the tub until the water starts to feel cool. I towel myself down, shave, brush my teeth and pack my rucksack. By the time I wander downstairs Martine is alone in the dining room, finishing off her croissant and coffee. Her hair is back to its coiffured best and she's wearing a blue roll-neck sweater and jeans. Her suitcase is standing by the breakfast table.

"Sleep well?" I ask.

Her eyes are red-rimmed and her voice is excited. "I was up most of the night tracking Benson. The guy's a complete weirdo. He travelled at a normal speed for a while before suddenly accelerating, then he pulled over for more than an hour and after that he started chuntering along, stop-start. At one stage he took two hours to cover ten kilometres. I've no idea what he was playing at."

"What route did he take?"

"Richmond to Darlington and then he headed south, eventually getting to London about half-past five this morning."

I order the full English breakfast with grapefruit juice, coffee and brown toast. "I think I've got it figured," I say between sips of juice. "He probably drove as far as Darlington and then caught a train to London."

"A train? Ten kilometres in two hours?"

"The British don't go in for TGVs. They prefer to admire the countryside."

"At three o'clock in the morning?"

I shrug. "Nice of you to wait for me, by the way. Thought you might've done a runner."

She twists her features into a grimace and pokes out her tongue. "You forgot to give me back my car keys, didn't you?"

"Did I? Oh, sorry about that!" When my breakfast arrives I flick out my linen napkin and place it across my knees before diving in. "Where did he go when he got to London?" I ask through a mouthful of toast.

"He wandered around in the vicinity of King's Cross station for a while, but he hasn't changed location during the past hour." She checks her gadget again. "I suppose he might have found a hotel and crashed out."

A thought strikes me. "If your tracker was never intended to leave French soil, how come it's programmed to handle every map reference from North Yorkshire to central London?"

"Search me." She frowns. "It's probably a test version."

Even though I'm not insured for her hire car, we agree to share the driving. She volunteers for the first stint because she doesn't want to face the London traffic and between Richmond and Catterick she almost writes the car off twice because she's paying more attention to the tracker than she is to the road. The pulse remains stationary, which is more than can be said for mine. I insist on taking over the wheel before we've even reached the A1.

The traffic on the way south isn't too bad and the device starts bleeping again as we're approaching the North Circular. The pulse wends its way from King's Cross, across the city centre, arriving at its destination just after half-past eleven and as we home in on our target I find myself threading through the familiar territory of Kilburn and Hampstead. Progress is painfully slow as we head towards the river and twelve-thirty is chiming when Martine announces we're within a hundred metres of Benson. Amazingly, I find a parking meter.

We walk the last stretch quickly and as we round the corner Martine refers to her device. "He's in there," she says, pointing towards the brown, marble-clad building straight ahead. I stop dead in my tracks.

"I recognise that building, Martine."

"What is it?"

I swallow hard. "MI6 headquarters."

She turns pale. "My bookmark's inside MI6 headquarters? Fucking hell!" She turns and stomps twenty metres in the direction of Vauxhall Bridge before spinning on her heel and storming back. "What bright ideas do you have now, smart-arse?"

"No need to take it out on me!"

"If you'd let me drive to London last night," she fumes, "I'd have been faced with the problem of recovering my bookmark from a hotel at King's Cross, not from fucking MI6 fucking headquarters!" She repeats her circular stomp. "Well? I'm waiting!"

I snap my fingers and grab her by the hand. "Come on! Quickly!"

"It's Thursday, Kathleen, so it must be chicken salad." Kathleen Morrison freezes with a forkful of lettuce in her hand as Martine and I sit down on the seats opposite her in the café.

"Frank... Frank McClure!" Her fork goes slack in her fingers. "What on earth are you doing here? What happened to your face?" She eyes Martine suspiciously. Who is she?"

"This is Martine Rubio. She's helping me track down Benson."

Martine gives a friendly smile and offers her hand. Kathleen drops her fork on to her plate and shakes Martine's hand as a reflex action without deflecting her stare from me. "This is too much of a coincidence."

"What is?"

"You – and Benson – on the same day!"

"You've seen Benson?" Martine interjects.

"I... I don't..." Kathleen is flustered. She inclines her head towards Martine. "Can we talk in front of her?"

"She's one of us," I state confidently. I'm not at all sure this is an accurate assessment, but it seems the reassuring thing to say.

"I don't know what I can tell you – " She pushes her salad to one side and shakes her head. "I shouldn't really be saying anything," she mumbles, tucking away a strand of loose hair. "But I've got to talk to someone." Having made her decision, it all comes out in a rush.

"I was in Mr Frobisher-Allen's outer office this morning when this – this *person* flounced up to me as if he owned the place. He was waving a silk handkerchief in the air and demanding to see Stanley. I mean to say – he actually referred to Mr Frobisher-Allen as *Stanley*. The cheek of it! God only knows how he got past security.

"There was something familiar about him, but I couldn't place it. Then it came to me – the photograph you faxed across from Montpellier. I told him he couldn't possibly see Mr Frobisher-Allen without an appointment but he just laughed in my face and barged straight past me. I tried to block his way, but the rude bugger – ” Kathleen breaks off and her cheeks redden. “Excuse my French. He literally pushed me to one side. I followed him into the office in high dudgeon but Mr Frobisher-Allen waved me away and told me to wait outside. He said everything was all right. My whole body was trembling when I got back to the outer office and I was still sitting in a state of shock when Mr Frobisher-Allen buzzed through a few minutes later and demanded two coffees. Demanded, mind you – not asked. He was terribly brusque.

“I don't know what got into me, but I didn't go for the coffees. Instead I hid behind the curtains. It was a crazy impulse. After a couple of minutes, when nothing had happened, I felt utterly ridiculous – and terrified that I'd be caught. I was about to sneak out and go for the coffees when I heard the office door opening and when I peered out I saw Mr Frobisher-Allen crossing to the wall safe. He and I are the only ones who have the combination. My heart was beating madly.”

All the time she was speaking, Kathleen was tugging strands of her hair loose, twisting them round her index finger and thrusting them back into her bun. “I saw Mr Frobisher-Allen take something from the safe and hurry back into his office. I ran all the way to the vending machine. When I took in the coffees, the brute was sitting with his feet up on the desk, puffing away on one of Mr Frobisher-Allen's havanas. Stanley told me to go for an early lunch. He was most curt.

“But then – then.” Her pace doesn't slow but her voice falls to a whisper and Martine and I have to crane over the table to hear. “I checked the wall safe. We keep a lot of cash in there.” Kathleen's eyes are out on stalks, her fingers tugging away at her hair. “Twenty thousand pounds in used notes was missing. Can you believe that?”

Martine refers to the tracker device and catches my eye. “He's still in there,” she nods.

Kathleen reaches across the table and grabs me by the wrist. “What's going on, Frank? What am I going to do?”

I take her hand and grip it tightly. "You can figure this out as well as I can, Kathleen. Benson has a hold over your boss. Your guess is as good as mine as to what that might be, but there aren't too many possibilities."

Kathleen's eyes narrow. "Such as?"

"Could Frobisher-Allen have a bit on the side and Benson's threatening to spill the beans?" Kathleen shakes her head furiously and her cheeks turn scarlet. "Perhaps Stanley boy's got a taste for high-class hookers and Benson's threatening to expose him?" Kathleen's glowering at me, tight-lipped, outraged. "Could he be doing drugs?"

"I've never heard anything so ridiculous in all my life!"

"Has he ever shown an unhealthy interest in small children?"

"Stop this! Stop it at once!"

"I'm sorry, Kathleen, but twenty grand ain't chopped liver." (As far as I know I have no Jewish blood in me, but I've always liked that expression). My fingers are getting crushed. Eventually Kathleen slackens her grip and starts blubbing.

Martine digs me in the ribs and thrusts the tracker in front of my face. "Look!"

"Kathleen, we've got to go. We've got Benson bugged and he's on the move. We'll do our best to nail him, but in the meantime you've got to tell someone in authority that Frobisher-Allen's a security risk."

"Who do you tell that the Director-General of MI6 is being blackmailed?" The tears are flowing thick and fast.

"I don't know. Isn't there anyone you can go to?"

She tugs out a tissue and wipes her eyes. "The head of security has access to the Home Secretary in case of emergencies." She sobs between sniffles. "But I couldn't do that. I couldn't go over Mr Frobisher-Allen's head."

"You have to, Kathleen. You have to blow the whistle. Frobisher-Allen's a JAP."

"A what?"

"A JAP. Junkie, Adulterer or Pervert."

154

Her sobbing degenerates into wailing. I give her arm a reassuring squeeze as I get to my feet. "I'll call you at home tonight."

Martine is already heading for the door, her eyes glued to the tracking device. "I've never heard of a JAP," she pants as we're sprinting towards the car.

"Neither have I."

CHAPTER 15

"Run that past me again!" Martine demands as I'm turning the key in the ignition. "You're an innocent bystander who got caught up in all this just because you happened to respond to an advert for a job in a Montpellier bookshop?"

I snap on my seat belt and rev up. "Put your belt on, Martine."

"I can buy that you might recognise MI6 headquarters."

"Concentrate on the tracker. We don't want to lose him."

"I could even accept that you happened to know the name of the Director-General of MI6." She turns side on in her seat to stare at me. "But how come you're on faxing terms with his PA?" Negotiating the heavy traffic isn't easy. "You know where and when she lunches. You even know what she eats on fucking Thursdays. Right?"

I turn off at the traffic lights.

She swivels back to face the front. "What did you do that for?" she yells. "You should've gone straight on there!"

"You said to go right."

"I fucking-well did not! Turn around."

"I can't. It's a one-way street."

"Shit!" Martine peers at the grid reference on the tracker. "Take first left, go round the block and get back on to – oh, for fucksake!"

I'm beginning to think that, for a Cambridge PhD, Martine's English vocabulary is rather limited. "What's wrong now?"

"It's packed in." She glowers at the device, shakes it and holds it to her ear. "The signal's gone. Both the pulse and the bleep have vanished."

"Where was Benson when you lost him?"

She studies the map reference. "South end of Vauxhall Bridge."

"Near the entrance to the tube?"

She checks again. "Yeah."

"Then he's probably gone underground. The tracking satellite won't be able to handle that."

"Bloody useless technology!" She flings the gadget over her shoulder on to the back seat. "What now?" she demands.

I pull over and drum my fingertips on the steering column. Feigning the lost, foreign tourist, I deflect the wrath of the traffic warden who bustles across by asking for directions to the nearest Hertz office and, as I drive away, I rattle off my plan. "Benson won't be out of satellite contact for long. We'll have a fix on him as soon as he emerges from the tube system, but we need to be more flexible. We'll drop off the hire car and pick up a cab."

As soon as we get to the Hertz office I phone for a taxi and by the time we've completed the paperwork it's waiting outside.

"Would you just cruise around for a while, please?"

"Sure. Anything in particular you'd like to see, mate? Houses of Parliament? Buckingham Palace? Tower Bridge?"

"Would you mind just driving up and down Oxford Street?"

"Mind?" He glances over his shoulder and shrugs. "You're the one who's picking up the tab, mate. If it keeps you happy, I'll drive up and down Oxford Street until the cows come home. Let me know if you're getting bored."

"We've hardly travelled a hundred metres before Martine starts up again. "Right. Now tell me about your relationship with the Director-General's PA – and I want the truth this time."

I've been rehearsing my response. "Don't make a mountain out of a molehill, Martine. There's really nothing to tell. I used to work in London and one day I bumped into Kathleen in that salad bar and we recognised each other from our school days in Ayrshire. It was a Thursday and we were both having chicken salad. She told me she always had chicken salad on Thursdays – we had a joke about it. While we were chatting, I mentioned I was going to Montpellier in the summer to work in The Book Cellar and some time later she happened to need some information from Montpellier and she remembered our conversation so she sent me a fax."

Martine's about to query something when I grab her arm and point at the reactivated pulse. "Waterloo Station!" I yell, prodding the cabbie on the shoulder. "As quick as you can."

"Pretty low boredom threshold, mate!" He locks into a tight U-turn and the traffic lights are in our favour as we speed down Regent Street towards Piccadilly Circus.

"Pound to a pinch of shit Benson's heading for the Eurostar," I whisper in Martine's ear. We cross the Thames at Waterloo Bridge and pull up outside the railway station. Leaving Martine to settle the fare, I grab her suitcase, sling my rucksack over my shoulder and sprint across the concourse until I'm close enough to read the departures board. I'm panting for breath as I check the train times against the station clock. It's twenty minutes before the next Paris-bound Eurostar is scheduled to leave. Martine staggers to a halt by my side. When her tracker confirms that Benson's already on board this train, I trot over to the ticket office and, using my *carte bleue*, purchase two tickets, specifically requesting seats in the rear compartment.

Martine and I clamber on board with five minutes to spare and the pulse tells us Benson is about forty metres in front of us – the length of a couple of carriages. I wait until the train is under way, then, armed with the tracker, I make my way up the aisle, keeping a careful eye on the diminishing distance. When the device tells me I'm within ten metres of Benson I stop at the sliding glass doors and peer through into the next carriage. Four rows up, on the right, I can see a puffy hand and thick wrist dangling over the armrest. A red, silk handkerchief is tucked into the expanding watch strap.

I make my way back to my seat and slump down beside Martine. "It's Benson all right. What do we do now?"

"I've been giving that some thought," she says. "I don't see why we actually need to do anything. The bookmark will soon be back in

French territory, so my head will no longer be on the block. Why don't we just leave Benson carrying the bookmark and let Verdu and his boys pick him up at their leisure?"

I shake my head firmly. "I'm not walking away from this. I want to know what hold Benson's got over Frobisher-Allen. Besides," I add with a sly grin, "there's a little matter of twenty grand in cash that I wouldn't mind getting my hands on." I sit back in my seat, close my eyes, and reflect on how the lure of filthy lucre can play havoc with one's positioning of prepositions.

The compartment lights are switched off as we emerge from the Channel Tunnel and gather speed prior to crossing the flat terrain of Pas de Calais and Picardy. Martine looks up from *Zen and the Art of Motorcycle Maintenance*. "Do you reckon Benson's heading back to Montpellier?" she asks.

"Search me."

She folds down the corner of a page and closes the book. "What are you planning to do?"

"I haven't got anything as grandiose as a plan." I balance the tracker on the fold-down table in front of me. "For now, I'm just going to stick as close to Benson as I can and hope the opportunity arises to relieve him of Frobisher-Allen's cash."

Martine flicks *Zen* open again and starts thumbing through the pages – much too quickly, in my opinion, to digest the subtle nuances. I'm about to pass comment when I notice her head is drooping, swaying and bobbing with the motion of the train. Her eyelids sink. I slip an arm around her shoulder and her head comes across and nuzzles into my chest. When I ease her hair away from her forehead, she sighs softly and snuggles in closer. I continue stroking her forehead for a while, then my fingertips drift down to caress her cheek.

Suddenly, the bleep starts sounding and the pulse indicates Benson's on the move. He travels about ten metres, returning to his seat after a couple of minutes. I surmise he's been to the loo. Half an hour later he moves again, forty metres, this time remaining stationary for half an hour before returning to his seat. I assume he's been to the buffet car and this makes me realise how hungry I am. However, I don't want to disturb Martine and, besides, it would be too much of a risk to walk through Benson's carriage to get to the buffet.

By the time we're on the approach to the Gare du Nord the pins and needles in my arm are having a field day. I'm still reluctant to disturb Martine but the guard's announcement does it for me.

She sits up straight and rubs at her swollen eyelids. "You shouldn't have let me sleep so long, Jérôme. I feel dreadful."

I lever my stiff arm across and try to massage it back to life. She grabs my forearm, ignoring my agonised yelp. "Benson!" she shouts. "Is he still there?"

I prise her fingers away from my arm. "Somewhat surprisingly, he seems to have made no attempt to jump off a train travelling at two hundred and forty kilometres an hour."

She yawns and stretches. "You know what I mean."

"Not really."

"Fuck off!"

Paucity of vocabulary – definitely.

Our taxi keeps Benson's cab in sight as we thread our way along the Boulevard de Magenta, across the Place de la République and down past the Bastille to the drop-off zone outside the Gare de Lyon.

Martine sidles up to the ticket booth and overhears Benson book a single ticket to Montpellier on the next TGV. Once again, we opt for seats in the rear compartment and this time we stock up with magazines, sandwiches, water and beer before boarding. Martine gives me the choice and I opt for the window seat. The journey is uneventful, Martine and I taking it in turn to monitor Benson's movements on the tracker while the other dozes or reads. I nudge Martine as we're pulling into Montpellier station, just before midnight. She gets to her feet groggily and struggles to tug her case down from the overhead rack.

"Let's wait here until Benson gets off," I say. "I don't want to risk him seeing me on the platform."

She sinks back down on her seat and eyes the tracker. "He doesn't seem to be in any hurry." She leans across my body to rub at the steamed-up window with the heel of her hand, then she flattens her nose against the glass to watch the steady stream of passengers filing down the underpass towards the station exit. I feel a pleasant, warm sensation from the contact with her body. The stream has reduced to a trickle and Benson still hasn't made a move. "Do you think he might have fallen asleep?" Martine asks.

"How the hell should I know?" I'm tired and the tetchiness is showing in my voice. We sit in silence for another few minutes, staring at the stationary pulse. "I don't like this, Martine. Something's not right. Come on." We scramble to our feet and I grab the tracker and our bags and lead the way up the train, stopping to peer through the compartment door when we reach Benson's carriage. The pulse tells me he's six rows up on the left hand side, but I see no sign of life. I sidle up the aisle and steal a glance over the back of the seat.

"Your gadget's worse than fucking useless!"

Martine peers over my shoulder to check the pulse. "You're standing right over it?"

"What are you talking about?"

Pushing me to one side, she gets down on her hands and knees and tugs open the small waste paper bin underneath the window, then she pulls herself to her feet and hands me my wallet.

We're the only people on the deserted platform as I check the contents. I've recovered my address book and, of course, the bookmark but, hardly surprisingly, no cash. "He was bound to dump your wallet sooner or later," Martine says. "It's a pity he didn't think the bookmark was worth holding on to." I stuff the wallet into my jacket pocket.

"Where do you think he'll head for now?" Martine asks.

I sit down on her suitcase and scratch my head. "Let's try to get on to his wavelength. He won't go anywhere near the bookshop – as far as he knows I might still be there. That only leaves Le Vigan, but to get there he needs transport. He can't have left his car close to the station, everywhere around here is metered. The nearest free parking's a good twenty minutes walk away, so, if we hurry, we can get probably get to Le Vigan ahead of him if we take a taxi to your place and pick up your car. Are you game?"

Martine looks anything but convinced. "What if he doesn't go to Le Vigan?"

"Where else can he go?"

She gives a long drawn out yawn. "I was sort of hoping we might be going to bed." She stretches and twists her neck. "But if this *really* is your preference....?"

"Do you do rain checks?"

She looks up at the star-studded, night sky and shakes her head. "Not a rain cloud in sight."

We're not half way to Le Vigan and already I'm having misgivings. What if Benson doesn't show up? How long should we hang around waiting for him? Even if he does put in an appearance, what exactly am I going to do?

There are no lights on in the farmhouse. I lead the way up the dark, overgrown drive. "Fucking hell!" I let out a scream as I'm pitched headlong into a yawning, dark, bottomless abyss. At least that's what it felt like.

"Jérôme? Are you all right?"

I get to my feet and gingerly feel up and down my body but there doesn't appear to be any significant damage. I seem to be in some sort of crater, about two metres long, a metre wide and almost a metre deep.

"Jérôme? Where are you?" Martine's whisper is insistent. "Right in front of you. Be careful! There's a bloody big hole." She edges forward and grabs hold of my wrists to help me clamber out. I brush myself down. "This sodding pit wasn't here last week," I grumble.

"What's Benson been up to? Recovering buried treasure?"

"God only knows!" I carry on round to the back of the building and find the empty, spooky caravan in darkness. I make my way back to the car, giving the trench a wide berth.

"What do you suggest we do now?" Martine's tone is of the annoyingly superior, 'I told you so' variety.

"We'll wait for him," I state confidently. "Park down the road out of sight of the house, but close enough to see his car headlights when he arrives."

We get back into the car and she accelerates a hundred metres down the road.

Spinning round in a handbrake turn, she douses the lights and switches off the ignition. "Thirty minutes – absolute max," she states. "After that, you're on your own."

Dawn is breaking, Martine's asleep, I'm knackered. I ease open the passenger door and slam it shut, at the same time digging Martine in the ribs with my elbow. "Quick, Martine! I've got the twenty grand. Let's go!"

"What...? What's going on?" She's gabbling in a mixture of French and English as she struggles to assimilate where she is. "Where's Benson?" Her fingers grope for the ignition. "You managed it, Jérôme?" She fires the engine. "What happened?"

"Not a lot." I let out a sigh. "If you really want to know, he didn't show up."

She looks at me uncomprehendingly, then she cuts the engine and glares. "Very fucking funny!" Her whole body is shivering. "What time is it?"

I glance at my watch. "Nearly six."

"So we spent the whole night here for bugger-all?"

"That is one way of looking at it."

Not a word is said on the way back until we stop at a set of traffic lights on the outskirts of Montpellier. "Where would you like me to drop you off?" The tone is glacial.

"Anywhere near the centre would be fine." She drives on in stony silence and pulls over close to the railway station. "What are you going to do?" I ask.

"*I'm* going home to *my* bed."

I lean over to the back seat and pull over my rucksack. "Thanks for the ride, Martine. I'll give you a call later."

"I shouldn't bother."

I trudge up Rue Maguelone, cross the almost deserted Place de la Comédie, and trudge up the hill towards The Book Cellar.

I remember I'd promised to phone Kathleen and even though seven o'clock in the morning isn't the most sociable of hours I decide to try anyway. Her phone rings out for a long time but there's no reply. I don't like that one little bit. I crawl into the camp bed and within minutes I've crashed out.

It's early afternoon before I regain consciousness. A late lunch in a brasserie, then I pick up a six-pack of beer and head back to the bookshop. Reaching into my pocket for the shop keys, I discover I've still got Martine's tracker.

When I go inside, I sense that someone's been in the shop since I left. I look around, but nothing is obviously out of place, however, the feeling that someone's been here doesn't go away. I take Martine's bookmark from my wallet and zip both it and her tracker into the side pocket of my rucksack. At least this gives me an excuse to go round to her place to return them, but I think it might be advisable to leave her to cool off for a while.

I tug the ring-pull from a beer can and, as I'm badly in need of some light relief, I look for the video of the nymphets and the pool attendants, but I'm not able to find it. The other two brown paper packages, which were addressed to customers in Spain, have also disappeared. Has Benson been here to get them while I was out? I kick a few things round the shop in frustration, then I go to the storeroom and stretch out full length on the camp bed. I empty the can down my throat, close my eyes, and conjure up a mental image of small, tanned breasts and long, shapely legs.

I wake with a start and glance at my watch. It's almost five o'clock. I'm considering what to do when it dawns on me that today is Friday. Fitzpatrick's? Why not? There's nothing to lose – and there might be some gossip about Benson. I hurry to the Hertz office beside the station and pick up a hire car, then I call in at a fancy dress shop nearby and select a few random items; a convincing short, black wig to cover my give-away red hair, a realistic black beard, which will serve to hide my damaged chin, and a pair of clear-glass, steel-rimmed spectacles. When I get back to the bookshop I don the garb and check my appearance in the mirror.

I pack all my belongings into my rucksack and stow it in the boot of the car. Having found a space in the underground car park beneath the Place de la Comédie, I buy a copy of *Paris Match* and head for Fitzpatrick's, installing myself adjacent to the British Expatriate Club table just before seven o'clock.

Somewhat unusually, Emily Abercrombie is the first to arrive. She tut-tuts loudly and flicks the length of the bench seat with her lace handkerchief before sitting down. The tight, wizened mouth takes in a miserly quantity of Pimms, then she takes her reading glasses from their case and pulls a thick, hardback book from her shopping bag. Tracy and Anna arriving doesn't cause her to raise her head and only when George Davies appears does she condescend to stop reading and join in the conversation, quickly getting into her stride with some snide remarks about Linda's latest hairstyle.

The phone rings out behind the bar and I hear the barman chortle as he shares a joke with someone. He replaces the receiver and starts pulling a pint of Guinness and he continues pulling until there are three pints lined up on the counter. Every muscle in my body tenses.

CHAPTER 16

I'm doing my best to ignore the crap Linda's spouting while I try to figure out what to do. My mind's racing.

The guffaw is unmistakable as Charles walks through the door and he waves across to the BEC table before waddling up to the bar to collect his three pints. Linda is stunned into open-mouthed silence and all the colour drains from Tracy's face. I bury my head in *Paris Match* as the stooped figure staggers towards the table, balancing his tray.

"It's – it's great to see you, Charles!" George Davies stammers, scrambling to his feet. "There have been some pretty bizarre rumours flying around, I don't mind telling you. What on earth happened?"

Charles takes the seat at the head of the table and the first pint of Guinness gurgles its way down in one swallow. He burps noisily and wipes his moustache with the silk handkerchief dangling from his wrist before selecting another glass. "A most unpleasant business, George. Most unpleasant. That Dumas character turned out to be a right nasty piece of work." Confirmatory rumbles run round the table.

"I thought Jérôme was all right," Tracy states in what I consider to be quite a firm tone.

"Don't be ridiculous, my dear." Emily Abercrombie's lace handkerchief is flicked dismissively in Tracy's face. "The man doesn't even play bridge."

"Did you know that we all had a visit from Les Renseignements Généraux, Charles?" George asks. "They grilled us about your disappearance."

Charles licks his lips and nods. "Let me tell you what actually happened, George. Dumas intended to murder me so he could get his hands on the bookshop. It seems he spiked my tea with something or other, then forged my will and reported to the authorities that I'd had a fatal skiing accident in Estonia. Can you believe that?"

A collective *wow* runs round the table as another pint sloshes its way to oblivion. I'm having a real problem letting the bastard get away with this.

"The shitehound drove my drugged body up to my house at Le Vigan. The police reckon he was planning to bury me alive." Another collective intake of breath. Charles smacks his lips noisily. "Fortunately, I have a pretty strong constitution. When I came round I found myself slumped in the back seat of my car and when I peered out of the window I saw Dumas digging my grave, right in front of my eyes."

An even louder, elongated *wo....ow*. He has his audience on the edge of their seats.

"What's a shitehound, Mummy?" Anna asks, and gets her ear clipped for her trouble.

Charles is milking it for all it's worth as he starts on his next pint. "George, be a good chap and get a round in so I can carry on with my story."

George Davies signals frantically to the barman and Charles holds up his arm straight and waves three fingers in the general direction of the bar. "Fortunately, I had the presence of mind to realise what was happening, though I was in no fit state to take Dumas on. The man's a powerful brute. I could see the keys were still in the ignition so I forced myself to lie doggo until Dumas was deep in the trench and all I could see was the blade of his shovel glinting in the moonlight as the earth came flying out from my intended grave."

"Oh my God!" Linda squeals and clasps her hands to her face. "That must have been terrifying for you, Charles."

"Believe me, Linda, it was." A pause for maximum dramatic effect while the silk handkerchief dabs a layer of froth from the clotted moustache. "I waited until the last possible moment, then I staggered out the rear door and threw myself into the driver's seat. There was no

167

feeling in my legs. I fired the engine, over-revving like mad because I had no sensitivity with the pedals. When Dumas heard the roar of the engine he came out of the trench like a bat out of hell and charged towards the car, shrieking at the top of his voice, wielding his shovel above his head like some manic, whirling dervish.

"Somehow, I managed to find reverse gear. I screeched back down the dirt track away from the house but the crazed creature was closing on me with every stride, screeching like a banshee. I hit a tree stump and ground to a halt. Dumas was on to me in a flash, flailing at the windscreen, shattering it with his shovel." Linda lets out an agonised yelp. "In sheer desperation I slammed the car into a forward gear and hit the accelerator. The car lurched forward, knocking Dumas aside. I was starting to get some feeling in my arms and legs – I suppose it must have been a surge of adrenalin – and I wrenched the steering wheel round and roared away. You wouldn't believe the things he screamed after me as I made my escape." Charles shakes his head and wipes his brow with his soggy handkerchief. "I couldn't possibly repeat what he shouted, not in front of you, Mrs Abercrombie."

Emily Abercrombie gives a prim, tight-lipped, self-satisfied nod. "I knew that conniving Frenchman was a blackguard, Charles. From the very first moment I laid eyes on him."

The table dissolves into animated conversation as Charles lumbers towards the bar with his empty tray. Anna follows him, tugging at his trouser leg, demanding to know what a shitehound is. While Charles is up at the bar, Linda holds court on how I'd kidnapped her and Daniel at gun-point and held them prisoner for forty-eight hours without food or water. As soon as Charles returns with his laden tray the buzz of conversation dies away.

"Is Dumas under arrest?" George asks.

"By now, almost certainly. I spoke to Verdu an hour ago and he told me his men were closing in on him. Apparently he went over to England for a couple of days, but for some inexplicable reason he came back to Montpellier. God only knows what he's up to. The guy's clearly unstable. Verdu advised me to steer clear of the bookshop for the time being because he reckons Dumas might show up there."

"You can stay at our place, if you like, Charles," Linda says. "At least until you're sure the police have Dumas in custody."

Charles nods towards Linda and smiles. "Very kind, Linda. Thanks. I'll take you up on that." As another pint of Guinness disappears, I decide it's time to make myself scarce.

I hurry towards the car park and as soon as I'm behind the wheel I rip off my spectacles, beard and wig and throw them on to the back seat. If the vulture pack is closing in, then the bookshop's off limits. That only leaves the gîte at St Martin so I decide to head for there. When I spot a phone booth on the way out of town I pull over to try Kathleen Morrison's number. I let it ring out for a long time, but there's still no reply. I dial Martine's number, but think better of it and hang up before the connection is made.

I park in the drive outside the gîte and search in my pockets for the front door key. The house feels chilly and slightly damp and my fingers are fumbling for the light switch when suddenly the lounge is ablaze with light. Perched on the settee, wrapped in a long, black coat, sits Verdu. I spin round and see Sinègre standing by the door to the kitchen. Two other men I've never seen before are leaning against the fireplace. Verdu taps a filter-tipped cigarette from his packet and lights up. Taking a long, slow drag, he gets to his feet.

"Jérôme Dumas, you are under arrest for the kidnap and attempted murder of Charles Benson. Further charges relating to trafficking in pornography and paedophilia will be filed in due course. In the meantime you are not obliged to say anything, but – " He breaks off to suck hard on his cigarette, then chuckles evilly. "But a full confession would make things an awful lot easier for you." His three cronies guffaw on cue. Verdu picks up his black stetson from the settee and settles it firmly on the crown of his head, the brim nestling on the points of his pixie ears. With a curt signal to his men, he strides out of the door.

It's late on Saturday evening and I don't know where I'm being held. I was driven back to Montpellier last night in the back seat of a Renault, jammed between two of Verdu's heavies, while Sinègre followed in convoy, driving my hire car. I lost my bearings when we wove through districts I didn't recognize.

The only items of furniture in the cramped room are a single bed and an upright chair. There's a small, barred window high in the wall and the door opposite the foot of the bed leads to a bathroom which has a toilet, a wash hand basin and a shower with no curtain. My clothes and possessions were confiscated on arrival and I was given a loose fitting sweat shirt and a pair of track suit trousers. I've not been allowed any phone calls. I'm lying stretched out on the bed, my hands cuffed in front of me, my eyes closed. Although I'm physically drained, my brain is churning.

My eyelids flicker open when I hear the scrape of a key turning in the lock. I've been interrogated three times during the past twenty-four hours and Sinègre now yanks me to my feet again and leads me down the same narrow passageway towards Verdu's office, the soles of my bare feet leaving sweaty imprints on the cold, tiled corridor. Despite the fact I'm exhausted, I'm made to stand to attention in front of Verdu's desk while Sinègre hovers behind me, a long truncheon strapped to his right wrist.

"I've had as much of this nonsense as I'm prepared to take," Verdu snaps. "Now for the last time, are you going to tell me who you are?"

"Jérôme Dumas," I mumble. Sinègre prods the back of my knee with his truncheon, not particularly hard, but enough to make my knee buckle painfully. Verdu sucks angrily on his teeth. "Where are you from?" he barks.

"Alsace." The truncheon nudges into my other knee.

"Where, precisely, in Alsace?"

"Near Strasbourg." Every time I gave an answer Verdu doesn't like I get the truncheon treatment.

"Describe Strasbourg Cathedral."

"What?"

"Where's the railway station? What's the name of the football ground? What's the Palais de l'Europe used for?"

"I… I don't know the place very well. I was brought up on a farm about twenty kilometres outside the city." The next prod with the truncheon makes me lose control of my wobbly legs and I sink to my knees.

Verdu springs to his feet. "Do you think I was bloody well born yesterday?" he roars. "Never in my life have I been subjected to such a load of preposterous claptrap!" He slams his fist into the open palm of his hand, his glare telling me it won't take a lot more incitement for him to slam it somewhere else. "We've checked your papers, *Dumas* – your *carte d'identité*, your passport, your driving licence," he rants. "Every one's a bloody forgery!"

I gaze at the floor, tight-lipped.

Verdu sinks back down into his seat. "We can prove beyond any shadow of doubt that you forged Charles Benson's will." His voice is back under control as he flicks open the folder lying on his desk and refers to his notes. "How do you explain the fact that the earth samples from the shovel we found in the garage at St Martin de Londres match the soil of the grave that was dug at Charles Benson's farmhouse?" We've already been through this during the previous cross-examinations. I squat on my heels and gaze up at him blankly. His expression isn't pitying – that emotion is probably beyond him – it's more like contemptuous.

"I've already told you. I can't explain that. I don't know how that could've happened. I don't know anything about a shovel or a fucking grave! Someone must be trying to frame me."

He sneers. "Oh, by the way, on a wild hunch, I had the earth stains on your jeans analysed. Surprise, surprise! They also match the soil in Benson's intended grave."

"That, I can explain. I accidentally fell into a hole when I was up at Benson's place."

"How terribly convenient!" Verdu waves his hand dismissively and refers again to his notes. "When we raided The Book Cellar we confiscated a pornographic video tape which had your prints all over it, as well as two parcels containing similar material, addressed to people in Spain. In addition, the Spanish police intercepted tapes of a paedophile nature which had been posted from Montpellier and the fingerprints lifted from the packaging match yours."

He closes the folder and fixes me with a cold, supercilious stare. "This lot adds up to at least twelve years, so why don't you save us all a lot of time and trouble?"

"And how do you propose I might do that?"

"For a start, you can tell us who you're working for, Mr McClure." He pauses to let the bombshell sink in. "It is *Mr McClure*, isn't it? Mr Frank McClure?"

My stomach is turning somersaults and my tongue feels as if it's stuck to the roof of my mouth. "I'm… I'm not working for anybody," I croak.

"If you confess to kidnapping and attempted murder," he continues in a nonchalant tone, "I'm prepared to drop the other charges. You'll probably get eight years and, if you're lucky, half of that might be suspended. Keep your nose clean and you could be out in three. However, if you persist in sticking to this preposterous story," he growls, "I'll throw the book at you and you'll go down for twelve years without remission."

"How often do I have to tell you?" I scream, grabbing hold of the edge of his desk with my cuffed hands and hauling myself to my feet. "I didn't try to murder Benson. Talk to Martine Rubio, for Christ's sake! She'll corroborate my story."

"I wouldn't bet my life on that." Verdu gives Sinègre a knowing wink. "Not even twelve years of it, eh Serge?" Sinègre falls about laughing.

"I want to talk to Martine."

"All in good time. As soon as you've signed the confession."

"Bring her here now! She'll testify on my behalf." Sinègre goes into convulsions.

"Wise up, for Christ's sake, McClure," Verdu snaps. "How do you think we uncovered your true identity? How do you think we discovered your hideout in St Martin de Londres?"

My exhausted, confused brain is struggling to deal with these questions. Of course Martine knows my identity, but she doesn't know about the gîte. Then it dawns on me. Of course she bloody well knows about the gîte! Didn't she follow me home one night from Fitzpatrick's?

I stare up through the barred window at the gathering dusk. I think it's Sunday evening, though I'm losing sense of time. Hunger pains are griping at my stomach. I've been given nothing but water and dry biscuits since I've been here. I hear the key turn in the lock and Sinègre drags to me feet. I've lost count of the number of times I've been through this routine. I'm marched, half-walking, half-staggering to Verdu's office where I'm propped up against his desk.

Verdu gives a signal to Sinègre who, for the first time in forty-eight hours, unlocks my handcuffs. I massage my aching wrists. "That will be all, Mr McClure," I hear Verdu say breezily. "You're free to go now. Thank you for helping us with our enquiries."

I think I'm starting to hallucinate.

CHAPTER 17

"Free? To go?"

"I do believe that's what I said."

"What….. what about the charges?" I stammer.

"You must have misunderstood, Mr McClure." Verdu's tone is incredulous. "There never were any charges. You just agreed to help us with our enquiries."

I look from Verdu to Sinègre and back again, trying to figure out if I'm being set up in some variation of the 'good cop / bad cop' routine. They're both poker-faced.

"You'll find your clothes and your possessions on your bed. Your car is parked at the rear of the building," Verdu states casually. "You can pick up the keys from reception. Thank you again for your co-operation."

Sinègre strolls from the office, whistling tunelessly, while Verdu ostentatiously turns his attention to dealing with the pile of paperwork in his in-tray. I sidle towards the door and Verdu doesn't look up when I glance back. My instincts tell me to get the hell out of here while the going's good and worry about trying to figure out what's going on later. I hurry back to the cell and find my clothes laid out neatly on the bed, my wallet and my papers lying beside them. I change as quickly as I can. The uniformed officer at the reception desk hands me my car keys without being asked and I stumble down the steps and, moving as fast as my shaky legs will allow, I scuttle towards the car park.

I drive around in circles for some time, trying to get my bearings, and I pull over when I spot a phone booth.

"Martine's not here." I assume this to be either Philippe or Bernard. "Can I take a message?"

I hesitate. "Yes. You can take a bloody message!" I fume. "Tell her

Jérôme Dumas called. Tell her I want to thank her for squaring things with Verdu!" I slam down the receiver and kick the phone booth, then I pluck up the handset and dial again.

"Hello," she yawns. "Who is it?" It sounds as if I've woken her up.

"It's Frank McClure, Kathleen. Sorry about phoning so late, but I had to talk to you."

"No problem, Frank." She yawns again. "I was having an early night, but I'm glad you called." She sounds calm, her voice assured. "I assume Verdu has released you from custody?"

"Yes! How on earth did you know about that?"

"It's a long, complicated story, but everything's straightened out now. I can't go into any details over the phone. Are you planning to be in London in the near future?"

"Planning is not high on my list of capabilities right now, Kathleen. I've had a pretty traumatic forty-eight hours."

"I understand that, Frank, but I can assure you it's all behind you. When you're next in London, I'll explain everything."

"I need some time to recover."

"Of course you do. Why don't you go back to Kilbirnie for a few days?"

"Kilbirnie?"

"Why not? Relax for a while on home ground. When you've had a chance to unwind, come down to headquarters and I'll fill you in. Give yourself a treat. Fly business class. I'll authorise it."

When I eventually get my bearings, I make my way to the car park beneath the Place de la Comédie and I pick up a baguette from an all-night *boulangerie* before trudging back to the bookshop. I prepare a sandwich and open a can of beer, but fall asleep in a chair before I've touched either of them.

I'm wakened by the laughter of children passing by on their way to school. My legs are suffering from cramp, my neck's stiff and I've got a thumping headache. I stretch for the phone.

"Is Martine there?"

"She won't talk to you, Jérôme." Pascale sounds adamant.

"Is she there?" I insist.

There's a pause. "She's in the kitchen."

"I have to speak to her, Pascale."

"You're not listening to what I'm saying, Jérôme. She won't talk to you. It's not negotiable."

"I need to know what she told Verdu."

"I can't help you with that."

"Pascale!" The line goes dead.

I take Kathleen at her word and phone Air France to book a business class ticket for the afternoon flight to Paris and an onward connection to Glasgow. I collect my car from the underground car park and, having checked to make sure my rucksack is still in the boot, I stop off at the fancy dress shop and return my disguise before driving out to the airport and dropping off the car keys at the Hertz desk.

I could get used to champagne in the middle of the afternoon. At Glasgow airport I pick up a top of the range hire car to drive to Kilbirnie and by the time I reach the outskirts of town it's starting to get dark and steady rain is falling. When I turn into the High Street I'm astonished to see the bright, neon pub sign lit up and when I walk into The Plucked Pheasant I hardly recognise the place. The lounge has been given a fresh coat of paint, the tables and chairs are new, there's piped music in the background and, the most amazing thing of all, there's a buzz of conversation from the customers – there must be at least forty of the buggers – at six o'clock on a Monday evening.

Lachlan is holding court behind the bar but he breaks off when he sees me walk through the door. "Frank!" he roars. "Why did you no' let me know you wis comin'?" It takes me a moment to tune in to the accent. For the first time I can ever recall, Lachlan is smiling. I notice he's put on weight, especially around his glowing cheeks, and his blonde mane has been cropped. Grabbing a bar towel, he wipes his hands on it before stretching across the counter to envelop my fist in a firm grip. He sets up a large Glenmorangie and a pint of lager on the bar.

I climb on to what had been my father's favourite barstool – I'm pleased to see it survived the refurbishment. Picking up the whisky tumbler between thumb and forefinger I swill the drink round in the glass before throwing back the contents in one gulp. Grimacing, I wipe my mouth with the back of my hand, then I tip the whisky dregs into my lager and take a long, slow swallow. "You've certainly got this place on its feet, Lachlan, my boy." My gaze travels round the crowded bar. "Lager's in nice condition, by the way."

He nods his appreciation. "Best day's work I ever did, movin' in here. But it's a' doon tae her," he says in a whisper, jerking his thumb in the direction of an attractive, petite redhead who is pulling a pint at the far end of the bar. "Dae you no' recognise her?"

I look the girl up and down. "Sort of. I'm sure I've seen her before, but I canny place her."

"She's yer next door neighbour."

"It's never Shellagh McGarrity?"

"The same."

"She's put on a bit of weight."

Picking up a sparkling pint tumbler, Lachlan polishes it furiously with a tea towel. "Shellagh straightened me oot. When I first moved in here, we bumped intae each other in the street a couple o' times. Wan day, she invited me in fur a coffee an' it jist took aff frae there. It wis her idea tae open up the pub fur business. Wi'oot her pushin' me, I'd still be spendin' hauf the day in ma pit. But she willny let me smoke," he whispers into the back of his hand. "Nuthin'. No' even a bloody fag!" Lachlan hangs the towel over the rail and I notice the hangdog expression is back. "But a' good things must come tae an end." He gives an audible sigh. "I suppose you'll be wantin' tae claim back yer birthright?"

I look him straight in the eye. "Lachlan, pal, I've nae idea whit I want." I hold out my whisky glass for a refill.

I spend the next few days soaking up the atmosphere and visiting my old haunts. There's a match at Somerset Park but it's a disappointing performance from Ayr, going down three-one to Greenock Morton. After the game I walk for miles along the beach in the incessant drizzle.

In the evenings, I help out behind the bar and on my second night back, during a lull, Lachlan pulls me to one side. "Frank, I've got a confession tae make."

"Whit's that?"

"I'm tradin' in your name."

"Whit are you on aboot?"

"I didny dare apply fur a pub licence. They'd never huv gi'ed me wan. So I've been forgin' your signature for everythin' – orderin' beer, buyin' furniture, payin' the decorators. I huvny dared tell Shellagh, but. She'd go ballistic if she found out."

I smile. "I can live wi' that, Lachlan. As long as you're plannin' tae pay ma tax bill."

He grins and uses both hands to try to part his non-existent mane. "Fair's fair."

"Now you tell me somethin', Lachlan. Have you ever heard of someone called The Pheasant Plucker?"

He falls about laughing. "O' course. That wis your nickname at school."

"Wis it?"

"Did ye no' ken?" I shake my head. "It wis a' yer faither's fault – callin' his pub The Plucked Pheasant. Whit else can you expect? Yer auld man hud a grand sense o' humour, but. He used tae run a tongue-twister competition in the pub every Saturday night. You hud tae repeat the rhyme five times, as fast as you could." Lachlan takes a deep breath, closes his eyes, and taps out the beat with his foot as he chants: "I'm no' the

178

pheasant plucker, I'm the pheasant plucker's son – an' I'm only pluckin' pheasants till the pheasant plucker comes." He opens his eyes and grins. "I canny say it quick. Yer faither used tae gie a pint o' heavy to whoever could say it five times the fastest – wi'oot pluckin' it up, o' course!"

It's Thursday evening and I almost drop the pint of lager I'm pulling when I see Sadie Mason walk through the door. She's hardly changed. The same peroxide-blonde hair with the prominent dark roots, the cheery grin, the slightly smudged, ruby-red lipstick. When she strides up to the bar I notice several deep wrinkles etched into her forehead which weren't there before.

"I heard you wis back in town, Frank."

"Good news travels fast, Sadie." I feel a sense of foreboding. "How aboot a drink on the house fur auld times sake?"

"Never been known tae turn doon an offer like that."

"Is it still gin an' tonic?"

"Still large wans. An' you can take that worried look aff yer face, you daft bizzum." She grins at me. "You're far too auld fur me." Unbridled relief surges through my body. "Anyway," she says, standing on tiptoe on the bar rail and leaning across to whisper in my ear. "Even in yer prime, you couldny haud a candle tae wee Tommy in number thirty seven." She cackles. "Did I say *wee* Tommy?" Her mascara-caked eyes are dancing. "We're talkin' serious candles here." Sadie is convulsed in laughter as she tips the bottle of tonic into her gin. I join in the laughter.

It takes me a few days to admit to myself what I've known all along. I phone Kathleen Morrison and arrange to meet her for lunch on Monday.

I fetch a stepladder from the basement and climb up to the loft to recover my battered biscuit tin from underneath the tarpaulin. Having spread the contents out on the bed, I wrap each item in tissue paper before stowing it carefully in the zip-up pocket of my rucksack. I stretch out on the bed with my hands clasped behind my neck and, when I close my eyes, a sexy giggle rings in my ears and I imagine the powerful scent of Rive Gauche invading my nostrils.

I wander into the salad bar and do a double-take. It's Kathleen's table all right – it's Kathleen, but she's barely recognisable. Her hair is short, streaked with blonde highlights and stylishly cut in a scalloped fringe. Her make-up is flawless. Dark blue eye shadow and matching mascara set off her eyes and her black spectacles have been replaced by mother-of-pearl designer frames. A light foundation with a suggestion of blusher counterbalances the striking red of her lipstick. She's power-dressed in an extremely sexy outfit; three-piece, blue-pinstripe trouser suit, white satin shirt and a grey thong tie. As I sink down on the bench opposite I notice there's an open sandwich on the plate in front of her.

"Hey, it's Monday! What happened to the tuna salad?"

I'm greeted with a broad smile. "I'm undergoing a lifestyle reassessment, Frank." She sweeps her hair back from her forehead and points to the sandwich. "Smoked Scottish salmon with mayonnaise on whole wheat baguette. I'm even thinking of trying a different restaurant," she adds in a whisper, having first checked to make sure the waitress is out of earshot. "But I can't handle too many changes all at once." She takes a sip from her glass of white wine. "How are you getting on?"

"Okay, I guess." I call across the waitress and order a tuna salad and a Perrier. "Thought the kitchen staff might appreciate a bit of continuity."

Kathleen smiles. "I notice quite a change in your accent."

"I can revert to Kilbirnie, if you prefer."

"I'm quite taken by your Home Counties."

"My curiosity's killing me, Kathleen. What's been going on?"

"I'm afraid you'll have to wait till we're back in the office, Frank. It's much too sensitive to discuss in here. By the way," she adds, "I have a new boss now – Stephen Atherton-Loring."

"Quite a mouthful."

"Mmm…." There's a far away look in her eyes as she dreamily runs her tongue round the tip of her baguette before sinking in her teeth and wrestling off the end. Putting down the sandwich, she unfolds a paper napkin to dab away the dribble of mayonnaise running down her chin. "He's actually rather dishy. He's very young to be in such a senior position. Divorced." Her blusher darkens a shade. "But no children," she adds quickly. "He involves me in absolutely everything and he trusts my judgment implicitly. The decision to authorise you to fly business class?" She shrugs her slight shoulders and points a perfectly manicured, red-varnished fingernail at her pouting chest. "Mine and mine alone. Didn't even have to consult Stephen about that," she says, teasing a strand of hair loose and tucking it neatly behind her ear. "With Mr Frobisher-Allen, my financial authority never extended beyond signing the occasional chitty for coffee and biscuits."

My lunch arrives and we indulge in small talk about the weather and the horrors of commuting in London while we eat.

"Coffee back in the office?" she suggests.

"Suits me."

Kathleen waves across to attract the waitress' attention. "Put both meals on my tab, Jennifer," she says as she's getting to her feet.

A light shower of rain starts falling as we're crossing Vauxhall Bridge and we break into a trot for the last fifty metres. When we're back inside the building we take the lift to the second floor and pick up two coffees from the vending machine. Kathleen has moved office since I was last here and she's now installed in a spacious office, adjacent to the Director-General's suite, with a superb view across the Thames.

"Okay," she says when we're seated, "let's take it from the last time I saw you, which was when you and Martine Rubio turned up in the salad bar. As soon as I got back to the office that afternoon I asked at reception why that frightful Benson character had been allowed into the building. I almost died when the guard told me he had a permit signed by the Director-General himself.

"When I heard that, I went straight to the head of security and told him what I – what *you* – suspected, about Frobisher-Allen being blackmailed. I told him about the twenty thousand pounds that had been taken from the safe and about Frobisher-Allen giving Benson a pass to enter the building. Things moved quickly after that. I was whisked off to a hotel where I was cross-examined by God only knows who for hours on end. I was kept there for two days."

"Which explains why I got no joy when I tried to phone you. I called several times, but there was no reply. I was worried about what might've happened to you."

"Sorry about that. Well, apparently, Frobisher-Allen had been under suspicion for some time. The National Audit Office had raised concerns with the Home Secretary about MI6 funds being misappropriated and mine was the confirmatory evidence they needed."

I nod in satisfaction. "I knew all along he was a JAP."

Kathleen shakes her head. There's a mischievous twinkle in her eyes and a smug, *I know something you don't know* grin is smeared across her features. "Are you ready for this, Frank? Stanley Frobisher-Allen is not a JAP." She pauses for effect. "He's a brother."

"A what?"

"When confronted with the facts, he broke down and confessed. The person we both know as Charles Benson is Stanley Frobisher-Allen's brother."

I stare at her, wide-eyed. "You have got to be kidding!"

"I thought that might come as a bit of a surprise!" She's grinning like a Cheshire cat. "It appears that Stanley Frobisher-Allen started out life as Stan Hawkey, but he changed his name by deed poll when he applied for a vacancy as a clerical officer with the Civil Service. He thought a double-barrelled name would improve his chances of selection. Obviously it didn't do them any harm because he got the job and over the following years he worked his way up through the ranks, eventually attaining the elevated position of Director-General of MI6 and for the past five years his sole motivation in life has been to get a peerage on his retirement. It became a fixation with him. Everything he did was geared towards that end. However, his younger brother, Arthur Hawkey, whom you know as Charles Benson, stuck his nose in and put a spoke in the wheel."

It crosses my mind to comment on this potentially painful mixture of metaphors, but I decide to let it pass.

"Arthur Hawkey has spent the past twenty-odd years wandering around Europe," she continues, "making his living by flogging marijuana to British expatriates. He'd been hounded out of Germany and Spain and Stanley knew he'd been operating in France for some time. Arthur had an eye for the main chance. He knew how desperate his brother was for a peerage and he realised he had him over a barrel. He sent Stanley an e-mail in which he threatened to sell his memoirs to the tabloids unless Stanley bought him off – *MI6 Director-General's Brother Peddles Pot to the Populace* – that sort of thing. Stanley could see his prospects of ermine going up in a puff of marijuana smoke."

Kathleen's phone rings and she checks the display panel. "Excuse me, Frank. I have to take this call. It's my boss." She snatches up the hand set and listens attentively. "Yes, Stephen," she states confidently. "If push comes to shove, we can concede another two million, but no more. That's the absolute limit the budget will stand.

"Sorry about that," she says, replacing the receiver. "He wanted to check what our position should be in a some delicate negotiations we're involved in. Now, where was I?"

"You were saying that Charles Benson, a.k.a. Arthur Hawkey, was threatening to throw a spanner in the works regarding Frobisher-Allen's peerage."

"Ah, yes. Well, Stanley decided he needed to nail Arthur once and for all and to that end he started diverting an incredible amount of MI6 resources towards tracking him down. He knew he was operating in France, but he'd no idea where, so he activated the whole of the MI6 network to search for his brother. Every time there was a possible sighting, Stanley would send someone in on a fictitious surveillance mission to try to get confirmation. The blurred photo you faxed across from Montpellier was the clincher. Frobisher-Allen swung into action.

"His objective was to get Arthur locked away in a French jail for a few months, long enough for him make sure his peerage was in the bag. Stanley knew that Arthur made his living by flogging marijuana and he suspected his source of supply was somewhere in England, so he contacted the major shipping companies and discovered that Chronopost had a contract to make regular deliveries to The Book Cellar in Montpellier. He instructed his men to intercept these shipments and thus discovered that Arthur was working a scam with their Uncle Godfrey who was growing marijuana in his greenhouse in Yorkshire and shipping it out to France, concealed in packages of books. However, Stanley realised that reporting this to the French authorities wasn't going to get them over-excited. A ticking-off for a bit of low-key marijuana peddling, perhaps. Possibly a fine. That wasn't good enough. Stanley decided to up the ante. Knowing that his brother was allergic to paying taxes, he dropped a hint to his counterpart in the French Secret Service that they might want to check out Arthur's tax returns. He followed that up by using his influence with Customs & Excise to obtain a batch of confiscated videos on the pretext that he needed them to bait a sting operation, then he instructed Special Branch to intercept Uncle Godfrey's book shipments before they left the country and substitute paedophilia and hard core pornography for the pot. When these consignments were en route to France, Stanley tipped the wink to Verdu that Arthur was trafficking in paedophilia and porn in the hope that this would be enough to get him incarcerated."

I'm struggling to keep up with all this.

"However, before Verdu had the chance to intervene," Kathleen continues, "Arthur phoned Stanley out of the blue and announced he was in England. He insisted that they should meet and he instructed Stanley to send him an MI6 security pass, care of their Uncle Godfrey.

When Arthur turned up at headquarters he breezed into Stanley's office and offered him a deal; he would agree to adopt a low profile in Montpellier and keep his mouth shut if Stanley gave him twenty thousand pounds in cash and got the French authorities off his back with regard to tax evasion. If not, he threatened to sing his head off to the *Sun*. Stanley went along with this. Arthur was given the cash and Frobisher-Allen fobbed Verdu off with some cock and bull story about there being a mix-up over Arthur's tax affairs. Arthur was never aware of the fact that consignments of pornography were en route to the bookshop and, to avoid this blowing up in his face, Frobisher-Allen told Verdu that *you* were the person responsible for trafficking in paedophilia and pornography."

"Charming!"

"As a result of all this, Stanley realised that you were now a much bigger threat to his peerage aspirations than Arthur. If you were to start sounding off about MI6 undercover agents operating on French territory, or start squealing about being framed on trumped-up pornography charges, he'd be up the creek without a paddle, so he concocted a plot to have you arrested for attempted murder and he talked Arthur into going along with it. Stanley sent his boys in to dig a pseudo-grave at Arthur's place in Le Vigan and then plant the incriminating shovel in the garage of the gîte in St Martin."

"What *boys?*"

"Don't ask, Frank!" Kathleen throws both her hands in the air. "Don't even ask! Some of the things that have been going on in the name of MI6 don't bear thinking about. As an aside," she adds, struggling to stifle a smirk, "I'm led to believe that you managed to fall down that selfsame hole and get soil stains on your jeans. That was an unexpected bonus for the Hawkey brothers."

"Just my luck!"

"Stanley then gave Verdu the address of the gîte in St Martin so he could apprehend you and he also tipped him the wink about the incriminating shovel that had been planted in the garage."

I interrupt her in mid-flow. "Just hold on one minute, Kathleen. Are you telling me that it was *Frobisher-Allen* who directed Verdu to the gîte?" Kathleen nods. "Not Martine?"

"I don't know anything about Martine's involvement in any of this, but I do know that Frobisher-Allen informed Verdu that your real name was Frank McClure and he also told him you were a notorious paedophile who was listed on the sex offenders' register in the UK."

"Bloody hell!"

"I know this for a fact because Frobisher-Allen's phone was being monitored by this time and I was the one designated to listen in on his calls. He was so desperate for you to be locked away until his peerage was in the bag that he was prepared to resort to just about anything.

"Well, I think that's about it, Frank," Kathleen says, closing the folder on her desk. "When Stephen, my new boss, found out you were being held in custody in Montpellier, he leaned on Verdu's superiors and organised your release."

My head's reeling. "What happens now?" I ask.

"To Frobisher-Allen?" Kathleen shrugs. "He'll retire a few months early – on health grounds. Pressure of work and all that."

"And his peerage?"

Kathleen shakes her head dismissively. "He was deluding himself. If he'd been thinking rationally he would've realised that was never on. Life peerages for time-served civil servants are a thing of the past, but his ego wouldn't allow him to accept that."

There's a sharp rap on the office door and Kathleen breaks off as a tall guy in his mid-thirties walks in.

"Am I disturbing anything?" he enquires.

"Come on in, Teddy." Kathleen waves him across. "I asked Teddy to drop by, Frank," she says. "I believe you two know each other?"

I eye him up and down. He's tanned, solidly built, and wearing an open-necked pale-green shirt and a pair of well-cut chinos.

"We've met," he announces in a slow drawl as he takes my hand in a painfully firm grip, "in a manner of speaking. More a case of having bumped into each other." I can see the muscles rippling up his forearm underneath his shirt sleeve as he crushes my fist. I recognise his face from somewhere, and there's something familiar about the jagged scar running from his temple to his earlobe, but I've no recollection of us ever having met.

Kathleen sees the confusion in my eyes. "Let me introduce Commander Teddy Monagle, Frank. He's the one who tackled you outside the Scetbons' house. He was staking out the place when you put in an appearance."

Monagle takes up the story. "I'd been briefed by Frobisher-Allen that you'd been assigned to Montpellier and when I saw someone skulking around in the bushes outside the Scetbons' house, I recognised you from your photograph. I called Frobisher-Allen for instructions and he told me to render you inoperational."

"Meaning what, exactly?"

"He told me to incapacitate you and arrange for you to be locked up out of harm's way for a while. However, just as I tackled you, someone intervened – I still have no idea who it was – and hit me up the backside with a stun gun. I was out cold for a couple of hours. When I came round I found myself lying in the undergrowth. I couldn't sit down for a week," he says, rubbing at his left buttock. "It still stings."

"I know who did that."

"Really?"

"A friend of mine," I nod. "Martine Rubio. She gave you a blast with her anti-rape device."

"Extremely effective! Remind me never to try to rape her."

"A hundred thousand volts, no less."

"Bloody hell! No wonder it still hurts."

"Talking of hurting, I wouldn't like to run into you on a rugby field, Teddy. I've never been hit by a tackle like that."

"I have my rugby blue from Oxford," he says. "As well as my black-

and-blue from Montpellier," he adds, rubbing hard at his left buttock. I laugh along with him.

"Hey!" I turn to Kathleen. "How come Commander Monagle had a cell phone and I wasn't issued with one? You've no idea how useful a mobile would've been over there."

"Teddy's experienced in transmitting coded messages, Frank. There's no risk of a security breach if one of his communications happens to be intercepted. Besides, Frobisher-Allen wanted to keep tabs on you," she adds. "If he'd let you loose with a cell phone you could have been calling in from anywhere. Without one, you had to use telephone kiosks and our computers are programmed to pinpoint the location of a call from any telephone booth in France within five seconds. Didn't it strike you as odd that there was no phone in the gîte?"

"Sort of, but I never really questioned it."

"And you wonder why we had you marked down as gullible?" Kathleen teases. "Frobisher-Allen had the phone removed from the house before you arrived to make sure you couldn't make any incriminating calls which Les Renseignements Généraux might intercept and trace back to the gîte."

"Was that to protect me or his holiday arrangements?"

Kathleen grins as she glances at her watch. "Sorry to break up the party, boys. but I'll have to leave you to it. Stephen and I are briefing the embassy staff at two-thirty on the latest developments in the Middle East situation, but you're welcome to carry on using my office. Frank, would you please drop back in to see me later this afternoon – any time after four. There's a few things we need to sort out."

"Fancy a coffee, Frank?" Monagle asks as Kathleen is leaving.

"No thanks, Teddy. I just had one."

Monagle settles down on Kathleen's chair. "According to the rules," he confides, "what I am about to tell you should be divulged only on a need-to-know basis, but I think you're entitled to know what you've been mixed up in, even if you don't strictly have a need to know.

However, what I'm about to divulge must go no further than these four walls." I nod my concurrence.

Monagle gets to his feet and crosses the room to close the office door before returning to his chair. "I was in charge of Operation Damp Squib at the Montpellier end," he begins. "Let me explain what that entailed. About a year ago, we broke the internet codes for an international racist group's communications network and we were able to monitor their activities. As they were doing nothing more than exchanging racist propaganda we decided to let them have their head for a while so we could identify as many of the morons as possible before we pulled the plug on them. Daniel Scetbon was a small cog in this very big wheel. We knew he'd been in cahoots with Gerry Madill for some time. They first teamed up when they were both involved in Arab-baiting in Toulouse when England played there during the 1998 World Cup."

"They do say football fosters international co-operation," I interject.

"For a long time they did little more than exchange racist propaganda over the net," Monagle continues, "but after the 9/11 strikes on the World Trade towers, Madill came up with the warped idea of taking indiscriminate revenge on the Islamic community on some future anniversary of September the eleventh and, after the outrages in Madrid and London, we discovered that they intended to make it happen this year. I believe you know the outline of their plan?"

"All I know is that they were going to bomb a dozen Islamic targets and the initial letters of the places involved would spell out an unsubtle message concerning Bin Laden."

"That's the gist of it. Their objective was to create mayhem, while at the same time sowing panic throughout the Islamic communities in Britain and France. They had compiled a distribution list of the mobile phone numbers of several hundred prominent Muslims in both countries – clerics, politicians, local councillors, doctors, teachers, etc – and they intended to send them all a text message at exactly twelve noon on the eleventh of September containing only the letter 'F', while at the same time blowing a mosque in Fulham to smithereens. Five minutes later, another text would be sent saying 'FU' while a target in Uxbridge was going up in flames. And so on, with a message every five minutes, until they'd spelled out 'FUCK BIN LADEN' and obliterated targets in Carpentras, Kidderminster, Bradford, Islington, Nantes, Lyon, Avignon, Derby, Edinburgh and Nîmes."

"My God!"

"Apart from the carnage, you can imagine the panic this would have engendered. The elapsed time of the whole exercise would've been just one hour and throughout that period news flashes would come filtering through about bombs going off in mosques and schools. The recipients would see the pattern emerging on their mobiles, but be powerless to intervene. At twelve forty, for example, they'd receive a text saying 'FUCK BIN LA' at the same time as a bomb was being detonated in Avignon. They would know exactly what message was coming next, but they wouldn't have a clue as to whether the next explosion was about to erupt in Dundee, Derby, Dunkirk, or somewhere else."

"How sick can these morons get?" I shake my head.

"Fortunately, one of our agents had managed to infiltrate their Birmingham cell, posing as an ex-Balkans mercenary," Monagle continues. "He let it be known that he could get his hands on a supply of Semtex. We provided them with a few grams of the real stuff for test purposes, but it was our intention to fob them off with inert plastic when it came to supplying Semtex for making the bombs. However, that idea came unstuck when we found out Madill planned to travel to France himself and build the bombs for the French attacks over there. Madill's ex-army bomb disposal and he was never going to be fooled by a few lumps of plastic, so we had to think again. After a lot of angst, we decided to supply inert plastic for the British bombs, but provide Madill with live Semtex for the French attacks on the assumption that we would be able to intercept the bombers before anything nasty could happen."

"That was one hell of a big assumption!"

"I couldn't agree more. However, from the messages we had intercepted on their communications' network, we knew their plans down to the last detail – their schedules and their targeted locations, although most of the names of the people involved were in code – so it was deemed a risk worth taking if it meant we could nail them red-handed and close down all the cells."

"Frobisher-Allen gave me the impression that he didn't know a lot about Gerry Madill or what he was up to. A racist football fan and an ex-member of the BNP, but not much else."

"He knew the score all right, but he would be playing his cards close to his chest, as was his wont," Monagle states. "In fact, he had to give his personal authorisation before Madill was allowed out of the country carrying Semtex. Can you imagine the furore if a mosque in France had been blown up by racists using Semtex obtained in England – never mind supplied by MI6!"

"I can see how that might have put a bit of damper on the *entente cordiale*," I state. "Do you think Frobisher-Allen would've given his approval for live Semtex to be used if Madill had been building the bombs for Islington and Bradford?"

"An interesting question! To which we will never know the answer. However, his decision to let Madill travel to France with live Semtex left me holding the baby. I was responsible for liaising with Verdu to make sure we swept up the Montpellier cell while, at the same time, making sure the Semtex didn't get within a mile of the target in Nîmes."

"Tricky situation! How did you resolve that?"

"When the Scetbons were driving to Nîmes to plant the bomb on the morning of the eleventh of September, they had a front wheel blow-out on the motorway as they were overtaking a removal van."

"Unlucky!"

"The odds were tilted slightly in our favour by the fact that the driver of the removal van was one of Verdu's agents and his passenger had a high velocity rifle. The motorway breakdown vehicle that arrived quickly on the scene was also manned by Verdu's guys and when they lifted the spare wheel out of Scetbon's boot, unfortunately for him, the tyre was deflated and the valve was irreparably damaged. Despite their protestations, the Scetbons were driven home and their car, with the Semtex stowed in the boot, was towed away to a garage."

"What happened in the other French towns?"

"Much the same routine. In each case, the would-be bombers were intercepted long before the Semtex got anywhere near the target."

"Which explains why there was nothing about foiled terrorist attacks in the newspapers?" Monagle nods. "Surely, when Madill got wind of these interceptions, he wouldn't think they were all a coincidence?"

"Of course not, but the news filtered through too late for him to call off the operation at the British end. We were waiting for the bastards in all seven UK locations and we let them plant their pseudo-Semtex before nabbing them red-handed."

"How come nothing about this hit the front pages?"

"We're playing it low key. We've taken the perpetrators into custody, but we haven't charged them yet and we haven't released any information about the arrests to the press. We'll get round to filing charges in our own good time. Someone picked up for handling Semtex in Derby one day, a racist hooligan arrested in Edinburgh a few days later, some hotheads disturbed while trying to damage a mosque in Bradford the following week."

"How long can you hold them without bringing charges?"

"As I'm sure Frobisher-Allen must have mentioned to you, Frank. We're MI6. We're leading edge." He grins. "Ninety-nine percent of our activities never get reported in the press – and thank God for that, otherwise, we'd spend all our time trying to justify our actions to a bunch of wishy-washy liberals. We don't exactly run a Guantanamo Bay operation over here, but we do have the odd location where people sometimes feel inclined to tell us about their misdemeanours after benefiting from a few days of our hospitality. However, the main reason we're spreading out the formal arrests is that we don't want to give their master plan the oxygen of publicity, otherwise some other nutters would be bound to jump on the bandwagon and try to copy the idea. It's also not in our interest to disclose the fact that the Semtex they were handling in the UK was fake," he adds. "That way, our undercover agent in Birmingham can remain operational."

"What about Madill?"

"On his way back from France he was stopped by custom officers as he drove out of the Channel Tunnel and a load of Semtex was discovered, concealed in the boot of his car."

"He didn't drop it all off in France, then?"

"Do try to keep up, Frank! Leading edge, remember?"

I shake my head and smile. "I thought I'd stumbled on to something important, but you had the situation under control all the time."

"Don't underrate your contribution. Knowing what they were up to isn't the same thing as proving it. Their e-mail communications were carried out using code names and, although we knew from the outset that Madill was a key player, we didn't have anything that would stand up in court until you sent across your recording. What with that, and discovering a load of Semtex in his car boot, we'll be able to put him away for a very long time. Tom Ivinson managed to amplify the sound track on your tape, by the way. We matched the voice prints to Daniel Scetbon and someone called Cecil Abercrombie. Does that name mean anything to you?"

"I don't think so."

"He's a real saddo. A middle-aged, English racist who lives with his mother in Montpellier."

"Ah! I do believe I know the mother."

"By the way, Verdu got in touch with us yesterday. He's holding Scetbon and Abercrombie and apparently they're both going to turn Queen's evidence, or whatever the French equivalent might be."

"I wonder how he managed to persuade them to do that?"

"Convincing arguments?" Monagle shrugs. "Truncheon up the arse? With Verdu, you never know."

It's three o'clock and I have an hour to kill before Kathleen's due back. I feel like going out for a walk so I ask Teddy Monagle to give me a pass which will allow me to get back into the building. The air has been freshened by the rain shower and I take advantage of being able to stroll around central London in the middle of the afternoon with time to admire the sights – with time to think.

"I took the opportunity to discuss your situation with Stephen after the Middle East meeting, Frank," Kathleen says when I'm back in her office. "He endorsed my recommendations. Here's the deal." She refers to her notepad. "We're planning to sell the St Martin gîte because it's no longer strategically useful to us now that Les Renseignements Généraux know of its existence. However, we believe next summer would be the best time to dispose of the property so, if you're thinking of going back to Montpellier, you can have use of the place until then."

"Thanks. And talking about disposing of property, Kathleen, I'm afraid I've got a confession to make." She looks at me enquiringly. "I flogged the Peugeot."

"You did *what?*"

I feel my freckles flush. "I needed to raise cash quickly, so I sold the car to Scetbon."

Kathleen furrows her brow and stretches across the desk to press the button on her intercom. "Sandra, have you sent the briefing e-mail to Verdu yet?"

"I'm just about to do it."

"Would you please add a paragraph to the effect that Daniel Scetbon stole a car – a Peugeot 206 – belonging to MI6?"

"Sure."

Kathleen releases the intercom button.

"Can we get away with that?" I ask.

"By the time Verdu's finished with Scetbon, a mere detail like whether he bought the car or stole it will be totally irrelevant. As a matter of interest, how much did he give you for it?"

"Three thousand euros."

"If that's not stealing, I don't know what is."

"Fair point."

"After the problems we had with the National Audit Office regarding Frobisher-Allen misappropriating funds," she says, "the last thing Stephen needs right now is to have to explain to the internal auditors why one of our agents sold off government property. Now where was I?" Kathleen adjusts her spectacles and refers back to her notes. "Oh yes. Frobisher-Allen gave you a twelve month contract, Frank. We're prepared to honour that commitment, which means you will continue on full salary until July next year. In addition, you'll be given a bonus of one year's salary, tax free, to compensate you for – how can I put it – unforeseen circumstances in the execution of your duty."

"That sounds eminently reasonable."

"However, I must remind you that you're still bound by the terms of the Official Secrets Act, which means you will never be able to disclose anything about Frobisher-Allen's activities or the racists' bombing campaign."

"I thought that clause had been blown out of the water by a couple of recent embarrassing court cases?"

She glares at me over the top of her spectacles. "It's a package deal, Frank. You accept the terms, otherwise there's no bonus."

"Swayed by the logic of your argument, I concur. Where do I sign?"

"No need." She fiddles with the buttons on the side of her watch. "I have your agreement."

"Touché! Talking of which, should I return my MI6 watch to Tom Ivinson?"

"Please. And if you would also hand in your French identity papers to the office, they'll give you back your British passport and driving licence."

I find Tom Ivinson alone in the technology unit. His jacket's hanging over the back of a chair, his shirt sleeves are rolled up beyond the elbows and he's perched on a high stool, huddled over a microscope, probing at a tiny object on a slide with a minuscule pair of tweezers.

I clear my throat and he looks up with a start. "I'm here to return your watch, Tom."

He pushes the microscope to one side. "How did you find it, Frank?" he asks, jumping down from his stool. "I'm always on the lookout for suggestions for improvements."

"It worked fine, Tom. I had no problems with it."

Tom takes the watch and puts it away carefully in his desk drawer before crossing to the office door and pushing it closed. "I heard you had problems of a different kind," he says in a hushed tone. "With old fish-face Frobisher-Allen," he mouths. I grin. "Don't worry," he says, "you can talk freely in here. It's the only room in the building that isn't bugged." He roars with laughter.

"Tom, I'd like to ask you a favour, but I don't know if what I'm about to propose is technically feasible."

"You really know how to get me going, Frank." He pushes his shirt sleeves further up his arms. There's a glint in his eye. "If there's one thing I can't resist, it's a technical challenge."

CHAPTER 18

I've been back in St Martin de Londres for a week now but I haven't tried to get in touch with Martine.

I've hired a BMW and although I've been hanging around the gîte most mornings, in the afternoons I've taken to driving to the Mediterranean coast and wandering along the shore. My favourite spot is La Grande Motte, a lego-land construction of concrete, pyramid-shaped, holiday apartments built in the nineteen seventies on marshland recovered from the mosquitoes. The holiday season is long since past and the peak summer population of over eighty thousand has shrivelled to the smattering of permanent residents and the odd hardy soul taking advantage of an out of season lease. The vast car parks by the beach are deserted and most of the restaurants are boarded up with only a few seaside bars remaining open, relying on the patronage of the occasional dog walker. The stretch of sand between La Grande Motte and Carnon reminds me of Ayr when the tide is out. I spend hours on end treading the sandy beaches and perching on the dunes, gazing out to sea.

My doorbell jangles as I'm preparing my mid-morning espresso. The postman asks me to sign for a recorded delivery package as he hands over a small parcel bound in heavy-duty tape. I sit down at the kitchen table, break open the wrapping and scan the enclosed note. Swinging my feet up on to the table, I sip at my coffee, lost in my thoughts.

"I can't do anything about it, Jérôme. If she won't speak to you, she won't speak to you."

"Put her on the line, Pascale. Please! Tell her it's very important."

"Martine!" she shouts out. "He says he has to talk to you. He says it's very important." There's a muffled background conversation. "Delicacy prevents me from repeating her exact words, Jérôme, but the précis is 'No'."

I hold my finger to the Scetbons' bell push until Inge appears wearing a loose-fitting, open-necked, purple shirt and matching flared lounging pants. The hand-rolled cigarette dangling from the corner of his mouth is giving off aromatic fumes.

"I'm afraid Linda and Daniel aren't here, Jérôme. The police pulled them in for questioning a week ago and I haven't seen hide nor hair of them since. I've no idea what it's all about – but come on in anyway."

"I was actually looking for Charles Benson. Is he still staying here?"

"Charles?" Inge's hands and eyebrows are launched towards the heavens. "I don't think we'll ever get rid of him." He takes a long drag, burning off half his cigarette, then he exhales slowly through clenched teeth. "Charles!" he calls out as he struts back down the corridor. "Someone to see you."

Benson appears in the hallway in pyjamas, dressing-gown and carpet slippers and when he sees me he starts backing off, his tongue flicking nervously at his moustache, beads of perspiration forming on his creased forehead. He clenches his flabby fists and starts to raise them. "If it's aggro you're after, Dumas?" His voice is croaky. "You've come to the right place."

I stare at him in silence, watching the globules of sweat furrow down his bloated cheeks. "I'm not looking for trouble, Benson."

Air expels noisily from his lungs, his fists relax and his hands drop limply to his sides. "In that case," he blusters, dabbing at his brow with his silk handkerchief. "Come on in and have a drink. Daniel does a very nice line in Cognac."

I follow the waddling frame into the lounge. Benson stops to re-tie his dressing-gown cord, then he pulls two brandy tumblers from the display cabinet and fills them from a crystal decanter.

"Sit yourself down." He hands me a glass. "How are things?" He sinks into the settee and I take the armchair opposite.

"Don't try pissing me about, Benson." I watch his eyes. "I know your brother, Stan Hawkey, otherwise known as Stanley Frobisher-Allen. I also know all about your marijuana racket and I've met your Uncle Godfrey."

The hooded eyes open wide and the head nods up and down reflectively. "Robert Pirsig? Right?" He gulps at his drink and nods again. "Uncle Godfrey told me someone called Pirsig came to see me in Richmond while I was down in the Black Lion having a pint, but I couldn't figure out who it was." He stretches for the decanter on the coffee table and tops up his glass. "You really shouldn't go around using aliases, you know. It makes life very confusing." He laughs raucously. "By the way, was that your bird who was nosing around Uncle Godfrey's place?"

"Not really."

"Shame! Godfrey said she was a right cracker. Anyway. Cheers!" He waves his glass in the air and hands me the decanter. Plucking a half-smoked cigar out of the ashtray, he strikes a match. "By the way, I was on to you right away, Jérôme – or whatever the hell your name is. Did you know that?" He leans back in his seat and blows a tight smoke ring. "From the very first day you walked into The Book Cellar, when I asked you if you preferred your tea weak or strong and you answered me in English. Mind you, with that frightful Jimmy accent, it was hard to be sure it was English!"

Charles is becoming more relaxed as the drink takes effect. "And how could you imagine for one minute that I'd swallow that cock-and-bull story about Jura malt whisky being available on a twinning arrangement in the Jura district of France? You're talking to a man who knows every cheap booze outlet in western Europe, and quite a few beyond." He sucks hard on his cigar and exhales a cloud of smoke. "I'd no idea what your angle was but I figured you had to be up to no good. That was why I implicated you in my disappearance."

"Was it you who left the anonymous tip-off for Verdu that I'd murdered you and forged your will?"

"All's fair in love and whatnot, old chap." His flabby shoulders heave. "Not a bad drop, eh? Drink up. There's another bottle in the sideboard."

Having no compunction about demolishing Daniel's Cognac supplies, I recharge my glass.

"By the way, it was nothing personal, Jérôme." We've made a serious hole in the second bottle and we're both slurring our words. "When I cracked you over the head in Paris and when I cut you up in the bookshop, it wasn't personal. How is your jaw, by the way?"

I massage my stubbly chin. "A lot better." I'm having a great deal of difficulty focusing. "Tell me something, Charles. Why did you take the risk of coming back to the bookshop in the middle of the night to recover a second-rate porn cassette?"

"I didn't know it was a porn cassette. I was expecting a shipment of marijuana from Uncle Godfrey."

"That makes it even crazier. Why take such a risk for a few measly leaves?"

"I wasn't after the contents. I needed to destroy one of the address labels." I'm sitting with a glazed look on my face. Charles empties his tumbler and his voice drops to a confidential whisper. "Former Cabinet Minister," he mouths. "My best customer. He's got a holiday home in Spain and I've been supplying him with marijuana, both in and out of office, for over twenty years. If the tabloids ever got wind of that!" Charles slaps his thigh and guffaws as he replenishes his glass. "When I opened up the package and found it contained a porny cassette, I knew there was something seriously wrong. No way Uncle Godfrey would ever have shipped out anything like that. And if someone had enough influence to interfere with the mail, it had to be my brother, so I went over to England and had it out with him. Stanley agreed to get Verdu off my back and he also slipped me twenty grand to adopt a low profile."

"And, between you, you set me up as the patsy!"

"It was nothing personal, Jérôme."

"I wish you'd stop saying that." I gulp another mouthful of Cognac. "What are you going to do now?" I ask.

He shrugs. "Haven't really decided. Obviously, I'm washed up here – and there's not much point in me going back to England. They probably wouldn't prosecute me. They can do without headlines like: *MI6 Boss Blackmailed By Brother.* However, they could make my life pretty uncomfortable and there's a little matter of twenty grand they'd like to discuss with me." He pulls hard on his cigar. "Might try Italy. Lots of Brits in Tuscany. I've been thinking for some time about opening up a delicatessen specialising in imported British produce. Might even do haggis!" He splutters into his drink. "The cops cleared out Uncle Godfrey's greenhouse," he says with a sly grin, "but they don't know about his allotment in Darlington. He's stockpiling supplies even as we speak."

"What about the bookshop?"

"What about it?"

"I want it."

"You serious?" I nod and swallow another mouthful. Benson tops up his glass while he considers. "If you take over the bookshop, you'd be responsible for the back rent and the outstanding invoices. I reckon the value of the stock should just about cover that."

"Agreed."

He leans across and takes my hand in his slimy, fingertips-only grip. "You've got yourself a deal."

I take the Cognac bottle from the coffee table and spill some more into my glass, then I look up with a start when I hear a loud grunt, echoed by heavy snoring.

I've been walking for hours and my feet are aching. I seem to have retraced my steps several times but I'm sure this is the Vietnamese restaurant Martine parked outside. I cross the street, cut down the narrow lane and round the corner towards the apartment block and I huddle in the shadows for the best part of an hour, suffering from a real cracker of a hangover, until someone finally comes out of the building. Moving quickly, I catch the heavy wooden door with my toe cap before it can swing closed.

I take the slow cage lift to the fifth floor and press the door bell.

Martine tries to slam the door in my face but I'm prepared for this and I use my shoe as a block. "Go to hell, Jérôme!"

"I will, I promise. Just give me five minutes."

"Fuck off!" She's repeatedly jerking the door open and crunching it against my foot. The next time she tries it I crash into the door with my shoulder, sending her tumbling headlong along the hall. I stand on the threshold, panting for breath.

"Five minutes, Martine. That's all I ask."

She scrambles to her feet and limps towards the lounge. I close the front door behind me and go in after her and find her perched on the settee, her feet tucked beneath her, the yellow-eyed, protective Brutus cradled in her lap.

"Why wouldn't you talk to me on the phone?" I'm being treated to a heavy silence. "I only wanted to straighten things out." Brutus stretches out a tentative paw and extends his claws in my direction. I can tell he's itching to have a go. "This is getting us nowhere, Martine. Why didn't you tell Verdu the truth?"

Martine snatches Brutus from her lap and planks him down beside her on the settee. Springing to her feet, she strides purposefully towards me. "What did you just say?" I haven't seen this feisty side before. Our noses are almost touching.

Under the circumstances, I feel it important not to back down. "Why didn't you tell Verdu the truth?" I repeat hesitantly.

I don't know if it's part of Les Renseignements Généraux's basic training, but her knee jerks up viciously and explodes in my goolies. I let out a strangulated yelp and crumple in a writhing heap on the floor. Brutus jumps down from the settee and, if a cat is capable of sneering, he's doing it right in front of my nose. I try pushing him away and get the back of my hand ripped open for my trouble.

Martine's glaring down at me. "Nothing too badly swollen, I hope? I wouldn't want to make a mountain out of a couple of fucking molehills!" She flounces back to the settee and flops down. Moaning and clutching at my aching groin, it's all I can do to get to my knees.

"Martine," I whimper. "Verdu told me you'd turned me in. I have to know the truth."

Her huge eyes are flashing. "Oh, it's the truth we're after, is it? Well listen to me, you pathetic, snivelling, little worm. Verdu says whatever it fucking-well suits him to say! And while we're on the truth kick – " She breaks off and starts mimicking my accent. "'I responded to an advert in the papers for someone to work in The Book Cellar. That's all there is to it'. Forgot to mention you were an MI6 agent on an undercover mission, eh? Just slipped your mind!" Picking up her book, she hurls it in my direction, catching me a glancing blow on the side of the head.

"Does the Official Secrets Act mean anything to you?" I ask, rubbing at my temple.

"Jesus Christ! I hope you're not going to try to tell me Benson's marijuana peddling was a threat to Britain's national security?!"

I sink back on to my heels and raise both arms in a gesture of surrender. "Does *sorry* get me any Brownie points?" I think I detect some softening in those fired-up eyes. She flicks a strand of loose hair away from her face.

"It's a start, I suppose."

That didn't sound too grudging. I struggle to my feet and hobble across to the settee and ease myself down gingerly on to the seat beside her. "You've got bloody hard knees, you know."

"You shouldn't have lied to me."

I pull out my handkerchief and wrap it round my fist to stem the flow of blood, then I gently massage my aching groin. "Had I realised the consequences, I'd have thought twice about it."

A smile softens her features. "Are you all right? Is there anything I can do?"

Although her concern sounds genuine, I don't think this is the opportune moment to suggest a blow job. "I'll just sit quietly for a while, if you don't mind."

"Fancy a coffee?"

"That sounds good."

She springs to her feet and hurries to the kitchen. By the time she returns with two steaming mugs the pulsating pain in my groin has eased.

"I really am sorry, Martine." I place my mug on a side table and stir in two lumps of sugar with one hand, my other hand still cradling my throbbing testicles. "I got caught up in the role and it seemed easier to stick to my story than try to unravel it."

"I suppose my initial behaviour on the train might have left something to be desired in the truthfulness stakes," she concedes. She points towards my crotch and grins. "Would you like me to rub them for you?"

I wince. "The only other time I've ever felt like this was when I got in the way of a football in Kilbirnie in sub-zero temperatures. 'Don't rub them, ref, count them', was the expression, I believe."

She laughs. "How about something a bit stronger to take your mind off it?"

My hangover has receded. "Yeah. Why not? Got any Armagnac?"

She trots to the kitchen and reappears with a bottle and two glasses.

"I brought these, by the way," I say, standing up and handing her the tracking device and the bookmark. "I thought you might want them back."

"Oh, God! Thanks a million, Jérôme." She plants a kiss on my forehead. "Verdu's been giving me a hard time about these. They're signed out in his name and there'll be hell to pay if they're not returned by the end of the week," she says, pouring two glasses of Armagnac.

"And," I add, keeping hold of her hand as I take the proffered drink, "I also brought a present for you."

"A present?"

I put my glass down on the coffee table and produce the gold locket from my jacket pocket. "I'd like you to have this," I say, placing it in her open palm. "It was my mother's."

"No! I can't take that!"

"Please, Martine. It would mean a lot to me." I flick open the locket and show her my mother's photograph.

"This is way over the top, Jérôme. Accepting this would imply a level of commitment I'm not prepared to give."

I close the locket, lift it from her hand and, ignoring her protests, string it around her neck. "I'm not asking for any commitment." I feel a lump at the back of my throat as I whisper in her ear. "I'd just like us to be able to start all over again." I fasten the clasp.

"Start all over again?" she echoes.

"How about dinner tomorrow night?"

She shakes her head quickly and steps away. "I can't. I'm going away for a while. On my own," she adds firmly. She's fingering the locket as if it's burning into her throat. "I need a break from everything – from everyone."

"Where are you going to go?"

"I haven't decided yet. That's not important. I just need my own space for a while."

"How long are you going for?"

"A week – maybe two. I'm not sure."

I move towards her, lift her fingers away from the locket and wrap her hand in mine. "If you promise to wear the locket while you're away, it means we'll meet again." She drops her eyes and squints to focus on the glinting gold nestling in the crook of her neck. "It suits you."

Those large, green eyes look up slowly and start to mist over as she stares at me. "I will wear it, Jérôme," she says. There's a slight tremble in her voice. She leans forward and pecks me on the cheek. "I promise."

It's been a hectic couple of days since I took over the bookshop. I've got an interior decorator coming round tomorrow morning to give me an estimate for redecorating the place from top to bottom and, as I won't have the St Martin gîte beyond next summer, I'm working on a plan to convert the storeroom into habitable living quarters. I envisage replacing the camp bed with a bed settee and, at a push, there should be room for a wardrobe, a small table and a couple of armchairs.

I've organised an announcement in the *Midi Libre* to the effect that the bookshop is under new management and there will be a formal re-opening on Christmas Eve. Through a small-ad in the *BEC Thunderer*, I made contact with Paul Tierney, a Montpellier-based Irish odd-job man and I've commissioned him to paint a new sign to hang above the shop front. The next item on my list of things-to-do is to go through the shelves and clear out all the books that will never sell to make room for new stock.

On an impulse, I phone my mother in Peking. "Hello, Mum? It's Frank. How are you getting on?"

"Frank?" She sounds confused. "Yer voice sounds awfy strange, son. Is it the line or is there somethin' wrang?"

I realise she's not used to my Home Counties accent so I switch quickly to French. "Is that better?"

"Much better."

"How's Peking treating you, Mum?"

"Everything's going great, Frank. Me Sung and I have made a fortune out of the real ale and karaoke business and we're selling franchises like hot cakes. We could retire tomorrow if we wanted."

"That's fantastic!"

"How about you? Are you still travelling?"

"I've settled down now, Mum. I'm going to be living in France from now on."

"France!" She squeals with delight. "Where?"

"Montpellier."

"That's amazing! Doing what?"

"I own a bookshop, Mum."

"A bookshop!" I can almost feel her pleasure purring down the line. "How absolutely wonderful."

"The official opening is at Christmas and I was wondering if there would be any chance of you and Me Sung making it across?"

There's a garbled dialogue in the background in what I assume to be Mandarin. "We'll be there, Frank." She breaks off again and I hear another burst of conversation. "Frank, Me Sung says if you're going to be living in Montpellier, we should buy an apartment there so we'll have a *pied à terre* when we come to visit you."

"Just like that?"

"Me Sung's very decisive." There's pride in her voice. "Could you keep an eye out for something suitable for us?"

"Of course, Mum." This strikes me as an excellent idea. I'll be able to put the apartment to good use when they're not in Montpellier – much more convivial than the cramped storeroom.

"Give me your phone number, Frank. I'll call you back when we've sorted out our travel arrangements."

I re-think my ideas for the window display for the grand opening. Logging on to the computer, I place orders for ten copies of *Ulysses*, *Finnegan's Wake*, *The Portrait of the Artist as a Young Man* and *Dubliners*.

I interrupt Paul and ask him to knock me up a centrepiece for the window – a wide banner, with reindeers and holly, proclaiming: *Christmas is here! Let us all read-Joyce!* That should be good for a two-bedroom flat at least.

Half an hour later Paul calls me across. "Your name plate's ready. Could you give me a hand to put it up?" He scratches his head and steps back to inspect his work. "I still think it's a bloody weird name for a bookshop."

We both climb up on stepladders to unhook The Book Cellar sign from above the shop front and then we carefully replace it with the new one. I scramble back down the steps and cross the road to study the large gold letters, picked out on a white background. "You've done a nice job there, Paul," I say, admiring the sign swinging gently in the breeze, proudly proclaiming the advent of *The Plucked Pheasant*.

CHAPTER 19

I'm crawling along as I negotiate the narrow, snow-covered, car-lined streets of the village. When I come alongside a group of laughing skiers attired in Stars and Stripes ski jackets, I lower the car window, allowing a flurry of snowflakes to come swirling into the vehicle.

"Can anyone tell me where I'll find a post office?" I call out in English.

"Take the second street on the right, buddy," one of the skiers shouts, pointing his ski pole in the general direction. "It's about fifty yards up the hill, on the left, just past the newsagent. You can't miss it."

"Thanks." I close the window quickly and turn the heater up a notch.

I double park in front of the post office and switch on my hazard warning lights while I nip inside to purchase a book of stamps, then I drive a few hundred metres further up the hill and pull over under the eaves of a large hotel. The receptionist, an attractive, young girl, dressed in lederhosen, gives me a welcoming smile.

"Do you speak English?" I ask.

"Yes."

"Could I have a room for tonight?"

"I'm very sorry, sir. I'm afraid we're full."

"Will I be able to eat in the restaurant?"

"No problem."

It's just after five o'clock and there's already an animated buzz in the large, open-plan bar as groups of steaming skiers, still attired in boots and salopettes, mill around recounting the exploits of the day while pouring back recuperative glasses of *glüwein* and *Jägermeister*.

I wander into the dining room to seek out the head waiter and present him with a generous tip to reserve the table in the alcove with a splendid view of the impressive mountain slopes before ambling back to the bar and ordering a large whisky. I add a splash of water to my drink and settle down in an armchair beside the blazing log fire from where I have an unobstructed view of the staircase.

I have my glass to my lips when she appears at the top of the stairs, looking absolutely stunning in a powder blue miniskirt with matching ankle boots and an open-necked, white silk blouse. Our eyes meet and lock and her mouth is agape as she limps down the wooden steps. I scramble to my feet and hurry towards her.

"Jérôme! What in the name of God are you doing here?"

"Martine! This is incredible!" I take her by the hand and lead her back to the armchair. She sinks down in the seat and I perch on the armrest. "Would you like a drink?"

She nods. "I need one. Whisky. A large one. This is truly amazing. What on earth brought you to Austria? And how on earth did you end up in Obergurgl?"

"You're not going to believe this! I decided to do some sightseeing. I'd always wanted to visit Munich because a guy I was at school with lives there now and he raves about the place. I was on the autobahn, about twenty kilometres from the Bavarian border, when a Mercedes with skis strapped to its roof overtook me and – I just don't know what got into me – I took a sudden, crazy notion to go skiing. I must be stark, raving mad. I've never skied in my life, but something drove me to put my foot down and follow the Merc – I hadn't the foggiest idea where he was going – and I ended up here." I continue to gaze at her in utter astonishment, then I burst out laughing. "I don't even have any ski gear, for God's sake. I just sort of assumed I'd be able to hire what I needed when I got here."

"There's no way you could have known I was here." She's shaking her head in total disbelief. "I made a last minute booking on the internet and I told no one where I was going – not even Pascale." She turns side-on in the armchair and stares at me. "There are dozens of hotels in the village. What on earth made you pick this one?"

"I was driving up the main street and I liked the look of it."

"This is way beyond coincidence, Jérôme." She takes my whisky tumbler from my grasp and tips the remaining contents down her throat. "This truly is fate," she says, handing me back the empty glass. Holding her hands over her eyes, she slowly spreads her long, slim fingers, peeking through as if expecting the mirage to have disappeared. "This isn't even the hotel I stayed in last night," she whispers in awe. "There was a mix-up with the bookings and my things were transferred here this afternoon while I was up on the ski slopes."

"That's unbelievable!" I call across the waiter and order two large whiskies.

"It must be cosmic forces that brought us together, Jérôme. There is no other explanation." Martine's uncomprehending eyes are wider and larger than I've ever seen them. Her sun-burnished forehead, cheeks and neck are glowing, but her eyelids, having been shielded by goggles, remain alluringly pale.

I take her hand in mine and grip it very tightly. "I noticed you were limping when you came down the stairs. Are you all right?"

"It's nothing." She shakes her head dismissively. "Twisted my ankle slightly, that's all. I came down off the slopes early as a precaution."

We talk about everything and nothing as we down several aperitifs before heading for the dining room and she's delighted when the head waiter ushers us to the table in the alcove. Time races by and I hardly notice what I'm eating as we laugh and joke our way through reminiscences of our trip to England.

"How's Verdu taking it?" I ask.

"He's not at all a happy bunny. He was badly miffed at getting messed about by Frobisher-Allen, but he got really pissed off when word came down from on high that you were an MI6 agent and all charges against you were to be dropped."

I lean across the table and gently finger the locket cradled in the crook of her neck. "I see you're wearing it."

Her face flushes. "I promised, didn't I?"

The bustle in the dining room gradually dies away and is replaced by a muffled, insistent beat coming from the discotheque in the basement. As the cuckoo on the wall-clock is chirping its eleventh cheep, Martine's hand stretches across the table. She strokes my fingers lightly before intertwining them with hers. "I'm afraid I won't be able to dance tonight – what with my twisted ankle and all that."

"Shame." I top up both our glasses from the bottle of Armagnac the waiter left on the table.

Martine glances over her shoulder to check no one's within hearing distance. She squeezes my fingers tightly. "Do you have a thingy?" she mouths, the mother and father of all grins splitting her features. I smile and nod. "Your room or mine?" she whispers.

"Yours," I state authoritatively.

"Number thirty-seven. Third floor." She gets to her feet, rather unsteadily. "Give me five minutes." She leans across the table and chucks me under the chin. "I need the loo." She's consumed by a fit of the giggles as she slaloms towards the staircase.

Some risks in life just aren't worth taking. Removing the tracking device from my jacket pocket, I place it inside a protective Jiffy bag which I've pre-addressed to the gîte in St Martin. I seal the package, stick on an excessive number of postage stamps, and take it to the reception desk where I ask the girl to put it in the mail. As I wander back towards the roaring, open fire in the bar, I pull a sheet of notepaper from my inside jacket pocket. My eye scans the typed page:

'*Dear Frank,*

I had no trouble creating a duplicate tracker, it's a pretty standard piece of equipment. Analysing the frequency of the microchip in the bookmark was also straightforward. However, replicating identical function on to a smaller module turned out to be a bit trickier than I'd imagined, but I eventually managed it. As you requested, I've inserted the miniaturised

module in the gold locket, behind the photograph. You'll find the
bookmark, your locket and both the trackers in the attached package.

   Regards and best wishes,

   Tom Ivinson.'

Crumpling the sheet of paper in my fist, I lob it on to the fire and watch it curl, crinkle and flare up as it's devoured by the licking flames.

   Hurrying across to the wide staircase, I take the wooden steps two at a time. Dachshunds, eat your heart out!